DEMON
WITCH

THE TERNION ORDER

BOOK TWO

DANIEL R. MARVELLO

Published by Magic Fur Press
An imprint of Logical Expressions, Inc.
P.O. Box 383, Ponderay, Idaho 83852, USA

This is a work of fiction. All names, characters, places, and events are either the product of the author's imagination or are used fictitiously. Any resemblance to actual persons, living or dead, business organizations, events, or locales is purely coincidental.

Demon Witch

ISBN: 978-1-61038-054-6 (paperback)
        978-1-61038-055-3 (EPUB)

Cover art by Susan C. Daffron
Print layout by Susan C. Daffron
Ebook formatting by Logical Expressions, Inc.

Demon Witch is dedicated to my lovely and
talented wife.
She is the real magic in my life.

Books by Daniel R. Marvello

<u>The Vaetra Chronicles</u>
Vaetra Unveiled
Vaetra Untrained
Vaetra Unleashed

<u>The Ternion Order</u>
First Moon
Demon Witch

<u>The Western Geomancer</u>
Geomancer's Bargain

CHAPTER 1

Leap of Fate

Amanda stood near the edge of a deep chasm. Hundreds of feet below, water crashed through the canyon raising mist that obscured everything at the bottom except the topmost branches of a few tall trees. On the canyon's opposite rim, a male figure paced back and forth.

Even from a distance, she recognized his shape and the way he moved. She would know her brother Reggie anywhere.

The canyon cut through the landscape for as far as she could see in both directions. There was no bridge or narrow place where she might cross. She missed Reggie so much. Her heart ached to hug him tight and hear his comforting voice rumble in his chest. After their parents' death, his warmth and love had sustained her. He'd given up everything to take care of her, and now she was failing him.

Tears streaming down her face, she stretched a hand toward him and called his name softly, knowing there was no way he would hear her over the noise of the river below.

Reggie cupped his hands and shouted her name. His so-familiar voice came to her over the roar of the river in a broken collection of syllables. He stepped back several paces from the ledge, and her mind froze when his intention to jump the impossible distance became clear.

"No!" she screamed.

Reggie sprinted forward and leaped into the gap between them. His trajectory carried him high, but with only a fraction of the velocity he needed to reach her safely. She watched in open-mouthed horror as he stalled and then plummeted, arms circling wildly in a futile attempt to slow his descent.

Amanda jolted awake and pressed her pillow to her face, letting it absorb the scream she couldn't contain. She curled into a tight fetal ball and cried into the pillow, pulling it away only to catch her breath.

As her sobs subsided, the aroma of fresh coffee intruded upon her consciousness. The familiar and welcome smell shredded the final heartbreaking images from the awful dream. She released the pillow and turned onto her back, panting and wiping tear-damp hair from her face. Taking several deep breaths, she collected herself.

The fright from her dream drained away, but a lingering sense of helplessness threatened to bring the tears back. But it was just a dream. Pressing her fists to her eyes, Amanda growled in frustration. She threw back the covers and padded to the bathroom.

CHAPTER 2

Amber Eyes

Kyle looked up from the magazine he was reading when Amanda shuffled into the kitchen wearing her well-worn blue terrycloth bath robe and a pair of moccasin-like slippers. Sensing something was amiss, he watched closely as she covered a yawn with the back of her hand and dropped into the chair opposite him at the small square breakfast table.

Kyle immediately got up and fetched her a cup of coffee. Over the past month, Amanda's weekend sleepovers had taught him she wasn't much of a morning person. He knew better than to start a conversation until she had some caffeine pumping through her veins. Setting a steaming mug in front of her, he kissed the top of her head and ventured, "Good morning."

The glance she gave him as he sat down declared that it was nothing of the kind. Her dark hair was drawn back into a pony tail, and the morning light through the window next to the table emphasized the pallor of her skin. Wayward strands of hair clung wetly to her cheeks, suggesting she'd rinsed her face without letting the water warm up. Her puffy eyelids and the red crackle of veins around her gray irises cued him to the probability that she'd been crying.

"What's wrong?" he asked, leaning forward. "Are you okay?"

Amanda cradled the mug in her hands, blowing on the hot liquid and sipping it as quickly as she dared. She nodded and answered, "Bad dream."

"I'm sorry. Do you want to talk about it?"

She stared at him over the top of her mug. "Not yet," she said and took another sip.

Kyle wanted to say or do something to fix whatever was wrong, but he knew better than to force the issue. She would talk when she was ready. If he sat there staring at her, waiting for her to tell him what was on her mind, he'd just piss her off.

He got up and refreshed his own coffee, more for the distraction than anything. His stomach grumbled. A glance at the clock told him it was seven-fifteen, which meant he'd been awake for more than an hour. He opened the refrigerator door and evaluated his breakfast options.

"Want something to eat?" he asked.

"Maybe later," came the terse reply.

Kyle shut the refrigerator and sat back down at the table. Not knowing what else to do, he returned to the magazine article he had been reading. His eyes wandered over the printed words, but none of them registered.

He wondered if her mood was simply a matter of morning surliness coupled with the residual funk of a bad dream or if it was something more.

More, his intuition insisted.

He glanced up to find her staring at him. Their eyes locked. He couldn't read her expression, particularly with her hands and the mug obscuring half her face. Was she angry about something?

"You aren't wearing your contacts," she observed.

A full sentence, Kyle thought. *That's a good sign.*

"I almost never do on weekend mornings unless I'm expecting someone. It's not like I need them to see." His brown-tinted contact lenses had only one purpose: to disguise his amber irises, hiding the strange mutation that had been a side effect of nearly becoming a werewolf. "It's nice to get a break from them."

He wasn't telling her anything she didn't already know. His wolf-like eyes never seemed to bother her before. What was going on?

"Do you want me to go put them on?" he asked.

Amanda set down her coffee and looked into the cup. She waved her hand and shook her head dismissively. "No, it's fine. My dream was about Reggie, that's all."

And his eyes were a disturbing reminder of Reggie's condition.

Kyle rose from his chair to go put in his contacts. Amanda reached out and touched his hand. "You don't have to do that. It was just a bad dream. I'll get over it."

He lifted her hand and bent to kiss it. "Until you do, let me do this small thing for you."

She looked up at him, letting her guard down so he could see the haunted vulnerability in her eyes. "Thanks," she whispered, squeezing his hand.

By the time Kyle returned to the kitchen, Amanda had refilled her coffee cup and seemed a little perkier. She had taken over his magazine and was flipping through it without stopping long on any one page.

He sat down and gulped a mouthful of his lukewarm coffee. He wanted to ask her about her dream, but forced himself to be patient. Turning to the window, he parted the sheer curtains and watched the chickadees flitting around the back yard. The day was sunny, which was rare for late October.

Having spent time at Hayworth Farm where Amanda lived, he viewed the small fenced yard in a new light. There was plenty of room to set up a veggie garden next spring although he'd need to tear out some of the sod. He would have to ask Bob Daily, his next-door landlord, if that would be okay. Did having a garden enhance the resale value of a home? He'd have to look into that as a possible argument in favor of his proposal.

Kyle's garden plans were interrupted by Amanda's soft voice. "I couldn't reach him."

She had closed the magazine, and her hands were in her lap. She looked up from the magazine cover, unshed tears glistening above her lower eyelid. She blinked, and two fat drops rolled down, launching off the curve of her cheekbones into her lap.

"He was on the other side of a huge ravine," she continued, "and he jumped to his death just before I woke up."

"That's horrible. I'm sorry you had such an awful dream."

She gave Kyle a weak smile. "I'm sure Lucille would have a lot to say about what it all means. It probably reflects my indecision about how to help Reggie."

Her mood and the dream were starting to make sense. About two years previously, Amanda's brother Reggie had been possessed by a *lupusdaemon*, also known as a werewolf demon. After the one-month acclimation period between full moons, the demon had taken Reggie's body over completely and joined the other local werewolves who were part of the Selkirk Pack.

Amanda had spent the past two years trying to find a way to get her brother back. With help from her coven leader, Amanda had traded on her skills as a witch to gain entry into a secret paranormal law-enforcement group called the Ternion Order. Taking advantage of Order connections and resources, Amanda was still researching a solution when she learned of Kyle and his predicament.

Kyle had been the unwitting victim of a lascivious *lupusdaemon* named Clarissa who seduced him and then shifted from her own failing body into his. She'd known her time was running out, and she chose his body for her next vessel. If not for Amanda and the exorcism rite she'd been working on, the true Kyle Nelson would have ceased to exist, and the *lupusdaemon* would have eventually taken over and returned to the local werewolf pack in his body.

Kyle's exorcism had been a promising first step toward saving Reggie, but there were still substantial problems to solve. Amanda had been wrestling with those problems unsuccessfully, and it was starting to take a serious toll on her peace of mind.

"I thought you had decided that it was too late for Reggie," Kyle ventured carefully.

Amanda sucked in a deep breath and wiped the tear tracks from her cheeks. "I never *decided* anything. I just can't figure out how to help him."

"We've talked about this." Kyle said, using his most reasonable tone. "I told you what it was like for me on those occasions when the demon took over. I was thrown into some kind of sensory deprivation otherworld. If Reggie has been in that place for the past two years, you may not want to meet what he's become."

Amanda narrowed her eyes at him. "Yes, but what you experienced happened before First Moon. The demon pushed you aside, but you could still return to your body. What Reggie is experiencing might be completely different. His mind might have been put on hold or something. If I could get rid of the demon, he might come back thinking no time had passed at all."

"Or he could be gone entirely." Kyle hated to say it, but she needed to be realistic in her expectations.

Amanda closed her eyes and took a deep breath. "I know that." Opening her eyes, she gave him a sullen glare. "It would help if you were a little more supportive, you know."

Kyle raised his hands in a gesture of giving. "I *am* being supportive. Do you feel comfortable talking about this with anyone else?"

Amanda shook her head, but said nothing.

"I'll help you do whatever you want, but if we don't get perspectives from anyone else, one of us has to play devil's advocate, pardon the expression. Anything we do will be dangerous, so we can't charge off filled with righteous fire and no contingency plan. You can't plan for contingencies unless you stop to think about what might go wrong, and that's all I'm trying to do."

Amanda sat back in her chair and folded her arms. "Well, pardon me for getting all emotional about my brother being taken over by a demon."

Kyle lowered his head and sighed. "It's okay to be emotional. But we need to be logical about this, too. Let *me* be the logical one. I'm a programmer. I'm good at it."

Amanda rolled her eyes. "You're such a nerd."

"Exactly my point."

One corner of Amanda's mouth shifted up into the beginnings of a tiny smile. "All right then, Mr. Logical. Riddle me this: how do we convince the *lupusdaemon* that's controlling Reggie's body to submit to an exorcism?"

"I've been thinking about that, and I don't think it's possible," Kyle answered. "And putting aside all angst about the condition and location of Reggie's consciousness, *that* obstacle has been the primary reason why you haven't been able to see a way forward."

Amanda leaned forward, anger widening in her eyes. "It's impossible? How is *that* being supportive?"

Kyle shook his head. "When one logic path fails, you don't give up; you move on to a different one. Sometimes a less desirable one." Her intent expression let him know he had her full attention. He drank the last of his cold coffee to postpone what he had to say next.

"Reggie's demon will never go along with your plan," Kyle explained. "If you want to help your brother, we'll have to do it against the demon's will. Somehow, we're going to have to abduct him and restrain him while you perform the exorcism. I doubt the Order will approve of that idea, and if you succeed, you will become a threat to the entire Pack, if not all werewolf kind."

"I'm already a threat," she said. "You're the proof."

"Not the kind of threat you'd be if you exorcise a *lupusdaemon* already in full possession of a body. It's never been done. Afterward, *none* of them will be safe."

Amanda stared out the window, unseeing. "You're right. I know all this, but I didn't want to face it. I still don't see a way forward. I've failed him."

Kyle paused before responding. Her mission to save her brother could get all three of them killed. The deciding factor for giving his support wasn't her misery although he hated seeing her in pain. And it wasn't that he owed her his life. What sense did it make to throw that gift away uselessly? It was that he had nearly been in Reggie's position. If Kyle were still locked in the abyss, he'd want Amanda to do everything in her power to free him, even if the only possible freedom was death. Of course, Reggie would never want his sister to get herself killed in the process of helping him, but taking that risk was Amanda's decision to make.

"You've only failed him if you give up," Kyle finally said, "so don't do that. I'm telling you all this because we have to be realistic about the scope of work. The problem is complicated, and the solution may not be obvious, but knowing what you want and committing yourself to it will get the ideas flowing."

Amanda rose from her seat and came over to Kyle's side of the table. She pushed on his shoulder until he shifted his chair back, giving her room to sit in his lap. She sat across his legs and wrapped her arm around his neck, giving him a tender kiss.

"See, *now* you're being supportive," she said, putting her forehead against his. "And you really are such a nerd."

Kyle angled his head for another warm kiss. When their lips parted, Amanda tilted up an eyebrow questioningly, invitingly. "Wanna go back upstairs for a little while?"

Kyle squeezed her close. "I like where your emotions are taking this conversation."

CHAPTER 3

Dominance

Adolphus Rutlinger, alpha werewolf of the Selkirk Pack and founder of the Rutlinger Foundation, stared into his glass of wine, enjoying the play of light on the crystal goblet and the luster of the dark-red translucent liquid that swirled within. The soporific fog that dulled his emotions and warped his senses was a clue that he had been drinking too much.

His alcohol consumption had increased when Pack member Iledaste, the werewolf formerly known in human form as Clarissa, had been sent howling back into the abyss a month ago. The loss and its implications had left the entire Pack depressed and restless.

The little witch Amanda had surprised them all. After her first attempt to exorcise Iledaste from the body of Kyle Nelson had failed, Adolphus allowed himself to believe that she wasn't up to the task. That had been too much wishful thinking on his part.

Amanda's second attempt had succeeded, thus resurrecting an ancient threat that he'd thought long gone. She had dusted off a Native American ceremony that was nearly a hundred and fifty years old, and against all odds, she'd modernized it enough to make it function. For only the second time in known history, a human had successfully exorcised a *lupusdaemon* before it could take full possession of its host body at *Erste Mond*.

He admired her ingenuity, but at the same time, he hated her for the uncertainty she'd introduced into the future of every *lupusdaemon*. The next time any of them switched to a new body, they would be vulnerable until the following full moon. He didn't dare think about how much further the witches of the Ternion Order might be able to take their new power.

Gulping the last of his wine, he berated himself for dwelling on the same depressing train of thought for the hundredth time. As he leaned forward and sat his goblet on the coffee table, the front door of the Rutlinger Foundation manor swung open, admitting a fresh breeze laden with pine scents from the forest outside.

Rutlinger looked up, expecting to see one of his pack members enter the room. The smile he'd affected to hide his maudlin thoughts slid from his face, and he jumped to his feet. Two strangers wearing dark-purple cloaks stood in the slate-tiled entryway.

He strode quickly to intercept them. "The Foundation is private property. You should have announced yourself at the front gate. Who are you, and what is your business here?"

The nearest figure lifted the hood of her cloak and let it fall to her back. She was a strikingly lovely woman with a creamy complexion, full red lips, and dark hair that cascaded to her shoulders in waves. Her eyes were the unmistakable yellowish-amber of a werewolf.

"Greetings, Woreblin. It's been a while," she said.

Rutlinger was momentarily stunned. For a werewolf from another pack to appear in the heart of his territory without advance notice was not only rude—it was a direct challenge to his authority. He might have attacked her right then, except for her casual use of his true name. He did not recognize her, but she apparently knew him well enough.

She folded her arms and waited with an insolent smile while he collected himself and worked out who she was. His nostrils twitched as he sniffed at the air, but the olfactory reflex was one of habit. The signature "scent" he detected came to him through his demonic senses.

"Iledaste," Rutlinger concluded. "This is a new look for you."

"It is," she agreed. "My new form is called Marcella." She waved toward the person who accompanied her. "This is my coven. Well, what's left of it."

The other figure dropped his hood as well. Rutlinger was not surprised to see that he was also a werewolf. He'd sensed it when he'd detected Iledaste's presence.

"Your coven? You possessed a dark witch?" Rutlinger was genuinely surprised. It was a risky choice and quite the opposite of keeping a low profile when it came to the Ternion Order.

She gave him a wicked smile. "Turnabout is fair play, as they say."

Her oblique reference to the exorcism put Rutlinger on alert. "Why have you returned, *Marcella*?"

"I'm here because you failed us, *Adolf*."

Rutlinger narrowed his eyes at her deliberate provocation. "You know I prefer *Adolphus*. And how did I fail you?"

"The exorcism, you fool." Marcella stepped forward, gaining his absolute attention. "It should never have been allowed to happen. Once it did, no one should have left the scene alive."

Rutlinger shook his head. "We tried to prevent it."

"You didn't try hard enough," Marcella accused in a sharp tone.

Rutlinger clenched his jaw, holding back his anger. She had no business accusing him. He had tried to control the situation, but the disaster was a result of *Iledaste's* bad timing and choice of victim. "We did not expect the witch to succeed. She had already tried and failed, and the Order were protecting her. We expected her to fail again."

"You're telling me that eight werewolves couldn't defeat a few human bodyguards?" she scoffed. "The pack is weak under your leadership."

Rutlinger ignored the insult. It was nothing new. She'd been saying the same thing for years, but she'd never had the strength or the guts to take action. As Clarissa, she'd chosen to live away from the Foundation where his leadership affected her less. Nevertheless, when she'd transferred to Kyle Nelson's body, he'd done his best to help her keep it.

"We could have overwhelmed them," he agreed with a nod. "But if we had, everything we've worked for here would have been lost. We would spend the rest of our days on the run from the Order. Not unlike you will, I might add."

The Order was known to be relentless in their pursuit of dark covens.

Marcella drew herself up, anger tightening the skin around her eyes. "Don't compare yourself to me. You're a disgrace. You and the others have cozied up to humans for so long that you no longer remember what you are."

Rutlinger stifled a surge of anger. Former pack member or not, she was pushing the limit of what he'd tolerate from her. Although she had a new body, she couldn't use the magic of the dark witch she'd possessed. She wasn't much of a threat, which was what made her choice of bodies so odd. Meanwhile, her partner was standing back with his arms folded, letting her make her move alone.

Rutlinger had to draw a line and be prepared to defend it. "I'll remind you that this is my territory. I'm alpha here, and I won't tolerate your insults."

Marcella moved a little closer to him, invading the unspoken personal space that would have raised his hackles if he'd been in wolf form. "Don't make me demonstrate who is dominant here. If I had any interest in ruling your bunch of weaklings, I could take them from you now." She moved back just far enough to be less threatening. "Lucky for you, all I demand is a bit of your hospitality."

"What do you want?" Rutlinger asked in a suspicious tone. *Finally we get to the real reason for this visit.*

Marcella glanced around the room at the opulent furnishings, not bothering to disguise her disgust. "I need a base of operations while I clean up the mess you've made. Your ridiculous *Foundation* will do nicely."

"If you make trouble, this is the first place the Order will look. And if they find you here, they will believe the rest of us are complicit. I will not allow it."

Marcella stepped forward and gripped his throat with one hand. "If you refuse, I'll tear out your traitorous throat and do what I want anyway. If you help me, I'll see to it that you are redeemed in the eyes of our kind."

Outraged that she would have the temerity to walk into his home and physically threaten him, Rutlinger reached up with both hands to grab her forearm and pry at her fingers. His intent was to break her grip and then possibly her arm, but his efforts were useless against the iron resistance he encountered.

Her incredible strength made no sense. Even though her new body was undoubtedly stronger than the one that had been failing her when she'd possessed the Nelson boy, she couldn't be *this* strong. Something was very wrong. Yes, Iledaste was in there somewhere, but he wasn't talking to Iledaste.

Rutlinger's flailing did nothing except bring a wicked smile to her face. She nodded when she saw the realization dawn in his eyes. "Hello, Adolphus. Meet the *real* Marcella.

With Iledaste's help, my magic is stronger than you can begin to imagine."

While Rutlinger clawed at her, Marcella squeezed until his vision began to dim. His attempts to remove her hand became more and more feeble as he gasped for breath and his knees buckled.

Just when he thought she would make good on her threat to kill him, she released his throat. He caught himself from toppling over and sat with his legs folded until his head cleared. Looking up into her eyes, he could see a determination that would not be denied. She was both witch and werewolf. To his knowledge, it was the first such pairing.

With a feeling of sadness for the future of his pack, Rutlinger admitted to himself that she had defeated him. He was no longer alpha. He remained on his knees and bowed his head, lowering his eyes. "We will do what we can to accommodate you," he said.

She patted his head in a patronizing fashion, making his face heat with humiliation. "Good boy. Now, perhaps you can give us a tour."

CHAPTER 4

Gathering

Amanda turned off the pavement and slowed her car for the bumpy climb up Gold Creek Ridge Road. Her Subaru Outback was a little older than the Toyota RAV4 it had replaced, but she liked the car-like ride, and the interior was nicer. She hoped the Outback would last longer, not that crashing into a tree had been her poor RAV's fault.

At the top of the ridge, she followed the winding road past everything from tiny cabins to sprawling mini-ranches. Tall evergreens bordered the road easement and the yards that had been carved out of the forest. Birch trees had grown into many spaces where the ground had been exposed to sun, their yellow fluttering leaves a hallmark of the season.

In spite of Kyle's pessimistic assessment that morning of the situation with Reggie, his suggestion that they start collecting information and exploring options made her feel like she could finally do something useful. His promise to help her once they came up with a plan of action was also reassuring.

Turning at Noreen's driveway, Amanda drove a short distance before entering a clearing filled with vehicles parked near a large cedar home. Usually, she was among the first to arrive. She grimaced as she pulled in next to Cara's sporty little red SUV. If Cara was there, she was *really* running late. Amanda hadn't yet adjusted to the longer drive from Kyle's house or the delays imposed by the man himself. At Hayworth Ranch, she was used to downing a bowl of cereal and driving ten minutes to the gathering. She hadn't planned for morning snuggle time with Kyle or the huge breakfast he insisted on feeding her afterward. Add the half-hour drive from his house in town, and she was lucky she'd made it at all.

She looked down at her full tummy pushing against the waist of her jeans. If she let him keep feeding her the way he did, her pants wouldn't fit for much longer. It was time to set some ground rules.

Amanda grabbed her canvas bag and hurried to the house, entering the front door without bothering to knock. Noreen would be expecting her. Impatiently, no doubt.

"Well, look who decided to join us," piped Cara's sultry voice. "New boy toy keep you up late?"

Amanda hadn't quite figured out why Cara was so fascinated by her relationship with Kyle. Cara's approach to men was to chew them up and spit them out. As an air witch, she had the power to attract any man she wanted, but she had no need for magic in that department. Men were irresistibly drawn to her petite but enviably proportioned figure and her glacier-blue eyes, which dominated a round face framed by long black hair. All she had to do was smile and crook her finger.

Jessie came to her defense. "Give her a break, Cara. You got here a whopping two minutes ago, and that was early for you."

"That's okay, Jessie," Amanda said. "I guess I deserve a little ribbing. Sorry I'm late."

"You haven't missed anything," added Tanya, the fourth of Amanda's coven-mates. She offered a shy welcoming smile that deepened the dimples in her dark olive skin. "Noreen is still getting drinks."

Since Cara had appropriated Amanda's favorite chair, Jessie shifted closer to Tanya to give Amanda space on the couch. The leather cushion creaked as Amanda sat next to the long-legged blonde. One of the things she disliked most about the slick upholstery was the unflattering noises it made every time she shifted around on it.

"Good. Everyone's here," Noreen said, carrying a tray of silver goblets into the room. An identical tray already sat on the table with an insulated tub of ice and the three beverage carafes Noreen prepared for every gathering. The red one held cranberry juice, the blue one water, and the yellow one orange juice. If you wanted something else, you had to bring your own although Noreen frowned upon soda pop or energy drinks.

The women took turns serving themselves. Cara swirled her cranberry juice and twisted her lips into a disappointed frown. "Now all we need is some vodka."

Jessie shuddered. "Bleh. Too early in the day for me."

It was 9:15 AM according to the clock on the thick mantle above Noreen's river-stone fireplace. Amanda echoed her friend's reaction.

Cara opened her mouth to make the inevitable snarky remark about how conservative or boring the others were, but Noreen interrupted her. "I have an announcement to make," she said, setting down her goblet.

Once all eyes had turned to her, she sat up straight in her high-backed antique chair and placed her hands on the gold-painted arm rests. "Elder Evelina Barritt is retiring from the Court of Elders, and I have been nominated to replace her."

Amanda and all of her coven-mates stared in shocked silence at the incredible news. The Court of Elders consisted of five witches who presided over the policies and guidelines for all practitioners of elemental witchcraft across the entire world. Only the most powerful witches were nominated.

All of the women extended their congratulations, and Noreen tilted her head in proud acknowledgment.

"But who will teach me?" Tanya asked in a pleading voice. She had asked to join the Gold Ridge Coven specifically because she wanted to learn from Noreen. Both women were fire witches, and Tanya had been learning the craft quickly from the respected adept.

Noreen waved the question away. "I haven't been elected, only nominated. It will be months before the Coven Conclave makes a final decision. By then, your apprenticeship could be over. It would be over already if you would stop holding yourself back."

Tanya lowered her gaze to her goblet.

"What will happen to the coven?" Cara asked. If the conclave elected Noreen to the Court of Elders, she would no longer have time to lead the Gold Ridge Coven.

Noreen looked around at all four women. "That will be up to the four of you and the conclave. Amanda or Jessie could petition for adept status and take over the coven." Noreen wasn't snubbing Cara by omitting her as a candidate. Cara had only recently been elevated from apprentice to crafter, and being accepted as an adept was a long way off for her. "Or you could disband and join other covens."

Ugh. Joining a new coven didn't hold much appeal for Amanda. It took time for coven members to work well together, assuming it *ever* happened. Their group had its problems, but the problems were known and everyone had managed to adjust. On top of that, most of the other covens in the area were already at or beyond the optimal five members needed for a full casting circle. Joining another coven would mean becoming an alternate, which would reduce her opportunities to practice.

Amanda looked at Jessie, whose expression of distaste seemed to mirror her own thoughts on the matter. Would Jessie be willing to lead the coven? It was a big responsibility and one that Amanda wasn't interested in taking on at the moment. She intended to put most of her energy into solving the Reggie problem, so she couldn't let the coven tie her down.

Cara didn't look very enthusiastic either. None of the options would look good from her perspective. If she stayed, she would chafe under Jessie's leadership, so joining a new coven might be the better choice. She adopted a mock-cheerful attitude and said to Noreen, "We'll just have to hope you don't get elected."

"That *is* the most likely turn of events," Noreen said sourly.

"Do you even want the position?" Amanda asked.

"If anyone else were retiring, I'd probably decline the nomination. But with Barritt gone, we'll need someone with sense on the court to balance the remaining opinions."

"Who else was nominated?" Jessie asked.

"I don't know yet," Noreen answered. She cleared her throat. "But that's enough about my nomination. Last month, we discussed Amanda's *lupusdaemon* exorcism spell. Does anyone have any final questions about that before we move on?"

Cara held up her hand. "I do." Looking at Amanda, she said, "I want to know more about the after-effects. Does Kyle still have the physical *enhancements* you mentioned last month, or have they started to fade?"

"He still has them." If one of the other women had asked the question, Amanda might have elaborated.

Cara gave Amanda a mocking smile. "Have you discovered any *other* special abilities since then?"

"Nope."

"Oh, come on, Amanda. You've been sleeping with the man for weeks, and his *lupusdaemon* was a slut. Are you sure it didn't leave him with any other special *attributes?*"

Noreen interrupted at that point. "If no one has any serious questions for Amanda, I'll consider the matter closed."

Feigning an innocent expression, Cara said, "But I'm completely and totally serious, Mistress. You're the one who is always telling us that we need to consider *all* of the consequences of every spell we cast."

Cara was right, and Kyle did have one residual attribute that Amanda hadn't mentioned the previous month. "Actually, there is something," Amanda admitted.

Cara leaned forward eagerly. In a conspiratorial voice, she said, "Oh, do tell."

"Kyle can see magical auras."

Cara sat back with a puzzled expression. The revelation was apparently not what her dirty mind had imagined.

Noreen, who was aware of Kyle's unexpected gift, frowned in disapproval. "You shouldn't have shared that."

The Ternion Order had requested that everyone who knew about Kyle's ability to see magical auras keep it a secret until they could learn more about it. If all *lupusdaemons* had the gift, then they had managed to hide it for a very long time. As with breaking an encryption code, knowing the opposition's secret was more useful while they remained unaware of your knowledge.

Amanda believed the covens had a right to know. If demons could detect the use of magic and identify the source element like Kyle could, they would have an advantage in any encounter with a witch who was unaware of that ability. Although they were both members of the Order, Noreen's loyalty to the organization was much stronger than hers. For Amanda, the Order were mostly a means to an end.

"Sorry, Mistress," Amanda said. "It kind of slipped out. I sometimes forget that not all of us are in the Order."

The excuse was a stretch. Technically, Amanda and Noreen were the only coven members who were in the order. Jessie was married to Jonathan Pesce, a journeyman in the Order's tactical discipline. Cara and Tanya were aware of the Order, but had expressed no interest in becoming members.

The look Noreen gave her showed that her coven leader wasn't fooled by the lie. "None of you are to discuss Kyle's ability here or anywhere else. Do you understand?" She looked around at the room and was answered by a chorus of "Yes, Mistress" from the other four women.

Jessie, ever the peacemaker, changed the subject. "Speaking of werewolves, Deputy Arpin brought Reggie into the hospital a few days ago. He had a nasty gash on his arm."

Amanda clutched Jessie's arm. "Was he okay? What happened?"

"He was fine," Jessie said, patting Amanda's hand. "He just needed a bunch of stitches."

"I thought werewolves could heal themselves," Cara said.

"They can," Jessie confirmed, "but the cut was practically to the bone. Although he would have healed on his own eventually, the stitches closed the wound and sped things along. I'll bet he was able to pull them out by the time he got home."

Jessie's reassurances only partially settled Amanda's concerns. She didn't care about what happened to the demon, but she did care about what happened to her brother's body.

Thinking about the hospital incident, her thoughts took a turn that made her mouth go dry. Whatever plans she might make for getting her brother back depended on her having access to his body. What if the demon left the area for some reason?

Worse, what if the demon transferred to a new body as Clarissa had done? When a werewolf took a new body at *Vollmond Ritus*, the Full Moon Ritual, the previous body always died. Always. It was one reason why everyone believed the original human spirit that inhabited the body was lost forever once the demon took full possession.

Her mission to save Reggie was on borrowed time. Two years had already been lost since he was possessed. How much longer did she have? There was no way to know. She might have years, months, or only weeks. Or it might already be too late.

While Amanda fretted silently, Noreen took control of the conversation. "Moving on, I have several ideas for topics we can explore next. I'd like to focus on Tanya's training, so we may have to cover some ground that is already familiar to some of you."

"You don't have to make special arrangements for me," Tanya objected. "We should work on something that will benefit everyone."

"It's *always* about her," Cara complained. "There are four of us here, and I think we all deserve consideration."

Jessie shrugged and said, "What's the difference? Anything we practice will improve everyone's skills."

Noreen's annoyed gaze flicked from speaker to speaker. Then she stared at Amanda with a raised eyebrow, waiting for her to chime in.

Amanda had an idea that might settle the matter. "Divination," she suggested.

Cara clapped her hands together. "Yes, please! That sounds like fun."

Cara liked the idea because divination was literally in her element: air. For most of the spell castings, she would be prime, the witch who performed the working, and the rest of them would be pillars, the supporting witches at each compass point on the casting circle.

Noreen gazed steadily at Amanda. She narrowed her eyes in consideration and then nodded. "All right, we'll start with divination. Did you have anything specific in mind?"

Divination covered a lot of ground, but for Amanda's purposes, there was one area that would be most useful in the near term. She tried to be nonchalant about her suggestion. "How about location spells?"

"Location spells," Noreen repeated. "That is rather specific. Do you seek something in particular? Or some*one* perhaps?"

Noreen undoubtedly suspected Amanda's true intentions. As her coven mistress and her former training master for the Order, Noreen knew Amanda far too well. The question was whether or not she would interfere. Noreen had opposed Amanda's exorcism of Kyle's demon because she thought it was too dangerous, but in the end, she had helped Amanda perform the ceremony.

As long as Amanda respected the needs of the entire coven, Noreen probably wouldn't get in her way. "We should probably practice object *and* person location spells. The spells work differently, and they're both useful."

Noreen stared at Amanda for a moment, debating the suggestion. She looked around the room and saw the eagerness in the faces of the other coven members. "All right. Location spells it is. We'll do object location first. Cara, you will be prime. Tanya, I want you to pay close attention because you will be prime for the second casting."

"Yes, mistress," Tanya responded.

Object location was generally easier than person location, so the approach made sense. Amanda could be patient and wait for the chance to practice person location, which was what she truly wanted. When the time was right, she had to be able to find Reggie no matter where he might be.

CHAPTER 5

Desecration

The next morning, the jarring ring of the phone awakened Amanda from a Sunday-morning sleep-in at Kyle's. After a disturbing and brief conversation with Lucille, Amanda and Kyle were out the door within minutes, driving to the farm as fast as traffic and safety allowed.

Amanda opened the passenger door and jumped out as soon as the Explorer's tires slid to a stop. Kyle turned off the engine and was right behind her as she hurried toward the farmhouse.

Lucille stood waiting for them at the screen door. Her glaring eyes and furrowed brow reflected the anger and concern Amanda had heard in her voice when she called to let them know that someone had broken in and ransacked Amanda's workspace. Amanda wasn't sure what to expect, but her heart was in her throat in anticipation of what she might find.

Amanda slowed in response to a nagging feeling and suddenly came to a stop. Kyle bumped into her and mumbled an apology. She held up a hand to silence him. "Wait. Something's wrong."

Hayworth Farm was a designated Order sanctuary, and, as such, it was warded against trespass. Amanda had set those wards herself, so their presence hummed reassuringly in the back of her mind whenever she was within their perimeter. Standing quietly, she sensed nothing. "The wards are down," she said.

Lucille frowned. "I suspected as much. When you come inside, you'll see why."

Amanda followed Lucille into the house and up the stairs to her office. She stood at her office door, stunned by the mess that greeted her. Every drawer and file had been dumped onto the bed. The thief had taken Amanda's computer, pulling free all of the cords and leaving all of the peripherals behind.

"Can you tell if anything is missing?" Kyle asked, looking over her shoulder into the room.

"My computer," she answered in a subdued tone. "I'll have to reorganize everything before I can tell what else they might have taken."

As Amanda walked farther into the room, a chill worked its way up her spine. She wrapped her arms tightly around herself and realized she was shaking. Thank goodness Lucille had taken an overnight trip to Spokane, and she had been at Kyle's house when the intruders broke in. Amanda whipped her head toward Lucille. "Could they still be here in the house somewhere?" she said in a whisper.

"No," Lucille answered without hesitation. "This has been my home all my life. I would know if anyone unwelcome were here. A stench lingers just from their passing through."

Amanda nodded and relaxed a bit, trusting her psychic friend's instincts. Then she jumped at the rumble of an arriving vehicle outside.

Lucille gave her a reassuring wave of her hands. "I called the Order. They said we shouldn't touch anything until their techs have had a chance to investigate."

Amanda nodded again and visually inspected the mess, hoping to spot a pattern that would reveal the thieves' intentions. One word immediately came to mind: *thorough*.

"There's more," Lucille said. She hesitated before adding, "They visited the moon shrine."

Dread gripped her heart as Amanda hurried past Kyle and Lucille to the attic stairwell. She ran up the steps and paused in the open doorway at the top. Her nose tingled from a metallic odor, and it was then that she became certain they weren't dealing with ordinary thieves.

The bench Amanda used for her altar had been tipped over, her glass water pitchers shattered into pieces across the wooden floor. Her bookshelves had been emptied of the tomes and artifacts she'd carefully arranged upon them. The books had been thrown haphazardly into a pile as if they were fuel for a bonfire. Every other item had been hurled against the back wall, the more fragile items reduced to a heap of broken trash along the baseboard.

But the state of her casting circle disturbed Amanda most of all. The five-foot-diameter circle was engraved into a two-inch concrete pad with round candle depressions at each of the cardinal compass points. When casting spells, Amanda poured holy water into the circle to purify the workspace and protect herself from dark spirits. Someone had filled the circle with a dark red liquid.

As Kyle came up the stairs behind her, Amanda took a few stumbling steps into the room. Unable to believe the scope of the desecration, she uttered a cry of despair. Her stomach lurched, and she dropped to her knees with her hands covering her mouth. Tears mercifully obscured her vision.

Kyle knelt next to her and put his arm around her. He probably didn't fully understand the depth of the violation he was witnessing, but he had no difficulty interpreting her reaction to it. "I'm so sorry," he said. "I can't believe someone did this. It seems so … extreme."

Amanda closed her eyes and forced herself to breathe evenly, fighting against hiccups. Kyle was right. What someone had done to her precious moon shrine was extreme. Hateful, even. And dark. Oh, so very dark.

In spite of the early afternoon sun pushing into the room through the glass cupola, the space was gloomy with shadows that seemed thick enough to taste. The blood that desecrated her circle had not only wiped away every vestige of her most recent consecration, but it had attracted dark spirits like a carcass attracted vultures. It would take days of cleansing before she could use the moon shrine again, and she'd probably need help to eliminate the spiritual stain.

While she stared sadly at her ruined casting circle, a flash of violet caught Amanda's attention. Crawling on hands and knees, she moved to the edge of the concrete pad. Sitting at the center of the circle was a small black figurine of a frog with tiny violet gemstones for eyes. The gems caught the light perfectly, reflecting it directly into her eyes.

Had something survived all the destruction? She didn't remember owning a black frog figurine. But it was beautiful, and she felt compelled to hold it. She reached out to pick it up, but Kyle's hand grabbed her arm when her fingers were just inches away.

An edge of panic tinged his raised voice, ripping her attention from the frog. "I said, don't touch it!"

Waking from the daze that had gripped her, Amanda snatched her hand back from the figurine and sat back on her heels. She turned her head and looked at Kyle uncomprehendingly. "Why are you yelling at me?"

Kyle waved his hand in front of her face. "Didn't you hear me the first time? There's something *wrong* with that thing."

"He's right. Stay back," said a male voice from behind them. Amanda and Kyle turned around to discover a tall figure standing in the doorway. He wore a knee-length black duster over black jeans and a black silk shirt. To complete the dark ensemble, he wore a wide-brimmed felt hat, also black.

All he needed was a white priest's collar and he would look like a refugee from a *Saturday Night Live* skit.

The man strode forward and knelt at the edge of the concrete pad. He muttered what sounded like a prayer and reached toward the frog. As his hand crossed the red-filled circle, a blood-freezing screech filled the room. An unseen force hurled the man backward. He hit the floor in a tuck and rolled smoothly to his feet, as if he'd practiced the maneuver dozens of times. He picked up his hat and brushed at his duster, giving the figurine a disdainful glance. "Cursed. Just as I suspected."

"Who *are* you?" Amanda asked, getting to her feet.

The man stepped forward and held out his hand. "Amanda Clark, I presume? I'm Father Guido Sarducci."

Amanda hesitated before shaking his warm hand. His deadpan expression and dark eyes gave no hint of a jest. "You've got to be kidding me," she said.

He winked at her and smiled. "Admit it. That's what you were thinking."

Amanda lowered her eyes and felt her cheeks heat. "Maybe a little."

He released her hand and shook Kyle's. "Nathaniel Blackstone of the Ternion Order at your service." Tilting his head toward the desecrated casting circle, he added, "Cleaning up this mess won't be easy."

"So it seems," Amanda agreed. After watching Blackstone get blasted half-way across the room, she was sure that *won't be easy* was an understatement. Amanda frowned at the frog and the sinister violet glint of its eyes, embarrassed at how easily it had beguiled her. "You said the figurine is cursed?"

Blackstone slowly walked around the casting circle, using the toe of his boot to kick aside the shards of glass and ceramic that littered the floor. "Indeed. A strong one, at that. Someone really doesn't like you."

Granted. But who?

The Selkirk Pack was the obvious answer, but the only magic the werewolves could command was their ability to heal themselves and to transform.

The desecration of Amanda's moon shrine appeared to be the work of a dark coven. Yet the Order had stamped out every known dark coven long ago. The few that were rumored to still exist were as secretive as they were rare. Invading a sanctuary of the Order and using dark magic so openly was like sending up a signal flare. It was as if they were daring the Order to come after them.

When Amanda turned her attention back to Nathaniel Blackstone, he had completed his circuit and was standing with one arm crossed under the other. His hand rubbed at his chin as he considered the figurine.

"What would it have done to me?" she asked. "Do you know?"

He shook his head slowly. "I'll know more when I dismantle it, but my guess is that it was designed to lure you and kill you."

Amanda's mouth dropped open. Her blood froze when she thought about how close she had come to falling into the trap. Kyle put his arm around her to comfort her, and she touched her hand to his to let him know she appreciated it. She'd been in some nasty scrapes, but no one had set out to take her life before. Circumstances were worse than she had imagined.

"What I'd like to know," Blackstone continued, nodding toward Kyle, "is how your friend knew about it."

Kyle hesitated and looked at Amanda for guidance. She nodded encouragement to answer since Blackstone was apparently there to help. He would need all the information they could provide.

"I can see an aura when magic is active," Kyle explained. He pointed at the frog. "That thing was drawing Amanda to it with some kind of violet energy."

Blackstone took a step closer to Kyle and looked directly into his eyes. "Interesting. Tell me, Kyle: does violet energy have special meaning to you?"

A brief look of confusion crossed Kyle's face. "How do you know my name?"

Blackstone smiled. "How could I not? You're famous. The first person to survive the werewolf's curse."

Kyle gave Blackstone a sidelong look. "You mean the second."

Blackstone scoffed. "*Technically* you're the second, but not from a practical standpoint. The first survivor of a *lupusdaemon* exorcism was murdered by the local pack three days later."

Kyle's face went pale, and Amanda returned his favor by slipping her arm around his waist. "How do you know that?" she asked Blackstone. "I couldn't find anything about the survivor of the first exorcism."

"I have … unique sources of information," he answered. "Which is why I'm surprised that I didn't know about Kyle's unusual ability to see auras."

"That ability is still under study, and the Order have declared it need-to-know," Amanda said, an apology in her tone.

"Indeed?" Blackstone said, tilting his head to the side as he considered her comment. "You disagree with that declaration?"

Blackstone was too perceptive for Amanda's comfort. She'd have to watch what she said around him. "As it relates to Kyle, I *do* agree. Kyle's ability might be something the demon left behind, or it might have been dormant, and the demon possession activated it somehow. What bothers me is hiding the information that *demons* might be able to see auras."

"Ah," said Blackstone. "I understand." He turned his attention back to Kyle. "I'd still like to know what made you wary of the figurine's violet energy."

"Different kinds of magic have different auras," Kyle answered. "Amanda's auras are green. Some enchanted objects have a white glow to them. The only time I've seen a violet aura before now was when a werewolf transformed right in front of us. When I saw violet energy stretching between the figurine and Amanda just now, it … disturbed me."

"Fascinating," said Blackstone. "You were wise to follow your instincts. The curse that lurks within that figurine and the glamour that lured Amanda are most certainly constructs of dark magic."

Amanda glanced toward the door to the moon shrine and then back to Blackstone. "I'm surprised the Order didn't send a full crisis team."

"Oh, I'm sure they have," Blackstone said. "I happened to be visiting with the director when the call came in. As I have some experience with hunting dark-magic practitioners, he accepted my offer to take a look."

Amanda withdrew her arm from Kyle and straightened her posture. If this man had a personal meeting with the regional Director of the Hunt, he was no ordinary hunter. Only master hunters were invited into the director's presence.

Putting his skills into context with her situation, Amanda made a mental leap. "Your presence in the area and what happened here aren't coincidences."

The man in black tipped his head down, concealing most of his face with the brim of his hat. A grim smile was all she could see. "I couldn't be sure until I saw what happened here for myself, but I believe you are correct." He lifted his head and his dark, shadowed eyes looked into hers. "It appears that my mission has led me to your doorstep, Journeyman Hunter Amanda Clark. I'm afraid your life is about to become *interesting*."

~

Amanda stopped to listen as the rumble of vehicles approaching the farmhouse filtered through the cupola windows. Seconds later, the front door opened, and Lucille's calm voice carried up the stairwell. "They're upstairs," she said.

"Upstairs?" retorted the angry voice of Master Hunter Noreen Thornquist. "Amanda knows better than that. She's going to get herself killed!"

Blackstone raised an eyebrow at Amanda and twisted his mouth into a half smile. Amanda sighed, disappointed that Noreen would undoubtedly find out how close she had come to fulfilling that prophecy.

Footsteps pounded up two sets of stairs, and Noreen entered the room in a huff. "Amanda. Take Kyle and—"

Spotting the man in black, she stopped with her command unfinished. "Blackstone," she breathed. Glancing at the ruined casting circle, she added, "Your timing is uncanny, as always."

"We meet again, Master Hunter Thornquist. I was just getting to know Amanda and Kyle."

"Hell of a place for introductions," Noreen chided.

Tilting his head toward the casting circle, Blackstone retorted, "Your description is almost literally accurate, all things considered."

Noreen folded her arms. "Yes, well, I would like to get Kyle and Amanda out of here until I can evaluate the damage and check for traps."

"Good idea," Blackstone agreed. "You'll find the cursed figurine at the center of the casting circle of particular interest."

Noreen leaned to look past Amanda. Spotting the black frog, she shifted her gaze back to Amanda's face. "Did you touch it?"

"No. Kyle stopped me when he noticed a magical aura coming from it." Noreen turned her intense gaze on Kyle. He just swallowed and nodded.

Good, Amanda thought. *He's finally learning how to deal with her.*

"Very well." Noreen waved her hands in a shooing motion. "I would like everyone to wait downstairs until I call you."

Blackstone stepped forward, placing himself directly in front of Noreen. "Before any more decisions are made, I would like to take command of this investigation. Do you dispute my authority to do so?"

Noreen's glare could have burned wood, but it didn't seem to faze Blackstone. After a stare-down that lasted several seconds, she lowered her eyes and took a deep breath. "I do not."

Amanda's estimation of Blackstone jumped up several levels. It was the first time she had ever seen Noreen back down from anyone without a fight.

"Thank you," Blackstone said. "I would like to have your cooperation and your team's assistance. The director is already aware of my interest in this matter."

Noreen narrowed her eyes at him. "What *is* your interest?"

"I should think that would be obvious," he answered, waving toward the casting circle. "The vandalism committed here has all the hallmarks of a dark coven."

Noreen shook her head slightly. "There's more. You anticipated this, somehow."

Blackstone was taken aback by the accusation. "Not true. Your confidence in my abilities is flattering, but I assure you that the boldness of this attack on Amanda's life is an unexpected and disconcerting surprise."

Noreen folded her arms. The set of her face showed she wasn't buying it. "So, you just *happened* to be in the area."

Blackstone glanced at Amanda and then his gaze held Kyle's. "Kyle, you have been indoctrinated into the Order, correct?"

"Yes, sir," Kyle answered.

"Good." Blackstone lowered his voice so it wouldn't carry. "Since you are both already deeply involved in this incident, I'm adding you and Amanda to the crisis team. Share nothing about what you learn during this investigation with anyone outside the team, including other members of the Order. Do you both understand?"

"Yes, sir," Kyle and Amanda answered in unison.

Blackstone turned his attention back to Noreen. "We will submit no status updates other than what I report to the director himself. At the conclusion of this investigation, you may prepare a standard incident report and allow the Order's analysts to debrief you."

Amanda was shocked at the level of secrecy he demanded, but Noreen simply nodded her head, apparently expecting it. Operating without status updates meant they would be working without the support of the Order's analysts and logistical resources. Only a few people would be aware of their activities.

Amanda came to a disturbing conclusion. "You think we have spies in the Order?"

Blackstone's expression was unreadable. "Every organization is susceptible to infiltration. The Order are very good at weeding out undesirables over time, but when dark magic is involved and the stakes are high, we can't afford to take intelligence risks."

That level of secrecy came with a price, however. Kyle was as quick to see it as Amanda. "So, we're on our own," he stated.

"Not at all," Blackstone said. "We can get whatever help we need, but we have to weigh that need against the risk of exposing the operation."

Blackstone stepped over to the door of the moon shrine and closed it. The shadows that filled the room seemed to strengthen, filling Amanda with dread and a strong urge to leave. She moved farther away from the casting circle, taking Kyle by the arm and pulling him with her.

Returning to the group, Blackstone addressed Noreen. "You are correct that I did not just happen to be in the area. I've been tracking an elusive dark coven for some time now. I was beginning to believe they had disbanded until I learned of several incidents attributed to dark magic in Western Montana that convinced me otherwise. Reports of dark magic are often exaggerated, but someone from my team always checks them out. I followed up the lead myself and found signature indications of the coven I've been hunting. I reported my findings and my intent to conduct an investigation to your regional director. I was in his office when operations informed him of Hunter Hayworth's call."

Amanda fidgeted through Blackstone's explanation. Frustration was building, and when she stopped to wonder at her own agitation, she realized what was bothering her. Getting caught up in Blackstone's investigation was going to be a major setback in her goal of saving Reggie. On the one hand, she could use the cloak of secrecy to access Order resources without explanation, but on the other, Blackstone would be monitoring every move she made.

Could she bow out of the investigation? No way. Working on an independent crisis team was a rare and coveted opportunity. Passing on that opportunity would raise too much suspicion. Besides the interlopers had destroyed *her* moon shrine and targeted *her* for assassination by frog. She wanted to know who had attacked her and why they had done it. The best way to get answers was to be part of the crisis team.

Amanda still had trouble believing someone was out to get her. Everyone was assuming she was the target. Was the enchanted frog really meant for her? Or was this whole incident part of some elaborate trap the dark coven had prepared for Blackstone?

Either way, she had to do her part to help with the investigation even if that meant postponing her plans to save Reggie. Having a dark coven in the area was a serious matter. If not for Kyle's intervention, she might have died. She couldn't help Reggie if she got herself killed.

"You still with us, Amanda?"

Blackstone's question derailed her train of thought. Everyone was staring at her.

"What? Sorry, this is just … so much at once."

Even Noreen sympathized with a nod and a glance around the room. "What happened here is intolerable. We will find who did this and punish them."

"In the meantime," Blackstone said, "I would like you and Kyle take a closer look at the damage to your office and tell me if anything is missing. This was not random vandalism. If we are to anticipate their next move, we must know *why* the perpetrators attacked your home."

Chapter 6
Connections

Kyle followed Amanda back to her office, where they found a hunter processing the scene for forensic evidence. Having nothing to do but wait until the man completed his task, Kyle suggested they grab a bite to eat. Lucille was busy feeding the rest of the crisis team and had sandwiches waiting.

"How does it look?" asked Journeyman Hunter Jonathan Pesce. Jonathan was sitting at the kitchen table with a few bites left of his lunch. His dark-green fatigues and the Kevlar vest draped over the back of his chair identified him as part of the tactical team. Although no insignia declared it, he was also the team leader.

Kyle grinned and stepped forward to shake his friend's hand. Jonathan had been the first to encourage him to join the Order and gave him temporary work at Pesce Marina when Kyle had been between jobs. "Good to see you. I've been meaning to come down to the marina, but my training has been intense."

"Don't worry," said Jonathan with a smile. "Things will settle down once the Order figure out where you fit best."

"You should go up and see what happened before the cleanup begins," Amanda suggested.

"That bad?"

"Worse." Amanda then explained what had happened in her office and the moon shrine.

Jonathan's blue eyes went cold when Amanda got to the part where she had almost touched the enchanted frog. He got up from the table and put his empty plate in the sink. Kyle sat in Jonathan's vacated space with his sandwich, and Amanda took the opposite chair.

Leaning against the kitchen counter, Jonathan folded his arms. "Do you know what would have happened if you'd touched the frog?"

"Not exactly. Blackstone seems to think it was a deadly curse."

Jonathan glanced toward the stairs with an alarmed expression. He moved over to the table and lowered his voice. "Master Nathaniel Blackstone is here?"

Taking Jonathan's cue to speak quietly, Amanda asked, "What do you know about him?"

"Very little," he answered, "and I think that's the way he likes it. Blackstone's team is strictly black ops."

"Noreen seems to know him," Amanda said. "I don't think they get along."

"Does Noreen get along with anyone?" Kyle contributed with a chuckle.

Jonathan glanced over his shoulder toward the stairway. "Watch it, my friend. She has an amazing knack for showing up right when you say something like that. Besides, I work just fine with her."

"That's because you have the patience of a saint," Amanda commented.

Jonathan shrugged. "I've been thoroughly trained in the art of patience by a twelve-year-old son and an eight-year-old daughter."

Amanda laughed and said, "Maybe we'll all get a chance to learn about the man behind the curtain."

"What do you mean?" Jonathan asked with an edge to his voice.

"Blackstone just took over the investigation," Amanda answered.

"With nary a quibble from Noreen," Kyle added.

Jonathan ran his tanned hand through his short, sun-bleached blond hair. "That's unfortunate."

"What's wrong?" Kyle asked.

"I don't know much about Nathaniel Blackstone," Jonathan answered, "but I do know that wherever his team goes, the body count tends to be high." He paused and looked from Amanda to Kyle. "On both sides."

Kyle thought that might explain why Blackstone attached himself to local crisis teams. "We're cannon fodder," he concluded.

Jonathan glanced over his shoulder toward the stairs again. "I wouldn't go that far. You have to understand that, for people like Blackstone, the mission is top priority because the stakes are always high. Since the mission is also usually dangerous, a certain amount of collateral damage is expected."

Kyle exchanged a look with Amanda. Her frown of resignation mirrored his own feelings. He brushed at some sandwich crumbs on his pants leg. "I guess we'll just have to help Blackstone as best we can without becoming part of the collateral damage."

Footsteps thumping down the stairs announced the arrival of the forensics tech. He came into the kitchen with his black metal case and accepted a sandwich from Lucille. "It's all yours," he said to Amanda. "I got everything I need for the lab."

Kyle and Amanda got up from the table so the tech could sit down.

"Thanks," Amanda said. "We'll get started."

As they walked up the stairs toward Amanda's office, Kyle said, "Good thing the Order have their own forensics team. Still, it's weird to have someone break in and *not* call the police."

"True, but imagine how much fun it would be to explain the moon shrine to local authorities," Amanda replied.

Kyle laughed. "Yeah, I can see it now. Well, officer, in my spare time I'm a good witch, and now we think an evil witch is out to get me. Oh, and don't touch the cursed frog."

Walking into Amanda's office, they assessed the scope of work. Kyle offered to straighten up her desk and collect all the items that had been knocked to the floor. He knew where most of that stuff went. Amanda took on the task of straightening up her files.

About half an hour later, Amanda swore. "I should have known," she said.

"What did you find?"

"It's what I didn't find. All of my notes about the exorcism are gone."

Kyle stared at her for a minute, processing the implications. "This is all tied together. The dark coven Blackstone is hunting and the *lupusdaemon* exorcism are related somehow."

Amanda shook her head. "That doesn't make sense. What would a dark coven want with the exorcism ceremony? Dark witches *summon* demons and practically worship them. They certainly wouldn't want to exorcise them."

"Maybe that's the connection," Kyle mused. "The dark coven doesn't want you or anyone else exorcising werewolves."

"Okay, but stealing my notes isn't going to solve *that* problem. I've archived a copy with the Order. Besides, I could probably reproduce the ceremony from memory if I had to."

"That's probably why they tried to kill you," Kyle interjected.

"Noreen helped with the ceremony," Amanda continued. "I think she could replicate it in a pinch. You and I went over it in detail. I'm sure you could reproduce it, too."

Kyle stared at her for a moment. "I think you just named their hit list."

"But why a dark coven?" Amanda insisted. "I could understand the Selkirk Pack coming after us. We've been expecting that to happen for two months now."

Kyle shook his head. "I don't know. Maybe they're afraid of your magic and need powerful witches on their side. Maybe they hired the dark coven to cover their involvement so they wouldn't draw fire from the Order."

"I'm glad I put you on the investigation team," said an amused voice from the doorway. Kyle and Amanda both jumped in surprise.

Blackstone stepped into the room. "I like how you two bounce proposals off each other without becoming enamored of one particular argument. Detached analytical thinking is rare and valuable in my profession."

Kyle wondered if being detached was what helped Blackstone sleep at night. Otherwise, it would be hard to live with all that "collateral damage" he allegedly left in his wake.

"He's better at it than I am," Amanda said, tilting her thumb toward Kyle.

"What can I say?" Kyle responded with a shrug. "I like problem solving."

Blackstone addressed Amanda. "Am I to understand that the interlopers stole the notes relating to your famous exorcism?"

Amanda nodded, throwing a handful of files back onto the bed. "Every one."

"But you followed protocol and archived a copy with the Order?"

"I did."

"Good. However, the thieves may not be aware of that."

"Surely they'd expect me to make copies," Amanda objected. "It cost me a lot to put that ceremony together."

"*Did* you make other copies?" Blackstone asked. "Placing one in a safe-deposit box, perhaps?" He glanced at Kyle. "Forgive me for jumping to conclusions, but do you keep a copy at Kyle's home?"

"No, sir," Amanda answered. Kyle was pleased to see that she displayed no embarrassment about their relationship.

"Once I gave the Order a copy, I didn't see a need for more," she added. "And yes, in answer to your unasked question, Kyle and I are a couple. Is that a problem?"

"Thank you for telling me," Blackstone said with a slight bow of his head. "And, no, it's not a problem unless the two of you make it a problem. So far, what I've seen of your working partnership is promising."

A boom rattled the house and an ear-splitting shriek came from the direction of the moon shrine. The light in the room dimmed as a shadowy stream flowed in through the doorway. It circled once and fled through the window, stirring the curtains as it passed.

As Kyle watched the shadow exit the room, the hairs on his neck and arms tingled. Four months previously, the sight would have thoroughly freaked him out. He still couldn't help his body's natural reactions to all the weird paranormal stuff that surrounded Amanda, but he was becoming more used to it.

Blackstone gave Amanda a grim smile. "It seems Master Hunter Thornquist has broken the dark coven's bindings on your casting circle. I can deal with the figurine now, and I'm sure she will want your help cleansing the circle."

As if on cue, Noreen yelled from the moon shrine. "Amanda! Get up here and help me. It's *your* damned casting circle."

"Direct and literal, as always," commented Blackstone with a chuckle.

Kyle had done what he could to help Amanda with her office. He would be of no use to her in the moon shrine. He hated to abandon her at the farm, but he'd had enough magic and shadows for one day.

"I feel like I'm in the way here," Kyle said glancing at his watch. "And I have a project I'm supposed to be working on, so maybe I should head home for now. Amanda, give me a call when you want me to come pick you up."

Kyle could see in her eyes that Amanda wished she could leave with him. She'd told him that his little house in town was like an oasis of normalcy in her unrelentingly paranormal existence. When he brought her home later, he would escort her to the couch and put a glass of wine in her hand. A little snuggle time in front of the fireplace would make her feel better.

But Blackstone had other plans. "That would not be a good idea."

Kyle waited for Blackstone to continue, but the master hunter's expression prompted him to figure it out for himself. *Why would going home be a bad idea?*

Thinking through it, Kyle frowned and said, "They don't know how many copies you made or where you put them. And they can't know for sure that the black frog worked as planned."

Amanda put her hand to her mouth. "They could be waiting for us at your house."

"Probably not waiting," Blackstone said, "but they may have left something nasty behind. We'll check it out with the entire team when we're done here."

Kyle reached out and squeezed Amanda's arm. "You do what you need to do. I'll try to make myself useful downstairs. Like Lucille says, there's always work to do on a farm."

"Speak to Hunter Pesce," Blackstone ordered. "We are going to use this sanctuary as our base of operations, so I want it secured. When we visit your home later, you and Amanda will gather what you need for an extended stay here."

"Yes sir," Kyle answered.

Kyle didn't mind staying at the farm for a while. Being with Amanda was the important thing—the location didn't matter. He could do his contract programming work from anywhere as long as he had his computer and an Internet connection. His training with the Order would undoubtedly be put on hold until the investigation was over.

The big problem was that he and Amanda would be under constant supervision, making it tough for either of them to work on Amanda's personal project. However, the dark-coven attack appeared to be related to Amanda's *lupusdaemon* exorcism. That connection might prove to be exactly the cover they needed to implement Amanda's plan to exorcise Reggie.

~

Jonathan's dark-green Toyota Sequoia led the procession that escorted Kyle's Explorer through town. Blackstone's enormous black Suburban filled his rear-view mirror.

Kyle tapped a finger on the steering wheel and said to Amanda, "If any of my neighbors see this, they'll think the FBI is busting me for something."

Amanda rubbed his shoulder. "They'll forget all about it when things return to normal."

Kyle glanced at her. *Sure. Like that will ever happen.*

She seemed to read his thoughts and laughed. "Okay. I mean normal in a relative sense. Or maybe in an *as-far-as-they-know* sense."

It was midday, so there was plenty of room along the curb for all three vehicles to stop together. Jonathan's rig blocked Kyle's driveway. As soon as the green SUV came to a stop, the doors opened and two men went swiftly around to the back. Jonathan and one other man approached the front. Kyle, Amanda, and Blackstone all stayed in their vehicles.

After peering through the windows, Jonathan signaled Blackstone as they'd arranged. Blackstone exited his Suburban and joined him at the front door. Once there, Blackstone bowed his head and put his palm on the door. After a few seconds, he nodded to Jonathan, who let them both in with the key Kyle had given him.

Kyle watched the shadows of the two men as they moved around in the house. After a quick tour, Jonathan came back outside and waved to Kyle and Amanda.

At first, Kyle thought all of their paranoia had been for nothing. Everything on the ground floor looked undisturbed. He ran up the stairs, skipping every other tread. Blackstone stood at the door to his bedroom.

"I'm guessing you had a safe here," he said, pointing toward the closet floor.

The question made Kyle's pulse race as he moved forward to take a look. Sure enough, someone had shredded the wooden closet floor and removed the small safe that used to be there. The lag bolts that fastened the safe to the floor weren't intended to stand up to a determined thief with a pry bar.

Kyle groaned. "Yes, sir." His landlord, Bob Daily, was going to throw him out for sure. First a fire in the bathroom and now this. The worst part was that none of it was his doing.

"Anything important in it?"

Kyle shook his head. "Nothing important to the Order. I had some spare cash, my passport, the title for my SUV … stuff like that."

"Do you have a computer here?"

"Of course," Kyle answered. "At least, I used to …"

Kyle hurried to the tiny second bedroom, which he had converted to an office when he started working from home. He had also added a second desk for Amanda to use when she visited on weekends.

Amanda was already in the room, surveying the damage with her hands on her hips. She looked over her shoulder as he entered the doorway. "They took both our computers."

"Dammit!" Kyle exclaimed. "Why are they doing this? I had nothing on my laptop that anyone else would care about. Replacing all of it is going to be a pain in the ass, not to mention expensive."

Amanda nodded in commiseration. "I know. Our notes on the exorcism were hand written. I intended to type them into my computer, but hadn't gotten around to it. They got nothing useful."

"Ah, but they did," Blackstone said from the doorway. "They learned that you probably didn't digitize the ceremony, which means you couldn't have disseminated it widely via electronic means. If you kept unprotected financial records on your computer, they also know where and when you spend money. They can deduce your habits, predict your movements, and find out who you spend time with."

Kyle gave Amanda a significant look. "It sounds like they don't have a specific plan yet. They're still collecting information."

Amanda's wry smile told him that she didn't miss the irony. She and Kyle were taking the same approach with regard to Reggie.

"That theory is consistent with what we've seen so far," Blackstone agreed. "Their immediate goal appears to be confiscating all records relating to the ceremony. To do that, they must figure out where all of the copies might be and who might be capable of reproducing it from memory."

Jonathan appeared behind Blackstone in the hallway. "We didn't find any evidence of electronic surveillance or timed explosives. I don't think this group is very high tech."

"Agreed," said Blackstone. "What they lack in technology, they make up for with determination and an unscrupulous use of magic."

Kyle shuddered at the thought of waking up in the middle of the night to the house exploding around him. His landlord would be *really* mad if that happened, but old Bob would have to satisfy himself with kicking Kyle off the premises in chunks.

It was as if Blackstone was reading his mind. "We're too exposed here," he said to Jonathan. "We need to get Kyle and Amanda back to the sanctuary. I think it's best if Noreen were to stay at the farm as well. I would also like you to double our tactical support."

Jonathan nodded and waved for Kyle to follow him. "Let's get you packed up."

On the drive back to Hayworth Farm, Kyle tried to make sense out of what was happening. On the surface, it was a straightforward problem. The Selkirk Pack, with the help of a dark coven, was trying to make sure a *lupusdaemon* exorcism never happened again. That meant eliminating all information sources related to it. At some point, they would have to figure out that the Order already had a copy, and going after Amanda would be pointless. Unless this was all about vengeance. But if that were true, why involve a dark coven?

There were too many variables in play. They needed to learn more about the motivations of their enemies. Until they did, they'd always be one step behind. When it came to Amanda's safety, being one step behind was unacceptable.

CHAPTER 7
Contingency

Dr. Adolphus Rutlinger stepped into the conference room Marcella had taken over in the Foundation's west wing. She stood at the table with a pile of papers laid out before her. Cyrus Fleming, her former coven's fire crafter, tapped away at the keyboard they'd attached to the computer they'd stolen.

Marcella glanced up at Rutlinger as she thumbed through Amanda's notes and diagrams related to the exorcism. "This is all very creative. I'm impressed with the bitch's ingenuity. If it weren't necessary to kill her, I'd have tried to convince her to join us." Something on one of the sheets caught her attention. She stopped to take a closer look, and then shook her head with disappointment. "She's an earth witch with a celestial affinity for the moon. Such a waste. She could have been useful."

Rutlinger was quite certain that Amanda Clark, the "bitch" in question, would never consider joining a dark coven, particularly one led by a werewolf. Amanda had proven that she was dedicated to the mission of recovering her brother, and that mission put her in direct opposition to Marcella, much to the young woman's misfortune. If Marcella's diabolical trap hadn't already killed her, it was only a matter of time.

"Have you found anything useful, Cyrus?" Marcella asked.

"No," the warlock answered in a surly tone as he opened up another document and started skimming it. "She has plenty of document files, and some of them relate to spells.

Her coven is apparently called the Gold Ridge Coven. I'm finding almost nothing about the exorcism or the Order."

Marcella gathered Amanda's papers and straightened them before slipping them into a manila envelope. "That's promising. If the laptops are equally devoid of information about the exorcism, it's possible we've arrived in time."

Rutlinger pursed his lips and gave her a doubtful look. "It's been nearly two months. Do you really think she hasn't transcribed them? Surely, her report to the Order would have included details of the ceremony, and if so, it's already too late."

Marcella curled her lip in disdain. "You'd like that, wouldn't you? If it's too late, then I'm wasting my time and might as well give up like the rest of you." She strode around the table and positioned herself in front of Rutlinger. "Don't get your hopes up. Even if the Order *has* made a copy of her notes, it may not be too late. The Order's paranoid secrecy and ponderous bureaucracy sometimes work in our favor."

Rutlinger's eyebrows rose in surprise at the implication. "You have spies in the Order?"

Marcella tapped her fingers on the thick envelope, apparently deciding how much to confide in him. "*Spies* might be too strong a word," she finally admitted. "Let's just say that one can often buy a breach of loyalty for the right consideration."

Reaching out his hand, Rutlinger asked, "Would you like me to dispose of that for you? It would make satisfying fuel for the fireplace."

Marcella stepped back, possessively tucking the envelope under her arm. "Absolutely not. If everything goes as planned, this will be the only remaining documentation. I will destroy it only after it no longer has value to me as leverage."

"Leverage for what?" Rutlinger asked, dropping his hand. It made him uncomfortable just having the papers in the building, much less seeing them in the possession of the dark witch. Would Iledaste allow Marcella to use the ceremony against her own kind if she perceived them as enemies? Could Marcella use it on herself to escape whatever bargain she'd made with Iledaste? It was all very confusing, and he didn't understand the situation well enough to predict the answers to either of those questions.

"Contingencies, Adolphus. I've been playing cat-and-mouse with the Order for a long time now, and it's always a dangerous game." Marcella tilted her head toward the envelope. "It would be foolish to throw away such a potentially valuable playing piece."

Rutlinger's discomfort grew in response to her cold and mercenary logic. Iledaste had always been a bit of a hot head, even for a demon. Now Marcella was the ice to Iledaste's fire. Together, they were bound to produce a flood of difficulties.

"I found something, Mistress," Cyrus interrupted. Marcella stepped behind him to look over his shoulder. He pointed at the screen. "Here is a list of everyone in her coven, along with contact information."

"Excellent," Marcella purred. "Figure out where those addresses are. If you have trouble, I'm sure Deputy Arpin can help you."

"I can save you some time," Rutlinger said. "Only Amanda Clark and Noreen Thornquist were present for the ceremony. The rest of the coven has no association with the Order that I'm aware of."

Marcella looked up and gave him a patronizing smile. "Let me worry about strategy. As you pointed out, it's been two months. Who knows what the witch shared with her coven. For all we know, they might have helped her research it."

Rutlinger nodded and casually left the room before Marcella could see the panic he felt building inside. If she murdered everyone in Amanda's coven and managed to destroy the Order's copy of the ceremony, the Order would be out for blood. And all of the clues Marcella was leaving behind would lead them straight to the Selkirk Pack. Her own mission accomplished, Marcella would probably disappear when things went out of control, leaving his pack as the only target of the Order's wrath.

CHAPTER 8

Protective Custody

A manda pushed aside the curtain at the sound of a car engine outside. Noreen's silver sedan came up the driveway, the tires picking up mud and spraying it along the side panels. Given her fastidious nature, Noreen would be cringing at the splattering noises. She was as bad as a recent California immigrant when it came to keeping her car clean.

Most North Idahoans quickly learned that it was a pointless effort, particularly if you lived on a dirt road. Idaho had four seasons: spring mud season, summer dust season, fall mud season, and winter slush season. If you timed a washing just right, your car could be clean for the two weeks in late spring when the roads had solidified but weren't yet dry enough to be dusty.

Amanda had been expecting Noreen—about an hour earlier, Lucille had rung to warn her what was coming. Lucille had received an anonymous phone call that claimed the entire Gold Ridge Coven was a target of the same group who destroyed her moon shrine. Lucille was with customers at her shop, *Rainbows and Butterflies,* so she couldn't go into too much detail. The bottom line was that Noreen was picking up the entire coven and bringing them to the farm.

The place was going to get crowded.

Amanda met the car at the front lawn where its passengers were unloading their traveling bags. "Welcome to Hayworth Farm," Amanda greeted them.

"You mean Hayworth Prison," Cara complained as she dragged her heavy suitcase out of the trunk.

"Don't be melodramatic," Jessie said. "We've all been placed in protective custody by the Order for our own good."

"I think *I* should be the one to decide what's good for me," Cara snapped.

Noreen stepped up behind Cara and ripped the suitcase from her hand. Heaving it back into the trunk, she said, "No one is forcing you to accept sanctuary. You should have said something earlier rather than pouting the entire drive here. It would have saved us both a lot of time." Noreen walked back around to the driver's side and opened the car door. "Get in."

Kyle had come onto the porch and opened the screen door. He stood at the top stair taking in the scene.

Cara looked from Noreen to Kyle and then back to Noreen. With an embarrassed duck of her head, she went around to the trunk of the car. "I'm sorry, Mistress. This is all just so sudden. If you really think I'm in danger, I'll take your word for it." She dragged her suitcase out of the trunk and flashed an apologetic smile at Noreen.

Noreen rolled her eyes and sighed. She flicked a glance at Amanda that warned her to be ready for trouble. It wasn't anything Amanda hadn't already been anticipating.

Might as well meet the issue head-on.

"Kyle, would you come over here?" Amanda called. "I'd like to introduce you to my coven."

Kyle hesitated for a second and then walked toward the cluster of women. Amanda introduced him to Cara, Tanya, and Jessie. She'd talked to him about the members of her coven, but it was the first time he'd met any of them other than Noreen. Jessie shook his hand and said she'd heard good things about him from her husband, Jonathan. Tanya gave him a shy smile and said it was nice to meet him.

Cara's gaze raked him up and down before settling on his face with a brazen grin. She cocked a hip and rolled her shoulders back, subtly emphasizing how well she filled her low-cut blouse. "It's so nice to finally meet you in the flesh, Kyle. Amanda has told us *all* about you."

Kyle blushed and seemed to be having difficulty keeping his gaze above Cara's neck. The slightly guilty glance he sent Amanda's way nearly made her laugh out loud. "Uh … nice to meet you too, Cara."

"Shall we go inside and get everyone settled?" Noreen's impatient tone made her question seem more like a command.

"Can I help carry anything?" Kyle asked.

Cara didn't miss a beat. She stepped forward and handed her suitcase to him. "How sweet of you to offer." After he effortlessly accepted the hand-off, she rubbed her hand over the curve of his bicep, squeezing lightly. "Ooh, somebody's been working out."

Kyle's blush deepened. He froze and looked toward Amanda. She wanted to step in and rescue him, but they were all going to be in close quarters for a while, and she wanted to see how well he'd handle Cara. So far, it wasn't looking promising. She folded her arms and lifted an eyebrow.

Kyle looked down at Cara, who stared back up at him with her light-blue eyes and dimpled coquettish smile. Amanda knew Cara had melted men a lot stronger than Kyle with that look. He took a breath and tried to rally. "Where should I take this?" he finally managed.

Cara's smile broadened. "Your room would be fine."

A flash of confusion crossed Kyle's face, followed by wide-eyed panic. "Uh … you do know that Amanda and I are together, right?"

Cara laughed and looked at Amanda. "Oh, Amanda. He's so adorable. Is he for real?" She looked at Kyle again and pursed her lips into an air kiss, making Kyle lean back in alarm. "Such an easy target," she said with a head shake.

Amanda finally took pity on Kyle and slipped her arm under his. Turning him away from the terrible little temptress whose shoulders were shaking from suppressed laughter, she led him toward the house. "It's only going to get worse," she warned him. "At some point, she'll corner you, and you'll be on your own. Think you can handle it?"

"Can't you do something?" he whispered.

"Not really," she answered truthfully. "We aren't exactly close friends, and that's just Cara being Cara. I've seen it before. By this time tomorrow, she'll have every male on the property eating out of her hand. Even gay men love her."

Kyle leaned his head toward hers. "But she's such a ..."

"Tramp," supplied Noreen as she strode up alongside them. Speaking to Amanda, she said, "Sorry to descend upon you like this. I assume Lucille told you about the anonymous call?"

"Yes. What made you take it seriously?"

"The caller knew to contact Lucille, so whoever it was obviously knows about the Order and our coven. What's more interesting is that the tipster must have inside knowledge about the dark coven as well."

Amanda had reached similar conclusions, but Noreen's experience often gave her deeper insights. The caller had to be close enough to the dark coven to be in on their plans. "An informant would be valuable," Amanda said.

Noreen waved a hand in frustration. "Assuming we could trust this person and had any way to get in contact. As it is, we must assume we will never hear from her again."

Lucille hadn't shared that detail. "Her?"

"The voice was altered and the message was only a few words, but Lucille is positive the caller was female."

Amanda smiled to herself. Such were the risks of contacting a psychic. Given a long enough conversation,

Lucille might have been able to assemble a complete image of the person on the other end of the phone. Which reminded her: "Could Lucille be a target?"

"It's impossible to know. If we believe the informant's warning, the dark coven is casting a wider net than we expected. I like that it implies they lack complete information about the exorcism and who was involved, but it also means they have to go after anyone who *might* know about it. I asked Lucille to close shop early today and remain at the sanctuary until this is over."

"I'll bet she didn't like that."

"I expected an argument, but she was unusually agreeable. I believe the break-in disturbed her more than she'll admit."

Amanda had to agree with that assessment. Lucille, who prided herself on her control and decisiveness, had seemed emotionally adrift after the dark-coven attack on her home. Amanda had restored the perimeter wards, and the Order had a strong tactical presence, but Amanda expected it would be a while before the farm would feel like a true sanctuary again.

~

Amanda wrinkled her nose as she stood next to Noreen in the moon shrine. Their efforts to remove all traces of blood from the casting circle had left a chemical odor of bleach lingering in the air. Revolted by the desecration, Amanda had been tempted to break the concrete pad into pieces and toss it, but creating a new pad would have been even more work than cleaning the old one.

With help from Noreen and Kyle, she had put the rest of her moon shrine back in order. The shelves were conspicuously empty and clean. Most of their contents had been shattered on the attic floor or otherwise damaged.

Blackstone had somehow disposed of the black frog figurine. He seemed to wield powerful magic although Amanda still wasn't sure where it came from. He artfully deflected every inquiry about his past or his skills. Noreen seemed to know something, but she was unwilling to discuss the matter.

"This might be a good opportunity for the coven to practice cleansing rituals," Noreen observed wryly.

Amanda's laugh trailed off into a sigh. "I think we'll have to do a bunch of them before I trust the circle for a serious working. This place is still a revolving door for dark spirits."

Noreen looked around the room using other senses than just her eyes. "It's better, now. We'll whip it into shape within a couple of days." Encouragement was a rare thing coming from her former master, and Amanda appreciated the effort.

Footsteps advancing up the stairway heralded the appearance of Blackstone with Kyle close behind.

Blackstone angled his head back toward the attic stairwell and the rest of the house below. "You appear to have multiplied in my absence." On his way up, he must have passed through the three coven refugees settling into their new environment. Lucille had closed her shop early as Noreen suggested, and she was back at home playing mother hen to her new brood of guests.

"True," Noreen said, "and we've run out of space to put everyone."

"You may have the living-room couch back," offered Blackstone. "My vehicle is equipped with adequate sleeping facilities, and I'm accustomed to using them."

"Thank you. We appreciate that."

"Bringing your coven here was wise," Blackstone added. "I should have suggested that myself. While I have doubts about the trustworthiness of the anonymous caller, we can't be too cautious." Turning to Amanda, he asked, "What other names might come to the attention of the dark coven? Did anyone else help you with the exorcism?"

"I didn't get much support from the Order. Everyone thought I was wasting my time, so I did most of the research myself. Noreen performed the ritual with me, and Kyle was there, of course. Lucille was at the house but didn't participate. I can't think of anyone else."

"What about Sherry?" Kyle asked.

"Who is Sherry?" Blackstone asked.

"She was my sort-of girlfriend when I ... had my werewolf problem," Kyle answered. "It's kind of a long story. Dr. Rutlinger invited her to stay at the Foundation under the guise of helping me get treatment, but she knows nothing about the supernatural stuff."

Blackstone looked sharply at Noreen. "The Order allowed this?"

"The Order wasn't informed," Noreen replied in a matter-of-fact voice, "though we later approved Amanda and Lucille's decision not to report the situation. The young lady went to the Foundation willingly and was supposedly free to leave at any time."

"So the only thing keeping her there was a lie," Blackstone said.

"You could say that, yes."

Blackstone's frown was disapproving. "Where is Sherry now?"

Kyle shrugged. "Last I heard, she was in California somewhere. We haven't stayed in touch."

Blackstone stood silently for a moment. Finally, he waved a hand in dismissal. "I doubt the dark coven will go looking for her if she remained ignorant of the true situation and wasn't at the farm when the exorcism took place. Besides, if *we* don't know where to find her, it's unlikely the dark coven would either." He turned his attention back to Amanda. "Anyone else? Perhaps someone who showed an interest in what you were doing or who helped you acquire the components you needed for your ritual?"

Amanda shook her head. "I get most of my components from Lucille or online."

"Except for the wolf skull," Kyle reminded her.

"Right, I got that from Derek Bell, a Native American artifact collector in Coeur d'Alene," Amanda explained. "He loaned me the wolf skull talisman that I needed to complete the ritual."

"This talisman was an integral part of the ritual?" Blackstone asked.

"Absolutely. The first time I tried the exorcism, it failed. The talisman seemed to function as a gateway to the abyss."

"Interesting. You returned the device to the collector afterward?"

"That was the deal," Amanda confirmed.

"Pity. I would have liked to have seen it. In any case, I doubt the dark coven would target the collector. The talisman is another matter. Mr. Bell might be in danger simply because it is in his possession. Did your notes reference him?"

"Yes," Amanda responded. When she had searched for a tool she could use in the exorcism, she had written down several possible contacts on a sheet of paper. That paper was in the file with the rest of her notes. She remembered circling Bell's name and writing "wolf skull" next to it. "My notes will lead them straight to him."

"Then I suggest you warn him," Blackstone said. "If you can convince him to loan it to you again, it might be safer for him and the artifact if we were to keep it here."

Amanda glanced at Kyle. Her excitement at the idea of getting access to the wolf skull was mirrored in the subtle details of his expression. The almost imperceptible nod he gave her seemed to say, "I told you so."

She had to admit that things were starting to work out the way he said they would. He had promised her that opportunities would appear if they kept their minds and their energy focused on saving Reggie. The wolf skull was a critical part of achieving that goal.

Blackstone interrupted her thoughts. "Then again," he said in a speculative tone, "perhaps it would be better if Mr. Bell could move it to a more secure and secret location." Blackstone watched Amanda intently, waiting for her response.

Aware of his scrutiny, Amanda suspected that he was fishing for a reaction. Had he noticed the silent communication between her and Kyle?

Amanda struggled to keep her voice neutral. "Wouldn't that put him in *more* danger?" she asked. "If we keep the talisman here, he can truthfully tell the dark coven where it is. If he hides it somewhere, they might force him to reveal its location."

Blackstone pursed his lips and nodded. The corners of his eyes hinted at suppressed mirth. "Good point. We might as well bring the talisman here. Hayworth Farm is already ground zero as far as the dark coven is concerned."

His comment was hardly reassuring. They had weighed the risks of putting everyone at the farm against the difficulties of trying to protect multiple locations. Concentrating their defensive capabilities in one place seemed like the best alternative. Ground zero, indeed.

"I'll give him a call," Amanda said as she turned toward the stairwell.

In her office, Amanda looked up Bell's number and placed the call. "Hi, Mr. Bell. This is Amanda Clark. I rented a wolf skull artifact from you a couple of months ago."

"I remember who you are." His voice sounded suspicious and unfriendly, which surprised Amanda. When she had returned the skull and told him of her success with it, he'd seemed thrilled to learn more about its powers.

"Yes … well … I need to tell you something that probably won't make you happy."

There was a pause on the line, and then Bell said, "I'm listening."

If Bell had been a *normal*, someone who knew nothing about the Order or the supernatural, Amanda would have hidden the truth from him and come up with some other excuse to borrow the talisman. However, while Bell was not a sworn member of the Order, he had contacts within the organization and frequently loaned artifacts from his collection to them.

"My exorcism has come to the attention of dark forces who seem to be gathering up everything they can find related to the ceremony. We suspect the Selkirk Pack is behind it, but a dark coven has also gotten involved somehow. The Order established a secure location for all of the people who participated, but it occurred to us that anyone who possesses the talisman would also be in danger. We were hoping to bring it here for safekeeping."

"A dark coven, you say?" His voice became more speculative than suspicious. "That would explain some things," he mused aloud.

Amanda's heart skipped a beat. "What do you mean?"

"You're too late," Bell answered. "The wolf skull was stolen last night. The police found no evidence of a break-in. Frankly, I think they believe I lost the skull or made up the story for insurance purposes. As if insurance money could replace such a treasure."

So much for Kyle's theory about opportunities. They'd certainly missed *this* one.

"I'm so sorry, Mr. Bell."

"My main concern is that the skull is now in the hands of a dark coven. Who knows what they might use it for?"

"I doubt this will make you feel any better," Amanda said, "but I'm afraid they intend to destroy the skull."

Bell sighed. "Well, at least you were able to save your friend Kyle with it."

Amanda hesitated before responding, and Bell read into her silence. "Did you have additional plans for the skull?"

Amanda glanced toward her open office door and answered in a soft voice. "I hoped I would have the opportunity to use it again someday."

Bell's voice took on a stern tone. "I can see why you would want to save your friend, but making a study of curing lycanthropy would be a dangerous hobby, as I'm sure you're learning."

Amanda could hardly argue with him about that. "Believe me, I know," she agreed. "But I don't want to cure lycanthropy. I just want my brother back."

"Your brother?"

"Reggie. He was taken by the Selkirk Pack a couple of years ago. I've been searching for a way to get him back since then. Kyle was the lucky first recipient of my research."

It was funny how most people talked in circles around the truth of lycanthropy. They spoke of it in terms of a disease, but it wasn't a disease. It was demon possession, and the "cure" was exorcism.

It was Bell's turn to be silent. "I'm sorry to hear that. I didn't realize your motivations were so personal." In a tender voice, he added, "But from what I understand, exorcism after First Moon could have tragic results."

He was kind enough not to spell out what everyone believed—that her brother's spirit was lost forever. She was used to doubters. No one had believed her exorcism would work on Kyle either.

"I can't give up on Reggie, even if everyone else has." The truth of her own words gave her some solace. "I don't know how yet, but I have to try to save him."

"I think I understand, Amanda. Good luck to you, and be careful. It seems you have already stirred up powerful opposition."

"Thanks, Mr. Bell. You should be careful too. We don't think you are in danger now that you no longer have the skull, but you might consider taking a long vacation somewhere out of the area."

Bell chuckled. "I'll take your suggestion under advisement. I could use a vacation, actually."

They said goodbye and Amanda hung up. Amanda was disappointed that the wolf skull was gone, but for some reason, the conversation had reaffirmed her commitment. Kyle would tell her it wasn't over yet. The talisman was just a tool. If necessary, they would find another to take its place.

CHAPTER 9
Loyalty

Marcella watched as Adolphus opened the front door and extended his hand toward the Foundation's living room. The last members of the Selkirk Pack, Baldur and Joslin Peri, had finally arrived.

They are rudely late, the demon Iledaste said with an impatient edge. Marcella accepted the comment without reaction. When she had first joined with the demon, it had taken days not to jump every time the multi-timbre "voice" spoke into her mind.

"Please, join us," Rutlinger said to the newcomers.

The couple entered and warily scanned the other guests in the spacious living area, which was approaching maximum capacity. Their eyes lingered on the two visiting strangers. Baldur cut his gaze back to Adolphus. "I understand we have new leadership," he said in a low voice that Marcella barely caught.

Adolphus held up a hand, suggesting patience. "We can speak later, if you wish. I'm sure many of your questions will be answered shortly."

Baldur narrowed his eyes briefly and then nodded. He took his wife's arm and led her toward the living room. Adolphus closed the door behind them.

The Selkirk Pack had seven members. Counting the two "guests," the Foundation was hosting a complement of nine *lupusdaemons*. The group milled around between the wine buffet along one wall and the two long leather couches that faced each other in the center of the room.

Marcella and Cyrus stood at one end of the couches, watching attentively while the others poured beverages and checked out the two visitors with furtive glances. Marcella was pleased by their subdued curiosity. It seemed that Adolphus had followed her orders and given them minimal information about who she really was.

After the guests had served themselves, Marcella called for everyone to take a seat. Although the long leather couches that faced each other could have comfortably accommodated everyone, Marcella and Cyrus remained standing.

"Thank you all for coming," Marcella said. "I asked Adolphus to call this meeting so I could introduce myself and discuss how we are going to deal with the exorcism threat that has been allowed to grow over the past few months."

Iledaste growled guidance. *Too polite. You are alpha. Command them.*

The demon was right. She had a role to play, and this wasn't a dinner party. It had coached her relentlessly on how to conduct the meeting.

"I thought that crisis was behind us," said Baldur Peri.

Marcella raked a disdainful gaze over Baldur and said, "You thought wrong. The crisis continues as long as we are at risk, and our pack should be the most concerned. The witch who succeeded in sending one of us to the abyss lives in our own back yard."

"You say *our* so casually. What would you know about it?" Baldur demanded.

"More than you think," Marcella answered in a smug tone. "In fact, you could say I had a front-row seat."

The room went silent while everyone stared at her.

"Iledaste," Baldur whispered. He shot a glance toward Rutlinger who confirmed the conclusion with a nod.

"So what?" Skyler Arpin snapped. "It's easy to second guess our actions after the fact. Most of us have been here for generations without a hint of trouble. No one could have foreseen what would happen as a result of *your* poor choices."

Insolent bitch, grumbled the demon.

"You didn't have to *foresee* anything," Marcella said. "You knew what the witch was going to do, and you did nothing to stop it."

"That's not quite accurate," Adolphus interjected. "Kyle Nelson proved to be remarkably resistant to your subconscious persuasions, so we brought him here at great risk to keep him away from Amanda Clark. Kyle escaped, but even if he hadn't, the Order was already pounding on the gates demanding his release."

Marcella shook her head, rejecting the excuse. "Bah. The Order. You worry too much about their petty little police force. We are stronger, faster, and smarter. You should have killed the witch the moment you discovered her plans."

Privately, Marcella did not entirely share Iledaste's characterization of the Order. She imitated the demon's derision mostly as a psychological ploy to play down the risk of her plans. There was nothing petty about the hunter who had tracked her coven the prior year. That hunter had paid for her perseverance with her life, but more of her kind would eventually follow. Although Marcella's skills with the dark arts were powerful, she hoped that her alliance with Iledaste would give her the additional edge she'd need to deal with future hunters. She would force the Order to reconsider the cost of trying to arrest her.

A Pack member who had introduced himself as Tim Osterberg ran a hand across his balding scalp and leaned forward to set his empty wine glass on the long center table that separated the two couches. A pink button-up shirt, tan slacks, and leather loafers were his concession to casual attire. As CFO of Northern Peaks Sports Equipment, he could afford to have expensive tastes. Tim sat back and crossed his legs, giving Marcella a disarming smile.

"The Order has a strong presence here," he said, "and you never did appreciate the political realities of that. If this is all about some petty revenge for the exorcism, I'm sure you'll discover exactly how foolish it is to antagonize them."

Iledaste surged forward in Marcella's mind with a snarl. Its fury overran her, curling her hands into claws and widening her eyes into an angry glare. Adolphus looked like he might applaud Tim's remarks, and his smugness fueled the demon's ire.

Marcella waited for the demon to subside and leveled an icy stare at Tim. "I'm well aware of the strengths and weaknesses of the Order. As a dark witch, I have had to evade their hunters for many years. Now I have the power to strike back."

"Just because you have a witch's memories doesn't mean you can think like her or control her powers," Tim scoffed. He gestured toward her body. "The witch *Marcella* may have evaded the Order, but *Iledaste* has been lounging around here, living off the largesse of the Foundation."

Adolphus sat forward, waiting for her response. He probably sensed that the moment to reveal the true nature of the Pack's new alpha was at hand.

If Marcella were going to convince the Pack that she had the power to command them and to stand up to the Order, she had to address Tim's remarks. Everyone in the room knew that, after full possession at First Moon, a *lupusdaemon* had access to the victim's memories for a while. Those residual memories made it relatively easy to step into the human's former life. But the demon did not automatically acquire the victim's skills, and *no* demon could command the mortal magic of a dark witch.

Marcella glanced at Cyrus, who raised a questioning eyebrow. She pursed her lips and nodded, subtly warning him of what was to come. If the Pack rejected them outright, they might have to fight for their lives.

She addressed Tim, but as she spoke, she peripherally watched the reactions of the entire group. "Marcella was no ordinary witch: she was a summoner."

Tim nodded with satisfaction. "So that's how you returned from the abyss." Then his brow furrowed as the implication sunk in. "But why would she let you take her body?"

"I didn't," Marcella answered.

The shock on the werewolves' faces amused Marcella, in spite of the dangerous tension her revelation triggered in their posture. Only Adolphus sat unsurprised as he monitored the reactions of the others.

"You *share* that body?" Tim said. "How is that possible?"

"I don't think it *is* possible *except* through a summoning. We struck a bargain that benefits both of us."

That's enough information for now, Iledaste warned. *Stay on task..*

Marcella put a warning edge into her voice. "How it happened doesn't matter." She raised her voice and addressed the entire group. "All you need to know is that I am both *lupusdaemon* and dark witch, and I am alpha. I expect your obedience, not your understanding."

The demon chuckled into her mind. *Good. You're learning.*

Tim's eyebrows went up at her unexpected reply. He appeared to consider saying something more, but stopped himself. Marcella's expression was that of an angry predator waiting for an excuse to attack. In a subdued voice, Tim asked, "What would you have me do?"

Marcella smiled. "That's better. The Order is still reeling from the speed of our attack, so we must act quickly to keep them off-balance. The only good thing about waiting two months for our retribution is that the delay has lulled the Order into complacency."

Marcella evaluated the Pack's reaction to her interaction with Tim. Skyler had retreated into the corner of the couch, clutching her wine glass to her chest. Reggie seemed bored, sitting back with his arms folded and his eyes half closed. Lawyer Fenris Kellen's keen attention followed the unfolding action with interest and some amusement, as if he were attending a boxing match. Joslin Peri shifted her gaze among the other occupants in the room, holding her husband's hand tightly all the while.

Baldur's frown had grown deeper while he listened. Finally, he was unable to hold himself back. "You mean *your* retribution. We've reached a balance with the Order. Most of the time, we get what we need, and they stay out of our way. You make it sound like the Order is about to embark on some jihad to rid the world of our kind. I don't believe it. What I do believe is that you are trying to manipulate us into supporting you on some personal agenda."

"I don't care what you believe, as long as you follow orders," Marcella said.

Baldur released his wife's hand and stood. "You don't scare me, and I want no part of your vendetta. Let's go, Joslin." He turned his back on Marcella and headed for the door, but he took only two steps before she started an incantation. Joslin, who was rising from the couch, fell back into her seat, her eyes wide.

Baldur's steps faltered at the sound of the incantation, and he turned toward Marcella with a daring glare. Finishing her spell, she gestured toward him with a twist of her hand.

Strands of purple lightning stretched from her fingers and broke free. A crackling ball of energy formed at the end of each twirling strand like a magical bolas. The strands whipped forward and wrapped around Baldur, shocking his body into spasms. He screamed and fell to his knees when the rounded ends smacked into him. They left scorch marks where they struck and the room filled with the odor of burning flesh and clothing. Unlike a real bolas, the strands continued to twist spasmodically, repeatedly bouncing the spherical ends against Baldur's twitching form.

In Marcella's mind, Iledaste cackled with glee while Baldur suffered.

"Stop!" screamed Joslin, jumping to her feet. She took a step toward Marcella, but Cyrus immediately moved to block her. "Please," Joslin begged, glancing helplessly at Baldur.

Marcella sent a mental query to Iledaste, and the demon responded. *You made your point. He'll heal, and he'll remember.*

Marcella closed her extended hand into a fist. The strands retracted into the balls of energy, which then disappeared with a loud zap. Baldur collapsed onto the floor, panting, and Joslin ran to his side.

"He'll be fine in a few hours," Marcella said with a dismissive wave of her hand. Addressing the rest of the group, she added, "I don't intend to control this pack with fear, but it was becoming obvious that you all needed a demonstration. You can thank Baldur later for volunteering himself."

"That was remarkable," Fenris said. The lawyer's expression and his tone showed admiration.

The reaction was unexpected and she wasn't sure if she should trust it. Iledaste had warned her that Fenris would be one to watch and that he was not easily impressed. He could be a valuable ally or a dangerous foe.

"We aren't here to talk about *me*," Marcella said. "We're here to talk about what I want from each of *you*. Have we established who is in charge here, or will another demonstration be necessary?" Marcella glanced around the room, but no one challenged her.

Meanwhile, Joslin helped Baldur back to his place on the couch where he collapsed with a grunt. His burns were already healing although pain still contorted his features.

Adolphus retrieved two open bottles of wine from the buffet and poured a glass for Baldur who accepted it gratefully. He then went around the table refilling everyone's glasses while Marcella spoke.

"For now," Marcella said, "I don't want any of you to do anything to compromise your cozy little lives. You'll sow more confusion by going about your business as usual. The Order knows a dark coven has visited the witch's farm, but they don't know exactly who it was or where we are now."

Adolphus stopped his pouring to chuckle. "How can they not assume your coven is here at the Foundation? Who else but our kind would have an interest in the items you stole?"

Marcella blinked at him as if the answer to his question were obvious. "I can think of many factions who would be interested in the ritual. Who among us has no enemies? Don't you think the ritual would have value to anyone who might want to seek vengeance against us or coerce us into doing their bidding?"

"Perhaps," he conceded, returning to his seat. "But even if you eradicate all record of the ritual, the proverbial cat is out of the bag. The Order knows it can be done. The witch Amanda is intelligent and resourceful, but she is not uniquely talented. Someone else will eventually reconstruct the ritual."

"Eventually, someone might," Marcella agreed with a nod, "given the right incentive." She glanced at Reggie. "But we know about the real reason for the witch's dedication. She had an uncommonly powerful motivation for constructing the ritual. If we eliminate the ritual and its creator now, we'll send a clear message that dissuades any casual practitioner from trying to duplicate it. It could be another hundred years before fate delivers someone with reason enough to try again."

"But for now, you want us to do nothing?" Adolphus asked.

"No, for now, I want you to go about your business as usual," Marcella clarified. "If anyone contacts you, claim that you know nothing about a dark coven. You can truthfully deny any involvement in our attack on the farm. The Order will have no reason to storm the gates, and we will have more time to act."

In response to Marcella's questioning gaze, every member of the Selkirk Pack nodded their heads in agreement with her plan. Even Baldur nodded grudgingly although she recognized a smoldering resentment in his eyes that might lead to future trouble.

Adolphus and the others probably thought she had let them all off the hook. For now, it was better to keep them out of her way and ignorant of her planning details. They would all get their chance to contribute to her mission ... once she ensured they had no other choice.

Chapter 10

Pyrotechnics

Marcella inspected a bundle of herbs tied to the fence post, taking care not to touch it. Her filtered and hooded flashlight cast a red beam, but she didn't need to see true colors to recognize the components. She sighed in disappointment. "Amanda Clark is still alive. Her wards are consistent, if unimaginative."

"Shall we tear them down again?" asked Cyrus.

"No. She would sense their destruction."

Marcella often included a feedback component in her own wards, and she assumed Amanda would do the same. Although the range was limited, it was easy to enhance a protection ward to alert the caster when someone triggered or destroyed it.

"We need to get closer," Cyrus complained.

"I know that," Marcella snapped. "Let me think."

Marcella took a deep breath to calm her edgy temper. Earlier that evening, she'd taken Cyrus and Fenris with her to visit all of the addresses they had uncovered for the Gold Ridge Coven, but every home was empty. They managed to sneak into the Pesce home undetected, but found nothing related to the exorcism. The wall safe might have given up something of interest, but Marcella wasn't willing to risk tampering with it yet. At that stage of their mission, stealth was essential, and she'd reached the conclusion that the entire coven had gone into hiding. For a while, she wondered if one of her pack mates had warned them she was coming. However, the move was not unexpected: it was typical for the Order to be overly cautious.

Guessing where the Order had stashed Amanda's coven mates wasn't difficult. The farm was an established sanctuary and relatively easy to defend. When Marcella had circled the grounds with her strike team, they discovered an abundance of vehicles near the farmhouse and Order hunters patrolling the area. It would be difficult to overcome their defenses with a direct physical assault.

Fortunately, Marcella had alternatives.

The wards were skillfully done, bordering on adept-level work. But they had a limitation she could exploit. Turning to Fenris, she said, "Transform now. If you do so inside the ward, it will be like lighting a bonfire to announce our presence."

Fenris nodded and closed his eyes. A glorious black cloud of writhing smoke encompassed him, flashing violet arcs of dark power and buzzing like a thousand swarming flies. When the cloud dissipated, a large panting wolf stood atop a pile of clothing.

Marcella didn't entirely trust Fenris, but she applauded his unquestioning obedience. When he had offered to assist her with her mission, Iledaste had spoken into her mind and insisted she accept. The demon argued that Fenris had been one of her few allies within the Pack when she had walked the mortal realm as Clarissa. Fenris's hostility toward Rutlinger certainly seemed genuine enough, as did his desire to eliminate the meddlesome witch.

Time would tell. The risk was low because she had no intention of confiding in the lawyer werewolf. If he betrayed her, she would send him to the abyss with Iledaste's blessing. In the meantime, he could prove himself by being useful.

Taking a vial of oil from a pouch attached to her belt, Marcella fumbled in the dark through a second pouch for a polished chunk of clear quartz. She spoke an incantation and dropped oil onto the stone and then rubbed it off onto the wolf's forehead fur. After repeating the spell, she rubbed the stone across Cyrus's forehead. She finally gave herself the same treatment.

She put the items away and waved a hand toward the fencing. "If you would, please. But be quick. The shield won't last long."

Cyrus bent down next to the fence and took out his own vial. He poured the salted water it contained down one of the vertical wires of the field fencing. Muttering an incantation, he touched the wire. Within seconds, it had darkened and crumbled to rust. Cyrus pulled the fencing aside, opening a triangular gap.

Fenris loped through without preamble and stopped to sniff the air on the far side. He disappeared into the underbrush along the fencing. Cyrus waved a hand toward the opening in invitation, and Marcella ducked through.

With Cyrus once again at her side, they crept through a copse of trees toward the farmhouse, trusting Fenris to return and warn them if their presence was detected. She couldn't guarantee that her mental shield spell would completely hide their presence. She felt confident the shield would mask their intent from the wards well enough, but it was less effective against a true psychic like Lucille Hayworth. If Hayworth foresaw their arrival or was able to sense a threat anywhere on the property, they might have to retreat in a hurry.

During their reconnoiter of the farm's perimeter, they'd identified three locations that would get them close enough to the farmhouse to complete the evening's mission. Unfortunately, two of those locations placed her team too close to the farm animals. The horses and goats would panic if Fenris approached in wolf form, so that ruled out the areas near the barn and the goat pen. The third option was to sneak through the trees in the empty horse paddock and perform their work from the corner of the pasture nearest the house. Unfortunately, that option exposed them to the Order's sentries although the timbers of the old wooden gate would help obscure their silhouettes.

Marcella sniffed at the cool damp air that had settled in after the recent rains. It would hamper their plans unless the eaves of the house had sufficiently sheltered the vegetation along the farmhouse foundation.

When they reached the gap between the dark shelter of the trees and the tenuous cover of the wooden gate, they practically crawled across the intervening pasture, watching and listening intently. The weak light of the quarter moon revealed only the silhouettes of the two patrolling hunters. She timed her forward movement by the direction of their pacing as the two sentries tried to stay awake and warm.

The tactic worked well until just before they reached the gate where Fenris was waiting for them. One of the sentries came to a sudden stop and then turned to walk in their direction. Marcella and Cyrus froze. Fenris, hardly more than a dark shadow against the backdrop of the meadow, crouched and leaped. He cleared the gate effortlessly and silently stalked toward the sentry.

The hunter didn't spot Fenris until the wolf was only a few yards away. The man unshouldered his carbine, but before he could bring it to bear, he went down under the savage pounce of a hundred-and-seventy-pound canine. The only noise to betray the attack was the hunter's body and rifle thudding to the ground.

Oblivious to his compatriot's fate, the second sentry continued his patrol in the opposite direction.

The wolf slunk away from the unmoving shape of the supine sentry toward the second guard while Marcella and Cyrus reached the gate and crouched facing each other.

Marcella plucked at the grass growing along the base of the gate post. "Too damp?" she whispered.

Cyrus shook his head and slipped his lightweight backpack off his shoulders. He extracted a wineskin and a black canvas bundle, which he untied and rolled open. Inside the canvas was a set of tools. With practiced speed, he pressed a spoked plastic ring into the dirt and used the compass built into the hub to align it. When he lifted the ring, it left behind a six-inch circular impression with marks at north, south, east, and west. Prying a cork out of the wineskin's spigot, he began an incantation and carefully poured a stream of salt into the circle.

Marcella watched the farmhouse closely while Cyrus worked. Casting dark magic inside the wards might alert the witch who set them even if the wards hadn't been designed with that purpose in mind. Additionally, the spells they were about to cast could easily overwhelm her psychic shield. But she was more excited than she was worried. Since she'd joined with Iledaste, her magic was more potent than ever. She had more power, strength, and stamina than any mere human witch or warlock.

When she glanced down to check on Cyrus's progress, he was placing a small silver chalice in the center of the circle, which was the final step of his preparations. At each compass point he'd already positioned a small talisman representing the appropriate element: a gemstone at north, a feather at east, a tiny brass incense burner at south, and a glass sphere of water at west. Each artifact touched, but did not disrupt, the perfect circle of salt. Cyrus finished his incantation, sealing the circle and protecting the working they were about to perform.

Cyrus handed Marcella a dried aspen leaf and raised an eyebrow questioningly. She watched the house for a moment, and then nodded her permission to continue. So far, the occupants seemed unaware of their activities.

Chanting softly, Cyrus dropped a piece of charcoal into the chalice and lit it, carefully using his body to hide the flare of the match from the sentry's eyes. The charcoal smoldered briefly and then began to glow.

Marcella joined Cyrus with her own incantation, concentrating on weaving her words in with his and calling to the dark spirits to help them against their enemies. She crushed the leaf Cyrus had given her and sprinkled the crumbs into the chalice. The leaf bits darkened and smoked, but did not catch fire immediately, just as she wanted.

Together, she and Cyrus focused on the farmhouse and intensified their call to the spirits. They had to keep their voices low so the sentry wouldn't hear them, but that wasn't a problem. Calling the spirits was about sincerity and resolve, not volume.

The column of leaf smoke rose from the chalice and bent toward the house. It streamed over the garden area and circled the foundation, rustling the weeds and wildflowers. Cyrus introduced new phrases into his incantation, and the flowers wilted under the increased heat. As Cyrus stepped up the intensity of his incantation, loose paint on the siding at the base of the house began to curl and tendrils of smoke began to rise.

Marcella watched while Cyrus increased the heat. When she estimated that conditions were right, she stopped chanting and blew gently over the chalice. As the smoldering leaves burst into flame, Cyrus uttered a completion phrase and made a sidearm throwing motion toward the house.

All of the vegetation along the base of the house as well as the lower section of siding instantly burst into flame.

They watched their handiwork for a moment and shared a celebratory grin as the sentries responded with yells of alarm. Cyrus quickly dumped the chalice and cooled it with loose soil while Marcella jammed the other items into the toolkit. Cyrus rolled up the kit and tossed it into his backpack while Marcella swept the casting circle away with her hand.

Their mission complete, the two arsonists ran toward the trees, counting on the chaos behind them to mask their departure. They reached the safety of the trees undiscovered and headed for the damaged section of fence. Fenris loped past, effortlessly weaving through the trunks and underbrush.

Once everyone was outside the fence, Fenris transformed back to his human form and the trio returned to their vehicle with smug satisfaction at a night's work well done.

As much as Marcella would have liked to stay and watch the hunters struggle with the conflagration, the pleasure wasn't worth the risk. The fire would either destroy the farmhouse and its occupants, or it wouldn't. They would find out soon enough how successful their attack had been. Either way, it would keep her enemies distracted and on the defensive.

CHAPTER 11
Teamwork

"Fire! Everybody out!"

Jonathan's shout and his fist pounding twice on the door startled Amanda awake.

Kyle sat up next to her. "What the ..."

Flickering orange light reflected against the window frame and billowing smoke rose past the window. The fire was right outside her room!

Amanda and Kyle leaped from the bed. Amanda wore a long flannel nightgown, but Kyle slept naked. "Hurry," she encouraged unnecessarily as he hastily pulled on a pair of pants and grabbed his flannel shirt from where he'd draped it over a chair. They both stuffed their feet into their slippers and left the room.

Downstairs, Jonathan was waiting next to a pile of jackets that had been yanked from the closet, hangers and all. Urging them forward, he said, "Take your jacket and go out through the porch."

"Where's Lucille?" Amanda asked as she bent down to retrieve her coat.

"She's already outside. Come on, you need to keep moving."

A wide-eyed Cara padded barefoot down the stairs in a two-piece pajama set made of red silk. Her dark hair appeared more windblown than slept on. Amanda couldn't help feeling annoyed that, even disheveled, Cara managed to look sexy. "What's going on?" she asked.

"There's a fire," Jonathan answered curtly, waving her forward. "Put on some shoes and a jacket and go outside."

Amanda slipped on her coat and followed Kyle out of the house.

The screened-in porch was wet from the water that had been sluiced over it. They dodged as another bucket was tossed onto the structure to keep the fire at bay. Amanda coughed as the wind swirled smoke around the corner of the house, stinging her eyes and engulfing her. Currents of heat threaded through the chill of the late October, pre-dawn hour.

Amanda and Kyle ran over to where Lucille, Noreen, and Jessie were huddled together away from the burning house. Tears streamed down Lucille's face as she watched her family home go up like kindling. "Everything … gone," she said weakly. Then she swallowed hard and started striding toward the barn. "There's got to be another bucket somewhere."

Noreen and Jessie started to follow her, but Amanda stopped them. "Wait. There's more than one way to put out a fire."

Amanda turned toward the house to see what they were dealing with. Flames licked up the siding all the way around. The sentries were keeping the porch area clear of flame by concentrating their efforts there, but the rest of the house was burning unchecked. Another few buckets weren't going to make a difference.

How could this happen? Someone would have had to pour accelerant around the entire house for it to all go up at the same time like that. But how could that person have evaded the sentries?

Noreen was staring intently at the fire and muttering calls to the spirits, holding one hand out toward the fire. Even without the support of her tools or a casting circle, she was a powerful fire witch and might be able to contain or direct the fire. "Dammit," she said, closing her hand into a fist and pulling it back to her side. "Something is fighting me."

Kyle nodded his head as he stared at the fire. "More dark magic."

"What did you say?" Noreen demanded.

Kyle squinted at the fire as if trying to make out some detail. "Dark magic is woven into the flames," he answered.

Jessie paled and put her hand to her throat. "Thank goodness we sent the kids to stay with my parents."

Amanda glanced at Noreen. "Magical accelerant," she concluded, and her mentor nodded in agreement. That explained why the fire nearly encircled the house.

Jonathan guided Tanya through a cloud of smoke as they ran coughing through the soaked porch and away from the house. Jonathan signaled to his men that the house was clear. The sentries turned their attention to sloshing water on the flames at the base of the house, but their efforts were too little, too late as the flames climbed the wall. They needed water everywhere at once, just as the fire was everywhere at once.

Cara joined the group of women, hugging herself against the chill. Tanya stumbled toward them as Jonathan went to help his hunters.

Amanda's anger and adrenaline pushed her mind into a hyper-aware state that slowed down everything around her. They needed to fight magic with magic. "I have an idea," Amanda said, "but we have to hurry." She waved the others closer. "Everybody gather in a Ring of Calling."

Amanda didn't have time for explanations or propriety. Fortunately, Noreen didn't question or argue under the desperate circumstances. The coven mistress simply positioned herself to the south of Amanda. Cara stood to Amanda's left and Jessie moved into position on her right.

With all four compass points covered, Tanya wasn't sure what to do. "Where do you want me?" asked the apprentice.

Amanda considered leaving Tanya out of the casting. She was inexperienced, and asking her to be prime was risky. But she was powerful when she didn't hold herself back. She might give them the boost they needed to succeed.

"In the center," Amanda answered. When the girl hesitated, she added, "Quickly!"

Tanya hurried into the center of the circle and the other women joined hands around her. "You want me to be prime?"

"Just follow our lead. I'll explain as we go."

Noreen narrowed her eyes and frowned, her doubt clear in her expression. Amanda couldn't blame her for her lack of faith. Casting an unpracticed spell was difficult under the best of circumstances. Orchestrating the efforts of five witches on the fly was next to impossible. But what choice did she have? It helped that their minds were already focused on the fire and the spell's objective was simple.

Amanda took an extra few seconds to ensure that everyone was aligned with their respective compass points, and then she started the purification ceremony. Her coven sisters knew their roles well, so it took only a moment to call the spirits of light and push away the dark spirits that had been drawn to the dark magic Kyle had sensed in the fire.

"Tanya, listen carefully," Amanda instructed. "Do what I tell you as best you can. Don't think. Don't question. Just do."

Tanya gulped and nodded. This was not Tanya's first time being prime for a casting, but during her previous experiences, Noreen had scripted and coached her in what to do. The strain in her features showed that she understood the gravity of the situation. With every second that passed, the flames ate deeper into the sides of the house and grew closer to the eaves. If the fire penetrated the roof or the walls, the house would be lost.

Amanda spoke swiftly but clearly. "We're going to take all of the water from the tank in the corral and put it around the house. Jessie will siphon it out of the tank and get it flowing. I'll make sure it doesn't soak into the ground. Cara will keep it from spreading out, and Noreen will strengthen the flow."

Tanya's brow creased in confusion for a moment, but when Amanda's jaw clenched in irritation, she blinked rapidly a few times and started to call the spirits. Amanda and the other witches joined her, reinforcing the spell with their individual elemental strengths.

The process was agonizingly slow at first. Water flowed over the edge of the corrugated metal tank and spilled onto the ground. It splashed uselessly until Tanya shaped Cara's air working into a tube. The approach worked so well that Amanda was able to abandon the task she'd set for herself and lent her strength to Tanya's efforts.

The tube of water stretched from the tank to the house, circling it at about waist height. Jonathan called his hunters back from the burning house, unsure of what the witches had planned.

Within thirty seconds, the last water had drained from the tank, and the circle around the house was complete. Tanya seemed to be having trouble holding the water in position, and she sent a panicked look toward Amanda.

"You're doing great," Amanda reassured her. "Now, blast all of the water at the house."

Tanya smiled and nodded. She concentrated on the water tube and called to the spirits.

Spells rarely behaved exactly the same way twice, even when practiced regularly. The mind of the caster shaped how the magic manifested in the real world, and that vision adapted to circumstance.

Tanya's impromptu vision for blasting the water at the house was nothing less than spectacular. With a deafening bang, she split the air tube and hurled the water toward the house with such violence that the liquid was nearly atomized. The result was unexpectedly effective: the destruction of the air tube acted like a detonation that shook the ground and extinguished much of the flame before the water drenched the siding. Several of Jonathan's men instinctively dropped to the ground.

The climax of the spell taxed Amanda's strength so swiftly that she swayed with dizziness. Jessie also sagged, nearly falling to her knees before she recovered and took a deep breath.

Lucille had been on her way out of the barn with an old feed bucket when the spell erupted. She froze and stared in shock at the farmhouse's smoldering siding. With a grateful smile toward the witches, she joined the sentries and helped throw water on the few spots that were threatening to reignite.

Tanya stood stunned in open-mouthed amazement. Then she lowered her head and blushed, giving Amanda a sheepish look. "Sorry. I've never handled that much power before."

Amanda grinned at her and said, "You did great." Tilting her head back, she began the incantation to release the spirits. Joined by her coven sisters, they shut down the Ring of Calling and dropped their hands.

Amanda stepped forward and gave Tanya a hug. "Thank you," she said, patting the young witch's back. "That was impressive."

"See what you can accomplish when you apply yourself?" A note of gentleness took some of the sting out of Noreen's typically caustic wording.

Amanda approached the house with Lucille and Jonathan. The siding was badly damaged, but most of the charring seemed to be external.

"Do you think we saved it?" she asked.

Jonathan looked up the two-story wall toward the eaves, which were darkened by smoke, but otherwise undamaged. "You may have stopped it in time. The fire department is on its way, and we'll watch for any lingering hot spots."

"We'll check the inside," Amanda said and started toward the house, expecting Lucille to follow her. When her friend continued staring at the siding, she touched the older woman's arm. "Are you okay?"

Lucille looked up and blinked a few times. "Yes … I'm fine. I just can't believe it. I've seen plenty of magic, but nothing like that. I was sure everything I owned was lost." Lucille's reserve cracked and a tear rolled down her weathered cheek. "Thank you for saving my home," she said before grabbing Amanda in a tight hug.

Squeezing her friend, Amanda smiled and said, "You're welcome, but it was a group effort." She turned toward the house, keeping her arm around Lucille. Catching Kyle's eye over her shoulder, she tilted her head, suggesting he follow. "Let's go see how it looks on the inside."

Amanda checked the interior from top to bottom with Kyle and Lucille, but they found no evidence of fire lingering within the walls or ceiling. The entire house smelled like smoke, but it was strongest near the entryway, indicating that most of the odor had originated from outside. While they searched, the fire department arrived.

Two firemen hurried inside the house and chastised them for going back in. In the end, the firemen didn't find anything to justify their concerns.

Lucille cringed at the sound of siding being torn away from the side of the house outside. When Amanda went out with her to investigate, they found that the firemen were making sure the fire wasn't smoldering within the walls.

The crew lieutenant lifted his helmet and literally scratched his head as his gaze followed the line of damage along the side of the house. "This is the strangest fire I've ever seen," he commented. "I can't tell where it started. It almost looks like it started everywhere at once." He glanced at Lucille. "I'd suspect arson, but I don't smell any accelerant."

Lucille drew herself up. "I did not try to burn down my own house, young man."

"Oh, I believe you, ma'am," the lieutenant answered quickly. "But I'd like to know what happened here. Do you have any thoughts as to how the fire might have started or who might want to harm you?"

Amanda's first reaction was to laugh, but she kept her expression under control. She was sure the fire had magical origins, and she had a good idea of whom to pin it on. She didn't share those thoughts with the lieutenant.

"It's an old house with old wiring," Lucille said with a shrug.

The lieutenant pursed his lips and shook his head. "If you think of anything else, let me know," he said, dismissing himself. He rejoined his crew and directed the paramedics who'd just arrived toward Noreen and the three younger witches.

"I hate lying to them," Lucille said after the lieutenant walked away.

"The truth wouldn't have made him happier," Amanda said.

"It rarely does." The deep sigh that followed Lucille's response hinted at a broader meaning. After years of giving tarot readings, she would understand better than anyone that truth seekers often needed to be careful what they wished for.

Kyle was speaking with the firemen who had gone inside. He ended his conversation and came over to stand with Amanda and Lucille. "Those guys are a little weirded-out by the fire," he said, glancing toward the lieutenant. "They can't make sense of it."

"We noticed," Amanda said, grabbing Kyle's arm. "C'mon, we're going to do a little investigating of our own." She guided him toward her coven sisters while she kept an eye on the firemen and paramedics. When she was sure that everyone had their attention focused elsewhere, she changed direction away from the house. She didn't want the paramedics to delay her while they checked her out.

As they walked, Kyle looked around. "Hey, where's Blackstone? His rig is gone."

"I have no idea," Amanda answered in a tone that revealed how little she cared. She had too many other things to worry about. Blackstone might have put Kyle and her on his team, but the man sure wasn't keeping them informed about what he planned or where he went. It wasn't the first time he'd disappeared without an explanation.

She probably should have informed Noreen of her intentions, but Amanda was getting tired of needing permission for every move. The fire had nearly destroyed her friend's home and could have killed everyone she cared about. She was going to get to the bottom of the incident while the evidence was still fresh.

CHAPTER 12

Private Eye

Nathaniel Blackstone adjusted his night-vision goggles and blew out a sigh of frustration. It was nearly impossible to find a good vantage point that would let him observe the Rutlinger Foundation from outside the block wall that surrounded the facility.

If he wanted to trespass, the wall wasn't much of an impediment. It wasn't designed to secure the grounds so much as identify the boundaries. He'd found more than one access point where natural features had been integrated into the perimeter, possibly to give wildlife access to the property.

The only wildlife he'd detected that evening had been a few deer and a large dog or, more likely, a wolf.

The canine had appeared out of nowhere while he debated crossing over a rocky prominence that interrupted the wall. They both froze at the same moment. He stood absolutely still, hoping the top of his head would blend in with the stones he hid behind. He prayed that the wind would not carry his scent to the animal. After more than a full minute of tense immobility, the creature finally sniffed at the ground and loped off.

The encounter had convinced him to stay outside the wall. If the dark coven was indeed hiding out at the Foundation, he couldn't afford to have them discover his presence just yet. The patrolling wolf would know he had been on the grounds even if he managed to get in and out without a direct confrontation. The last thing he wanted to do was spook the dark coven into changing location.

Amanda and Kyle had warned him that the Foundation was well hidden by the natural features of the mountain. The building rested in a glacial bowl near the base of a steep mountainside to the north. A sharp cliff sheared off the western edge of the property, and a jagged ridge protected the eastern boundary. An elevated plateau to the south offered the only vehicular access, with a gated road that wound through tall trees before sloping into the depression where the Foundation building was located.

After reviewing a topographic map of the area, Blackstone had concluded that the east ridge was his best bet for a clear view. It was a reasonable theory, but the sunken elevation of the building and the thick forest around it conspired against him.

Disappointed with his lack of success, he decided to call it a night and headed back toward his SUV.

He retreated as silently as he'd arrived, not wanting to alert the wolf, which could have been prowling anywhere. In spite of his high-tech goggles, negotiating the rugged terrain in the dark commanded all of his attention. He was so consumed with his cautious trek that he nearly stepped out of the forest and into the open before he spotted the glow of the floodlights at the front gate.

Easing back from the edge of the forest, he changed direction to travel alongside the driveway and stay out of range of the camera at the front gate. He'd only gone a few paces before the low rumble of an approaching car came from the direction of the county road. He paused and crouched behind a large tree. His position near the gate would give him a good view of whoever was returning.

The gate began to roll open as soon as the dark four-door sedan crested the plateau. The glare of the car's headlights prevented Nathaniel from seeing inside at first, but then the vehicle came to a stop while it waited for the gate to fully open. The floodlights angling into the passenger compartment revealed three profiles. Based on the dossiers Nathanial had acquired from the Order, the driver looked like Fenris Kellen, Selkirk Pack member and local litigation lawyer.

Blackstone's skin tingled and one corner of his mouth lifted in a self-congratulatory smile when he recognized the woman in the passenger seat. He had finally caught up to Marcella Pedroso, the dark witch who had murdered Donna Jansen, a talented member of his team and a good friend. Donna made the mistake of getting too close to the Red Claw Coven before backup had arrived. By the time Nathaniel had reached her, the Order's forensics team was already processing Jansen's cooling corpse, and the dark coven was long gone.

The dark witch turned her head to look directly at him, and he froze, holding his breath. He reassured himself that there was no way she could possibly see him. The floodlights would have ruined her night vision, and the contrast from the well-lit driveway would only deepen the cloaking shadows of the forest. However, there was no telling how sensitive she might be to the intense attention he'd focused on her.

After a quick scan of the trees, the witch turned to speak with Kellen. Nathaniel let out his breath slowly. As the car started to roll forward through the open gateway, he tried to identify the third passenger. Seated in the back, the male figure presented not much more than a dark silhouette, but he was willing to bet it was Cyrus Fleming. The dark warlock was reputed to be Pedroso's right-hand man and possibly her lover.

Nathaniel thanked God for delivering the confirmation that he'd been unable to manage through his own efforts. He may have failed to find a suitable location for spying on the Foundation, but his search for one had placed him right were he needed to be at the right moment in time. Some might call it coincidence, but he'd learned long before that his faith was most often rewarded by unexpected assistance while he was trying to solve problems for himself. It had made him a firm believer in the saying, "God helps those who help themselves."

As soon as the car was out of sight behind the wall of the Foundation, Nathaniel stood and resumed his journey back to his vehicle. As he walked, a sense of urgency took hold of him and he quickened his stride.

The Order, and his team specifically, had been hunting the Red Claw Coven for nearly a decade. The coven was extremely cautious and always moved secretly, often escaping the traps he laid for them with only minutes to spare. The dark witch would not have ventured forth from her hiding place without good reason. Where had she been? What had she been doing? What was her involvement with the Selkirk Pack?

Nathaniel reached the base of the Foundation's driveway and followed Pack River Road to the rough logging road where he'd parked. Along the way, his concerns grew about what the dark witch might have been up to. By the time his black Suburban came into view, he was practically running. He jumped into the huge SUV and started the engine. Throwing it into reverse, he backed up to the county road and then drove out of the mountains dangerously fast.

A strong feeling of foreboding pushed him to get back to the farm as quickly as possible. The dark coven had an astonishing knack for taking action when he wasn't around. Somehow, they had always managed to stay one step ahead of him.

But the game had changed … he knew where they were hiding.

CHAPTER 13

Evidence

Amanda skirted the side of the farmhouse with Kyle at her side and went past the garden. She stopped abruptly when a figure resolved out of the darkness.

"It's just me," said Jonathan. "One of my men is missing."

"Uh-oh," Kyle said.

"Yeah, that's what I'm thinking. He never showed up to help with the fire, and this is the first moment I've had to go look for him."

"We'll help," Amanda volunteered.

"Thanks. I'm guessing you're out here for another reason?" Jonathan asked.

"Whoever did this had to get fairly close."

"Could the spell have been planted when your moon shrine was vandalized and then triggered later?"

Amanda considered his suggestion, but then shook her head. "Unlikely. It took a lot of power to make that spell work the way your men described. That and the timing make me think it was a response to our bringing the coven here for protection."

"The fault is mine," Jonathan said bitterly. "I'm supposed to be keeping you safe."

"Don't blame yourself." Amanda placed a hand on his arm. "We're all facing new challenges here. It may take some time to figure out how to best protect ourselves."

"We'd better figure it out fast," Kyle put in. "This dark coven seems pretty serious."

"No kidding," Amanda agreed. "And the person with the most experience is our fearless leader Nathaniel Blackstone, who is conspicuously absent. Again. If I blame anyone for failing to protect us properly, it's him."

Jonathan nodded. "I'll sit down with him when he returns and come up with some improvements to our security." In a wry tone, he added, "We have all these witches hanging around. Maybe we can put some of them to work."

"Hey, I'm game," Amanda said. "I'm tired of sitting around waiting to be attacked. Maybe next time, we'll be ready for them and do more than just stamp out the latest fire."

"I hear that," Jonathan said somewhat absently as he looked over his shoulder. "But right now, I need to find Mike."

Jonathan walked through the damp brown grass toward the horse pasture. Amanda followed with Kyle close behind. The already dim landscape darkened as the moon went partly behind a cloud, and Amanda started to wonder if it was such a good idea for them to be out there all alone. What if the attackers were still nearby?

As if he was reading her mind, Jonathan drew his sidearm.

Kyle swore in pain as he stubbed his toe. "Do you have a night-vision spell or something?"

Amanda smiled. "Not with me."

Kyle was silent for a moment. "There really is a night-vision spell?"

"Sure. I tried it during my studies, but the tech solutions for night vision are more practical."

"How come?"

"The spell works by enhancing the sensitivity of your retina, which is fine if you can stay in the dark until the effect wears off. Normal light levels are excruciating until then."

"Bummer."

"Yeah. Night-vision goggles work better, and you can take them off."

The moon emerged again, and Amanda came to a stop. "Jonathan," she called, pointing toward a disturbed area of grass off to their right.

Jonathan hurried toward the spot she indicated and then swore in anger. He holstered his gun and knelt.

Amanda wasn't sure she wanted to see what he had found, but moved forward slowly after Kyle went past her. Standing at Jonathan's side, Kyle covered his mouth with his hand.

When she was close enough to see over the grass, she took a reflexive step backward and swallowed an urge to gag. Blood glistened in dark, thick droplets on Mike's cheek, and his neck was awash with it. He lay on his back with his head turned a little too far to the left for the pose to be natural. "Is he … ?"

Jonathan looked up into her eyes and simply nodded. Stupid question. Of course Mike was dead.

Jonathan took the radio off his belt and called for help.

Kyle came over and put his arms around her. "You don't need to see this," he said. "Let's go back to the house."

Amanda shook her head. "No. I'm okay." She swallowed hard, took a deep breath, and glanced toward the gate of the horse pasture. Anger swelled to replace her revulsion. "We aren't done here."

She eased out of Kyle's embrace and approached the pasture gate.

"You think they worked from here?" he asked.

"Probably. It's the closest spot to the house that has any kind of cover and isn't near the animals." Amanda slowly scanned the ground near the gate, but all she found was her own boot prints and the scrape mark from the gate being opened and closed.

"What are we looking for?" Kyle asked.

"Anything unusual. Watch where you step."

Amanda squatted and turned a pearl ring she wore on her right hand until the stone was reversed toward her palm. Although she was just starting to recover from the drain of her earlier efforts to put out the fire, the ring didn't take much energy to operate. She spoke a short incantation and the pearl began to glow. She adjusted the trickle of power she was feeding the ring until it produced enough light to clearly see the ground.

Cupping her hand to direct the light source, she searched for signs of interlopers.

"Check this out," Kyle said from a few feet away.

Amanda directed the light on the spot he indicated. It was a set of canine prints. Big ones. The edges of the prints were still crisp, indicating they were fresh. Some were oriented toward the gate and some away from it, and in both cases, they ended several feet away from the gate itself.

"I'll bet this is what attacked Mike," Kyle said, echoing Amanda's own thoughts. "It jumped over the gate, killed him, and then jumped back." He looked toward the copse of trees along the far fence line and his brow creased in concern. "I sure hope it's gone now."

Amanda rubbed her forehead with her free hand. "This doesn't make sense. The wards are still up. I'd have known if anyone had tampered with them. How could a werewolf have gotten past them without me knowing?"

"Are you sure they're working?"

"Of course I'm sure." Did Kyle really think she was that incompetent? "Remember Reggie's little visit a couple of months ago? When he sparked along the fence line, I felt that like it was nails on a chalkboard."

"Well, something changed," Kyle said in a musing tone.

"Brilliant deduction," Amanda said, letting her frustration tinge her voice with sarcasm. She immediately regretted her thoughtless comment. "Sorry. The whole point of the wards was to prevent what happened here tonight or at least give us fair warning. I guess I didn't do a good enough job."

Kyle silently processed her remarks and then gave her the look that always presaged a logical pronouncement. "This may not be about the quality of your wards so much as the strength and ingenuity of your opponent. The wards are important because they make things harder for our enemies, but we need to add another layer of protection."

Amanda nodded once, calmed by his objectivity. Kyle's support and passions often emerged in unexpected or unusual ways, but he always seemed to have her back. "Thanks. You're probably right." She turned back toward the gate. "Let's see what else we can find."

Inside the gate, Amanda finally discovered something of interest. Glittering droplets of clear liquid and a scattering of wet spots spread across a roughly swept area of ground. A partial hand print lingered at an edge of the swipe, and a faint outline hinted at the remains of a circular indentation. Unfamiliar boot prints marked the ground on either side.

"This where they set up," Amanda said, kneeling next to the evidence. As she watched, one of the droplets sunk into the ground leaving behind a wet spot. "But this liquid is strange."

Avoiding the prints, Kyle leaned over and touched his fingertip to one of the droplets. Raising his finger to his mouth, he tasted it.

Amanda looked at him incredulously. "Kyle! Yuck. We don't know what that is."

Kyle ignored her as he contemplated the flavor. "Salt," he concluded. "The crystals are absorbing moisture and liquefying. Then they soak into the ground. I'll bet you'll find a few whole crystals below the surface."

"That makes sense." Amanda pointed to the circular indentation. "They set up a small casting circle here and filled it with salt." She stood up. "Well, now we know how they got close enough to launch a magical sneak attack. I just wish I knew how they got past the wards."

Kyle pointed toward the boot prints and then toward more wolf prints inside the gate. "They left behind more evidence this time. Maybe the Order's forensics team can positively identify the attackers."

Amanda let her tone go cold as she glanced toward Jonathan and his unfortunate team member. "Maybe. But if we catch up to whoever did this, I doubt they'll ever see the inside of a courtroom."

"I thought the Order had a tribunal or something to handle cases involving the supernatural."

"They do," Amanda confirmed with a nod. "But remember who we're working with: Mr. High Body Count."

"Good point."

Two vehicles speeding up Farm-to-Market Road caught Amanda's eye. As she watched, they slowed and turned onto the driveway to the farm. The hunter who was guarding the entrance to the farm opened the gate for them. From the opposite direction, Blackstone's Suburban roared into view and followed the others onto the property.

"Speak of the devil," Kyle said.

The Suburban stopped near the house, but Blackstone didn't get out. Noreen went to the driver's side, and after a brief conversation, stepped back to let the vehicle roll forward. Amanda shielded her eyes against the headlights as it rounded the side of the house and headed toward her and Kyle.

Blackstone cut his lights as he approached, but then a bright spotlight split the darkness and lit up the trees in the horse pasture. Blackstone scanned the trunks slowly while Amanda squatted next to Kyle to stay below the beam. The spotlight went out and Blackstone finally emerged from his rig.

"Have you found something?" Blackstone asked.

Don't worry, we're fine, Amanda thought. *Thanks for asking.*

Suppressing her annoyance with Blackstone, Amanda pointed at the ground. "Here. It looks like the remains of a casting circle."

Blackstone came forward and knelt next to the area she indicated. He tasted one of the few drops of liquid that remained. "I concur." He stood and sniffed the air.

"Checking for brimstone?" Amanda asked in a wry tone.

Blackstone seemed to take the question seriously. "Not literally. However, the workings of a dark coven leave behind a singular residue. Not really an odor so much as a sensory impression. I find that taking a deep breath through my nostrils improves my ability to detect it." He turned his head to Kyle. "What about you, Kyle? Does your extraordinary vision reveal any lingering magical energy?"

"No," Kyle answered, shaking his head. "The fire was infused with dark magic, but I haven't seen anything like that out here. I think the auras only work with active spells."

"Interesting," Blackstone said, turning his attention to the copse of trees. "Let's go see how they managed to get this close." Without another word, he strode toward the trees, drawing a deep breath through his nose and adjusting his trajectory every few yards.

Amanda ran to catch up. "Are you sure this is a good idea? We don't really know that they've left. The whole Pack could be waiting for us in there."

"I know exactly who was involved and where they are," Blackstone answered. "After completing their misdeeds here, they returned to the Rutlinger Foundation, which is where I suspect they've been hiding all along."

Amanda's eyes widened at Blackstone's revelation. So, the Selkirk Pack was out for vengeance after all. Perhaps it had taken them a while to find and hire the magical support they needed. However, Amanda still found their wrath puzzling. After putting so much financial energy and time into building their foundation, and after decades of mostly peaceful coexistence with the human community, they had gone off the deep end because she took advantage of a once-in-a-century opportunity to save Kyle?

Or was it about something more? Did they know she intended to exorcise her brother? It wouldn't be a stretch for them to connect Kyle's exorcism with her desire to get her brother back, but the Pack knew better than anyone that Kyle's and Reggie's situations were different. Kyle's *lupusdaemon* had been exorcised during a brief period of weakness between initial possession and First Moon. For Reggie, possession was complete, and the demon's consciousness had replaced the human's. Game over. At least, according to theory.

Her research had turned up dozens of attempts to exorcise a *lupusdaemon* after First Moon by people who were far more qualified and powerful than her. It had never worked, and the Pack had to know that.

Had her success with Kyle spooked them so badly that they feared she'd succeed with Reggie? The idea was both encouraging and disappointing. Her chances of getting close to Reggie dropped to near zero if the Pack had truly joined forces with a dark coven and declared war on her. It was unlikely that both she and Reggie would survive to the conclusion of such a conflict, regardless of who was victorious.

Blackstone slowed as he entered the dark understory beneath the spreading pine branches. The trees were trimmed up to about seven feet, so there were few obstacles to avoid other than the tree trunks themselves. Amanda's hands had reflexively clenched into fists when Blackstone had arrived, blocking the light her ring projected. She stretched her fingers and cupped her hand again, feeding more power into the ring. A half-circle of light illuminated Blackstone and most of their path.

Blackstone looked over his shoulder and glanced at her hand. "That's helpful," he said, increasing his pace.

Upon reaching the corner of the property, they all stopped and stared at the compromised section of fencing.

"Well, that answers one question," Blackstone said.

Amanda stepped forward and inspected the ward charm tied to the corner post. Although the feedback sensations she received from the wards pulsed in reaction to the presence of so many visitors at the farm, the network of charms seemed intact. "I can't see how they tampered with it."

"Maybe they didn't," Blackstone said.

"Then how did they get past it without alerting me?"

"I'm sure there's more than one way to defeat a ward. What would you have done if presented with the same obstacle?"

"Some kind of cloak or shield, maybe?" Kyle interjected.

Amanda stared at Kyle, considering his suggestion. "I've never heard of such a thing, but I suppose it's possible. Personally, I've never tried to defeat a ward."

"Then your education is lacking," Blackstone said. His remark would have been offensive if it hadn't been delivered in such a matter-of-fact tone. "All defensive measures have weaknesses. Understanding those weaknesses allows you to layer defenses that work together. Knowing how a defensive measure has been defeated also gives you valuable intelligence about your enemies' capabilities, even if you never need to apply the skill yourself."

Amanda glanced at Kyle who shrugged and was smart enough not to look smug about Blackstone's agreeing with him. Blackstone was right. Her education *was* lacking. In her defense, dark-magic practitioners were rare, and she'd never had to defend against one.

"The Order needs to do a better job of mixing tactical training into all disciplines," Blackstone went on. "Crisis teams, which are a fairly new practice, are a step in the right direction. Unfortunately, the experience you gain from serving on a crisis team is hard won and sometimes too late to save you. Personnel should be regularly rotated into training teams and pitted against each other."

Blackstone's argument sounded well rehearsed, and Amanda guessed that he had delivered it on more than one occasion. The plan he proposed would be expensive, particularly since the Order were rarely faced with a crisis serious enough to benefit from it. But that didn't mean she disagreed with him.

"What you're saying makes sense," Amanda said, "but I can't wait around for the Order to implement a training program that may never happen. I need to up my game now."

"Excellent!" he responded with a grin. "I shall try to help you do that. We have a perfect opportunity right here in front of us." He spread his hands toward the fence opening. "Given what we know, how did our enemy penetrate your ward without triggering it?"

Amanda thought for a moment about the problem. "I like Kyle's cloaking idea best. Causing a distraction elsewhere along the fence might have also worked, but I didn't detect anything like that."

"What else?"

Amanda figured they'd covered the best options, but for academic purposes, she gave some thought about what else might have worked. "They could have done something to disable this ward while maintaining the continuity of the network around the farm."

"Like spray-painting the lens of a surveillance camera," Kyle added.

Amanda nodded. "Right. But I'm fairly certain they didn't physically tamper with the charm."

"Very good," Blackstone said. "We don't know exactly how, but they slipped through the fence and moved around within the ward without disrupting it or triggering it. Now, tell me more about how this ward works."

Amanda explained that the ward was mostly psychological. It deflected attention and made the farm appear unappealing from the outside. The protection aspect resisted the intrusion of anyone with bad intent toward the farm or its occupants. After a bit more back-and-forth discussion, they concluded that the intruders had shielded their minds somehow.

"Starting with that supposition," Blackstone said, "we can reinforce your protections, magical and otherwise."

Amanda pursed her lips dubiously. "But won't they try something different next time? They'll have to assume we figured out how they got in and have done something about it."

"Now you're thinking like a tactician," Blackstone approved. "We could patch the weakness or leave it in place as part of a trap, but either way, we must rethink the protections around the sanctuary. We are dealing with an unusually aggressive and capable opponent."

"You said you know who they are?" Kyle asked.

"Yes," Blackstone said. "I've been tracking the members of a dark coven called the Red Claw Coven. I believe that at least two of them are involved in this: their Mistress, Marcella Pedroso, and a warlock named Cyrus Fleming."

Deep in thought, Amanda followed Kyle and Blackstone back toward the farmhouse. They passed by the forensics team huddled with Jonathan over the body of the fallen guard. The guard Jonathan had identified as Mike was the first casualty of the war she'd started with the Selkirk Pack. She fought off a wave of nausea as they neared the farmhouse and entered a miasma of burnt wood and wet ash hanging in the air. A man was dead and Lucille had nearly lost her home.

Amanda frowned and bowed her head with guilt. This was all her fault. Her mission to save her brother was putting everyone who was close to her at risk. Her only consolation was that Kyle would have also been lost if she hadn't tested the exorcism on him. Of course, none of that would matter if he were killed in the aftermath. There was certainly no comfort in Blackstone's revelation that the last person to benefit from a *lupusdaemon* exorcism hadn't survived the ordeal for long.

Meanwhile, the conflict was escalating. Was there any way to put an end to it before more people were harmed? Reggie was probably already dead, for all practical purposes. She couldn't ask others to keep sacrificing themselves for her or her not-so-secret mission. What would it take to appease the Pack and end the hostilities?

She looked up to find Blackstone looking at her.

"What's on your mind?" he asked.

"Nothing," she answered quickly. But she needed to distract him with a more satisfying response: "Just thinking about ways we can reinforce our defenses."

His gaze lingered on her face in an assessing manner. He said nothing and finally looked away.

Kyle squeezed her shoulder gently. "Don't worry. We'll figure something out."

Sure they would. And then their opponents would come up with a fresh attack that they hadn't anticipated. Being on the defensive sucked. They were always reacting. Always one step behind. They had to go on the offensive if they wanted to take control of the conflict, but then even more people would die.

Amanda couldn't stand the idea of losing more friends. She had created this mess. Cleaning it up was *her* responsibility.

CHAPTER 14
Gone Girl

Amanda slid out from under the warm bed covers at 2:12 AM and waited silently by the bedside. Kyle didn't move, and his breathing remained steady.

Reaching under the bed, she slid out the change of clothing and shoes she'd hidden behind the dust ruffle earlier in the day. With a farmhouse filled with guests and Kyle sharing her room, it had been difficult to find a time when no one was around to observe her subterfuge.

As quietly as possible, she dressed herself. She froze when Kyle made a noise, but it was only the beginning of a soft snore. She sped up her preparations using the noise as cover. Slowly sliding open her nightstand drawer, she gently extracted her keys and wallet. She'd always hated carrying a purse.

Once she left her room, she had to sneak out of the house and get off the property as quickly as possible. She hoped she wouldn't run into anyone along the way because it would be hard to explain why she was dressed and had her keys in her hand.

Amanda stopped at the bedroom door with her hand on the knob, listening. The hallway outside was quiet. Gritting her teeth, she turned the knob slowly until the door unlatched. The old hinges groaned each time she pulled to widen the opening a little farther. Pulling faster would only make them squeak more loudly and at a higher pitch that would carry. If only she'd oiled them one of the hundreds of times she'd considered doing so.

She watched Kyle over her shoulder as she made her escape. She wished she could kiss him on the cheek or give him a hug since it might be the last time she would see him. As soon as the opening was wide enough, she slipped into the hallway and closed the door just as carefully as she'd opened it.

The house was strangely silent as she crept down the stairs. During the day, the place was endless noise and chaos. The house had seemed enormous when she had lived there alone with Lucille. Filled to capacity with her coven and the Order personnel, it had gone from spacious to cramped.

Guilt tugged at Amanda's heart when she thought about Lucille. After everything that had happened recently, her disappearance would be especially worrisome for her friend and mentor.

Kyle would be furious. He would feel betrayed that she didn't take him with her, and he'd believe she'd given up on their plans. In a way she had, unless going to the Foundation miraculously gave her access to Reggie as well as all the other things she needed to perform the exorcism.

Fat chance. Amanda already had a target painted on her back, and she was about to give whoever was hunting her a clear shot. But that was a risk she'd have to take if she wanted an opportunity to negotiate an end to the fight.

There had to be some kind of concession the werewolves would be willing to accept. She could promise that she'd never use her exorcism again and that she'd leave Reggie alone. She didn't believe her death was all they wanted because it would have been relatively easy to kill her *before* they put the Order on alert. Something else was going on, and she needed to find out what it was.

Amanda stepped off the stairs onto the ground floor and paused. A radio crackled in the living room, and a male voice asked for status. While the guards reported in, Amanda took advantage of the night commander's distraction to slip out the front door.

The next part would be the hardest. She had to reach her car and leave without causing a stir. The guards would want to know why she was leaving and might even try to hold her back until they received confirmation from someone in charge. If she could get to her car and start it, the rest wouldn't really matter. Once she was rolling, they wouldn't be able to stop her. She'd be long gone before anyone could follow.

But luck wasn't with her that night.

Of all the vehicles parked at the front of the house, one of the guards had chosen hers to rest against. Taking a deep breath, she readied herself to deliver the story she'd prepared.

When she was only a few steps away from her car, the shape leaning against it resolved from a vague silhouette into the tall dark form of Nathaniel Blackstone.

"Good evening, Amanda," he said. "You're up late. Or should I say early?"

Amanda suppressed a moment of panic. Talking her way past a guard was one thing. Getting through Blackstone was quite another. Her mind struggled to think of something that would convince him to let her go.

As soon as she opened her mouth to speak, he interrupted.

"Save it. I appreciate your noble willingness to sacrifice yourself for the greater good, but you would waste your life for nothing. Frankly, I expected better judgment from you."

Amanda's face heated with embarrassment and anger. How had he known her plan? And how the hell could he know she'd be wasting her life?

She couldn't let him talk her out of her plan. One man had already lost his life, and she couldn't stand the idea of anyone else getting hurt. "I can stop this," she said.

"No. You can't," he disagreed flatly. "I feel bad about what happened to Mike, too." It was like he was reading her mind. "The safety of this team is my responsibility. If you want to blame someone, blame me, not yourself."

"It's me they really want," she insisted.

"You're not thinking clearly. Our enemies have already demonstrated that they want to obtain or destroy everything and everyone related to your exorcism."

"I'll convince them that I'm the only person who knows how to perform the ceremony, and I won't do it again."

He shook his head. "You don't know our opponents like I do. Mercy and compassion are not qualities they possess. Until we resolve this conflict, anyone closely associated with you or your exorcism notes is in danger." Her distress must have shown on her face, for he paused and raised a hand in apology. "I'm not saying this to make you feel bad. It is what it is. Eliminating you is only one of their objectives. I would appreciate it if you didn't make that easy for them."

Amanda sighed. If Blackstone was right, then going to the Foundation wouldn't have accomplished anything. Her enemies would have checked her off their list and continued with their campaign. But she had to do *something*.

Blackstone wasn't finished with her. "We are all feeling frustrated and impotent because our opponents have had the initiative up to now. But we are going to change that, and to do so, I need your help *here*." He reached out and took her hand, holding her fingers with his and raising her hand between them as if he were going to kiss the back of it. "Can I count on you to help me save your friends and defeat the Red Claw Coven?"

The formality of their pose and the seriousness of his tone drove all confusion and duplicity from her thoughts. It was like his question triggered a light that chased the shadows of doubt, guilt, and shame into the far corners of her mind. It left only her determination and righteous anger gleaming at the forefront of her consciousness. She wanted to put an end to the attacks and get justice for her brother. Blackstone was the key to both.

"Yes," Amanda said without hesitation.

He released her hand. The moment of clarity faded, and her darker feelings emerged from their hiding places, but their influence was diminished.

Amanda shook her head and blinked. Had he just used magic on her? While he held her hand, she suspected that she couldn't have lied to him if she'd tried. If it was some kind of spell, it had somehow soothed her mental anguish at the same time it exposed her true feelings. It was both a balm and a violation. But how did he do it? She saw no jewelry that could carry enchantments, and he hadn't spoken an incantation. If he was using magic, it worked nothing like the witchcraft she was familiar with.

"What are you?" she asked, realizing how rude the question sounded only after she asked it.

Blackstone smiled. "I am a hunter of evil." He had answered casually, but his simple declaration was weighted with implication.

For the first time, Amanda thought about what it must be like to be Nathaniel Blackstone. He hunted the most vicious paranormals known to the Order. Although he was part of an elite team, the members often worked independently and in secret, drawing resources from the Order as needed. It was a lonely and dangerous existence, one that required discipline and a level of power Amanda could only guess at.

To him, she must seem like a spoiled amateur. He had seen right through her and given up a good night's sleep to deal with the little stunt she had planned.

"I apologize for acting so recklessly, Master Blackstone. I'll try not to make trouble for you in the future."

Blackstone chuckled as he put his arm across Amanda's shoulders and directed her back toward the house. "I appreciate your contrition, Hunter Clark, but don't make promises you can't keep. Our passions are part of who we are, and they fuel our thoughts and actions. The key is to channel them wisely. They can't be denied entirely, so if we don't control them, they'll control us."

"More insomniacs," said a voice from the deep shadows under the trees."

Blackstone's arm tensed around Amanda and then relaxed when one of Jonathan's guards stepped into the light.

"Sorry, didn't mean to alarm you," the guard said.

Blackstone ignored the apology. "Who else has been having trouble sleeping tonight?"

The guard started to answer, and then he looked at the ground with a confused expression. "I don't know."

His answer didn't make sense. If he didn't know, then why did he bring it up?

"I think I do," said Blackstone. "Was it Cara, the young dark haired witch?"

The guard opened his mouth to speak, but no words came out.

"Amanda, do you have the means to dispel a charm?" Blackstone asked.

Realizing what he was getting at, Amanda closed her eyes and sighed. Cara didn't normally need to use her powers to get what she wanted from men, but that didn't mean she wasn't willing and able to do so under the right circumstances.

Amanda stepped up to the guard and reached toward him. He ducked away from her hand. "What are you doing?" he demanded.

"A charm has been placed on you," Blackstone answered. "Allow Amanda to remove it."

Blackstone's tone made it clear that he was giving an order. The guard snapped to attention and held still.

Amanda easily recalled the short incantation for dispelling residual magic. She gripped one of her pentagram earrings between her thumb and forefinger. The small pentagram was weak protection, but she was removing a weak charm. Placing her hand on the guard's forehead, she chanted the spell and then snapped her fingers. Cara's charm unraveled swiftly, causing an unpleasant sensation as it dissipated. To manipulate the guard, Cara had used gray magic for her charm.

Cara's willingness to draw from the gray was a constant point of contention between her and Noreen. Using the gray was an acquired taste, so to speak: one that Amanda had never developed. One had to walk a moral tightrope to use gray magic, and it took great discipline not to fall off onto the dark side. Cara was not known for her discipline, and she hated being told what she could and could not do.

Blackstone resumed his questioning as soon as the confusion cleared from the guard's expression. "When did you see her?"

"Uh ..." the guard checked his watch. "A little over an hour ago."

Amanda looked around. All the vehicles she was familiar with were accounted for. "How did she leave?" she asked.

The guard looked down with a sheepish expression. "I loaned her my car."

Blackstone glanced toward the road and shook his head. "She could be in the next state by now. Or Canada."

"Maybe she's better off," Amanda said. "She said she feels like a target here at the sanctuary, and I can't blame her. All for a battle that isn't hers. Getting out of town may not have been such a bad idea."

Blackstone was unconvinced. "Perhaps. Assuming she left straight away and didn't do something unwise, like go home first."

"You think they could be waiting for her?"

"I don't know, and that's what bothers me. We have no idea what resources are available to our opposition. We have a patrol checking on everyone's homes and sweeping the area around the farm, but the mobile team can only be in one place at a time."

"If she did go home, she might still be there," Amanda said, turning back toward her car. "We have to talk her into coming back to the farm with us."

"No," Blackstone said, grabbing her arm firmly. "You are not leaving the sanctuary. We'll send the patrol to check on her. They will bring her back if they can convince her to return. If not, she's on her own."

Amanda pulled her arm free, annoyed by Blackstone's callous attitude. "We can't just leave her to the wolves," she retorted.

Blackstone raised an eyebrow, cluing Amanda in to her inadvertent metaphor. Then he shook his head. "Cara is not sworn into the Order; we can't force her to do *anything*. On the contrary, if she refuses sanctuary, we are required to respect her wishes."

"But it's for her own safety!" Amanda insisted.

"That argument has been made, and she has given us her answer." Blackstone placed his hand gently on Amanda's back, guiding her toward the farmhouse once more. "The only thing we can do now is have the patrol check on her. If they can't convince her to return, they might be able to convince her to flee the area. Perhaps she already has."

Amanda stepped away from Blackstone's touch, but continued toward the house. "What if the dark coven goes after her?"

"I think the odds of that are low. If they don't already know she has abandoned sanctuary, it will probably be some time before they do. If Cara is smart, she'll be out of their reach by that time." He paused, and Amanda glanced over to see a deadly smile on his face. "Besides, I intend to distract them with other matters."

More than anything, Blackstone's declaration made Amanda feel better about going along with him for the time being. Cara wasn't the only one who felt like a target, and Amanda was tired of being constantly on the defensive. She wanted to *do* something.

~

Amanda started up the stairs toward her room, although she doubted she'd be able to get back to sleep. She'd been awake for more than an hour and was too wound up. In fact, she was shaking a little from the tension that still hummed along her nerves. She and Cara were hardly close, but they were coven mates, and Amanda would feel terrible if something bad happened to her. Particularly since it would be partly Amanda's fault.

She'd waited by the radio with Blackstone and the hunter in charge of the night-time guard rotation while the patrol hurried over to Cara's tiny home. Cara rented a guest house from an elderly couple in the Selle Valley. The location was closer to the Rutlinger Foundation than Hayworth Farm, which didn't help Amanda's patience during the wait.

When the patrol arrived, Cara was gone. But it was obvious that she'd been home recently. The car belonging to the hapless guard she'd charmed was parked out front. The front porch light was on, as was the inside hallway light. After knocking, the team discovered that the front door was unlocked, so they entered the house and looked around.

Cara wasn't much for tidiness, so it was almost impossible to detect the signs of a hasty departure. Closet doors were open and a few clothes were strewn across the unmade bed, but based on Amanda's few visits to Cara's place, the same could be said for any day of the week. One good sign was that the patrol failed to find any luggage.

Amanda had almost been ready to accept that Cara had gone into hiding. The unlocked front door was bothersome, particularly since Cara was leaving for an unknown period of time. However, lots of people in remote areas didn't bother to lock their doors, and Cara may have simply forgotten to do so out of habit. But then the patrol had reported that Cara's SUV was parked in the carport next to the house.

Had Cara left with a friend? She might have talked someone into going on a sudden road trip with her. Getting a call from Cara in the middle of the night wouldn't be a surprise to someone who knew her well. Any *male* friend would probably have jumped at the opportunity to spend time alone with her, regardless of the hour.

With no trail to follow, they couldn't do much more unless Cara contacted the farm to let everyone know where she was. In the meantime, Amanda couldn't help but wonder and worry.

As Amanda reached the top landing of the stairwell, the door to her bedroom opened. Kyle emerged with tousled hair, tightening his robe belt. When he saw that she was fully dressed, he froze for a second and then stepped forward. "Are you okay? What's going on?"

Amanda shushed him and went to her bedroom door. She held it open and waved him inside. When they were both in the room, she shut the door and spoke in a quiet voice so as not to disturb the rest of the household.

"Cara took off. She charmed one of the guards and *borrowed* his car." She went on to describe how the patrol had gone to her home and found it empty. "It looks like she may have taken off with a friend, but we can't be sure."

"We should have seen this coming," Kyle said, rubbing his eyes with his palms. "She looked really upset after she found out about the dead guard and how the wards had failed."

"I know. I should have talked to her." She hung her head. "This is my fault."

"I wish you'd stop saying that. You haven't done anything wrong. You aren't in charge of security, and you aren't Cara's keeper."

"I know, but none of this would have happened if my exorcism hadn't started a war with the Foundation."

Kyle stared at her, his jaw clenching and the skin around his eyes tightening. "Then the solution is simple," he said in an annoyed tone. "We go back in time and you choose not to do the exorcism. You won't anger the Pack and I'll be dead."

"You know that's not what I want," Amanda retorted, a flash of anger heating her words.

"I'm not so sure anymore. All this self-flagellation is almost insulting. Your exorcism may have had unintended consequences, but it saved my life. The Order is backing you up right now because they believe you did the right thing. You have to start treating the rest of us like partners instead of victims. We're all in this together, and everyone knows it's going to be dangerous."

Amanda sat heavily on the bed. Kyle was right, but she couldn't just ignore the fact that she had started all this. "I don't want people to think I'm refusing to admit that I'm responsible."

"I think everyone gets that," Kyle said, sitting next to her and putting his arm around her. "We have a pretty high-powered team, and it's even stronger if we stay focused and work together."

Kyle released her and leaned away. His sudden silence and movement made her look over to find him staring at her.

"You were going to leave," he said, his voice reflecting shock and disappointment.

"What?" Amanda stalled for time to think while she pretended to be surprised by his accusation.

"After everything we've been through together," Kyle went on, "you were going to leave me behind?"

Amanda reached for his hand, but he pulled away and stood up, waiting for her explanation. She owed him an honest answer. "I thought I could convince Dr. Rutlinger that I was the only person who knew anything about the ceremony. That they could leave everyone else out of it."

Kyle folded his arms and stood silently for a moment. "What changed your mind?"

"Blackstone. He was waiting for me."

"Well, hooray for Mr. Perceptive," Kyle said as he started to get dressed.

"Where are you going?" Amanda asked. "It's three-thirty AM."

"Everyone *else* seems to be awake, and I'm too pissed off now to sleep."

"Okay," Amanda said, patting the bed next to her. "Let's talk about it."

"We'll talk later. After we've both had some time to cool down and think about what we really want."

Amanda didn't want Kyle to leave angry, but his mood was rubbing off on her. Some time alone sounded like a good idea, so she didn't try to stop him. He left and closed the door behind him without looking at her again.

In the silence of her bedroom, Amanda went over the conversations she'd had with Blackstone and Kyle. Blackstone had convinced her that sacrificing herself wouldn't help the rest of them. Kyle was right when he pointed out that their team was stronger if they worked together. She'd thought her plan was a noble act of sacrifice. Was it really a petulant act of self-absorption? She hissed aloud, irritated by her self-doubt.

Kyle said she needed to figure out what she really wanted. Her private mission had always been about Reggie. It was still about Reggie. If she had gone through with her plan to surrender, she probably would have failed her brother as well as everyone else. Her cheeks heated with shame when she realized how close she'd come to giving up on herself and her friends.

CHAPTER 15

Catch of the Day

Marcella waited while Cyrus unlocked the heavy metal-clad door. It swung open silently on well-oiled hinges, and she stepped into the chilly eight-by-eight room beyond. The basement storage room had originally been designed to function as a walk-in cooler, but according to Rutlinger, it had never been put into service.

Lucky her. It certainly made for an excellent prison cell.

The lone occupant had wiggled herself around so she could lean against the back wall. She huddled on the floor with her bound legs folded against her chest. Her hands were secured at the wrists, keeping her arms at her back. The captive wore black jeans and a matching jean jacket over a violet sweater. Her feet were clad in lightweight hiking shoes. A sack-like hood of dark- blue fabric covered the girl's head, held in place by a strip of leather around her neck. While Marcella observed, the young woman's only movement was an involuntary shiver.

Marcella motioned toward the prisoner, and Cyrus stepped forward to remove the hood. Lovely dark hair fell onto the girl's shoulders while static caused a few strands to float around her face. Her eyes darted around the room before settling on her abductors. Her ice-blue eyes reflected both fear and anger as she unfolded herself and slowly stood. She wobbled unsteadily from the zip-tie that held her ankles together and compromised her balance.

"Hello, Cara. I'm Marcella, and this is Cyrus."

Cara's gag prevented her from speaking, but her eyes revealed her wariness.

"Yes," Marcella continued, "I know your name. I also know you're an air crafter. If you agree not to try using your powers, I will remove your gag. The effort would be wasted anyway. Cyrus and I are quite well protected."

Marcella waited for Cara to respond. After a moment of staring, the girl nodded. Marcella waved Cyrus forward, and he removed Cara's gag.

As soon as the gag left her mouth, Cara shouted, "Who are you people? You have no right to treat me like this!"

Marcella rolled her eyes and responded calmly. "I think you know exactly who I am, and you have a good idea of why you're here. Now, are you going to calm down, or shall we gag you again?"

Cara glanced at Cyrus, who raised a questioning eyebrow. She shivered again, a reaction that probably wasn't due only to the room's chill.

"Can't you turn on the heat or something?" Cara whined. "It's freezing in here."

"I'll see what I can do," Marcella answered. "In the meantime, I have a few questions for you."

"But I don't know anything."

"Oh, I'm sure that's not true. For your sake, I hope it's not true."

Cara's eyes widened with fear. "What are you going to do to me?"

"That all depends on you, Cara."

"What do you want?"

"I want to know everything about your friend Amanda's exorcism."

"But I don't know much about it. I wasn't there."

That claim corroborated Rutlinger's belief that Amanda had not recruited the help of her coven, which was something

Marcella had difficulty accepting. It was foolish to attempt such a difficult and powerful spell without enlisting the entire coven.

"Who was there?" Marcella pressed.

"Just Amanda and Noreen. And Kyle, of course." Cara twisted her arms around to show her bound wrists. "Look, I'm being cooperative, right? Can't you untie me? My hands are going numb."

Marcella considered the request. Physically, Cara wasn't much of a threat. The girl's magic was her most potent weapon, but Marcella felt certain she could counter anything that might get past the protective charms she and Cyrus wore.

"All right. As long as you continue to answer my questions."

"Deal," Cara said without hesitation.

Cyrus opened a folding knife he kept in a sheath on his belt and cut Cara's bindings. The girl rubbed her wrists while Cyrus took a position in front of the door, his knife still ready in his hand. Cyrus wasn't a large man, but he had a werewolf's strength and speed as well as experience with using the knife he carried. Cara wasn't going anywhere.

Marcella continued her questioning.

"Why didn't Amanda use the full coven?"

"Noreen—she's our coven mistress—wouldn't allow it. We wanted to help, but Noreen said it was too dangerous. She also didn't think it would work. In fact, no one really did, except Amanda."

So, Rutlinger hadn't been the only one to underestimate Amanda. Marcella began to feel a grudging admiration for the young witch who had pursued her goal against the resistance of her peers. Once again she wished it was somehow possible to lure Amanda into the Red Claw coven, but she'd made a deal with Iledaste: Amanda Clark had to die.

"If your coven mistress thought it was dangerous and wouldn't work, why did she agree to participate?"

"Honestly? I don't know. I think it had something to do with Order business. There was some big showdown with the Selkirk Pack, and whatever happened really pissed off Noreen. I think she may have decided to help Amanda out of spite."

The negative undertone Cara had used when she mentioned "Order business" interested Marcella. "I take it you aren't part of the Order, and you don't plan on joining them?"

"God, no." Cara said, making a face. "Too many rules."

Marcella's interest in Cara sharpened. She needed new members for her coven, and surprisingly, her young captive was demonstrating some of the characteristics she looked for. However, she also wanted to know more about the Order's involvement, and Cara probably wasn't privy to that information.

Perhaps it was time for a broader inquiry. "Who else knows the details of the ritual?"

Cara thought for a moment and then shrugged. "I don't know. Amanda said she filed a copy of her notes with the Order. It's possible someone read through them, but I doubt anyone but a witch would learn anything useful."

The girl was deliberately playing down the potential exposure, but her statement might still be accurate. Marcella's contact within the Order also doubted that anyone else had read Amanda's notes. The notes were among a hundred other documents that some underpaid technician was expected to scan and store in the Order's digital-document archive.

It was sounding like Amanda, Noreen, and Kyle were the only people who could potentially reconstruct the exorcism after all. But Marcella still had trouble believing that everyone else in the coven was ignorant.

Watching Cara's reactions closely, Marcella said, "Amanda's unexpected success must have been a moment of celebration for your coven. Surely she shared some of the details about how she managed to save the young man."

Cara froze and blinked a couple of times. She probably knew her answer to the question might sign her own death warrant. Her eyes darted back and forth as she tried to formulate a response. When she spoke, she chose her words carefully. "We did talk about it in general terms, but nothing specific about how it worked. Noreen wanted to keep it a secret for some reason."

Marcella was certain that there was more the girl wasn't revealing. "Why keep it a secret? Amanda managed something that hasn't been done in over a hundred years. Her pride would demand that she share that accomplishment with her coven sisters. And the rest of you had to be curious about it."

"Oh, we were," Cara admitted readily. "I wanted to hear all about it. I wanted to know everything about how Kyle was recovering." Cara clamped her mouth shut suddenly. She'd apparently said something she hadn't intended. She hastily continued. "But our mistress wouldn't let us talk about it even though Amanda obviously wanted to. I got the impression that Noreen was waiting for permission from the Order."

Permission? Why would the Order want to keep the exorcism ritual a secret? Deep in the recesses of her mind, Iledaste virtually rubbed its hands together with glee. If the Order had locked down access to the ritual, their mission became a lot simpler: destroy Amanda's notes and eliminate the only three people who could re-create them. Cara's knowledge had proven to be useful after all.

The rush of excitement didn't distract Marcella from pursuing Cara's earlier slip. "What made Kyle so interesting to you?"

Cara blushed and looked down. "He's cute," she said with a slight shrug, as if that explained everything.

"And?" Marcella didn't buy that Cara's interest was strictly about lust.

Cara looked up. "While he was ... possessed ... he changed. Physically. I've known a lot of guys, but never someone with super strength and speed. Amanda and he were ... a couple, and I wondered what that would be like."

Marcella sighed in disappointment. Perhaps it was all about lust after all. Most air witches were naturally sensual, some more than others. Cara's femininity was powerful and unmistakable, a sure sign of an air witch who embraced and exploited her nature rather than trying to resist or restrain it.

However, Cara specifically mentioned an interest in Kyle's "recovery," and Marcella had wondered about that herself. She had theorized that Kyle would retain his strength, speed, and eye color because those attributes were physical alterations to his body that occurred over time. However, transforming into a wolf was pure demonic magic. When the demon left, so would that ability.

"After the ritual, did Kyle still have the strength and speed he stole?"

"Stole?" Cara said with a mild tone of offense. "I guess you could look at it that way. Not that he asked for it. But, yeah, last I heard, he's still strong and fast."

"Anything else?"

Cara's long pause indicated that she was holding something back. She made a show of remembering something more and said, "His eyes. His eyes are still wolfy." She leaned forward and stared into Marcella's eyes fully for the first time since their conversation started. She gasped and took a step back, bumping into the wall. Marcella was back-lit by the room's only bare light bulb, so Cara probably hadn't noticed until that moment that Marcella's eyes were also "wolfy."

Marcella smiled at the girl's reaction. "Yes, I'm more than a witch. I'm pleased to see that you were unaware of that."

Cara continued to stare in horror until she blinked away tears that tracked down her cheeks. She dropped her gaze to the floor. In a small voice, she asked, "You aren't going to let me go, are you?"

"Not just yet," Marcella answered. "But don't despair. As a reward for your honesty, I'd like to make you an offer."

Cara looked up with a mixture of hope and wariness in her eyes. "What offer?"

"I'm rebuilding my coven. If you join me, I could teach you things your current mistress never could. Would you rather learn from an independent air adept who has powers you can scarcely imagine or a stodgy fire master restrained by the Order and its 'too many rules?'"

Cara's mouth dropped open, but she didn't answer. The suggestion obviously took her completely by surprise.

"Think about it," Marcella said as she turned to leave. "You appear to have a clear schedule."

As Cyrus stepped aside to let her pass, Marcella added, "See if you can make our guest more comfortable. She may be here awhile."

CHAPTER 16

Purged

In spite of her agitation, Amanda managed to get a few hours of sleep. She awoke with a slight spacey feeling and a mild headache as reminders of her nocturnal activities. However, trying to sleep past seven o'clock was impossible with the buzz of morning activities filling the farmhouse. Also, the empty space where Kyle should have been spurred her to rise and see how he was doing.

After a quick trip to the bathroom to freshen up, Amanda entered her office where she found Kyle pounding away at the keyboard of the new laptop computer the Order had given her and cursing quietly to himself.

"What's wrong?" she asked.

"I think we have a problem," he mumbled, distracted by whatever he was doing.

"Another one?" Amanda stepped around a makeshift bed made from a thick piece of foam. The sheets and blanket were still tossed to the side exactly as Cara had left them. Amanda hoped her coven-mate had escaped to somewhere safe.

Kyle tore himself away from the monitor to glance over his shoulder with a strained smile. "I know. It seems problems are all we have lately." He punched a few more keys and then pointed at the screen. "Check this out."

Amanda leaned over his shoulder. Kyle was searching through the Order's document database. He had brought up a list of all documents bearing an "exorcism" tag. The list wasn't long: it included perhaps fifteen documents. She scanned the list, but one document was notably absent.

"Where is the *lupusdaemon* ritual?" she asked.

"Not where it should be."

Amanda took a deep breath and suppressed a moment of panic. "They must have misfiled it."

"That's what I thought too, but I've tried searching for it dozens of ways. I've searched by your name, by parts of the document title, and now by keyword tag. It's gone, and so are the backups. Whoever deleted it was thorough."

But that would mean the dark coven had influence inside the Order. Almost any member could *look* at the document database, but very few people could update it. With the amount of vetting the Order performed on their intelligence team, Amanda had trouble accepting that they had a spy that deep in the organization. There had to be another explanation.

"They probably haven't gotten around to scanning the physical copy yet," she concluded.

Kyle shook his head. "After the break-in, I checked on that. Your notes were already in the database. I should have downloaded a copy right then."

Kyle's news brought Amanda's feelings of futility back full force. The dark coven was closing in on them, and they were helpless to stop it. She sat heavily in a chair next to her desk, feeling Kyle's sympathetic eyes on her.

"There's still a chance the physical copy is filed somewhere," he said.

"If they had access to the database and the backups, they had access to the physical file as well, right?"

Kyle nodded. "We should verify that, but I wouldn't get my hopes up."

"I'll try to control myself," she said with a sigh. Then something else occurred to her. "What made you decide to check again?"

Kyle glanced toward the open door and lowered his voice. "We may still get an opportunity to use it." Letting his voice return to normal, he added, "Besides, I'm getting a little paranoid. Even though the document archive is supposed to be secure, I wanted to download a copy for my own peace of mind."

It heartened Amanda to know that Kyle hadn't lost sight of her goal, and in spite of his annoyance with her, he'd continued to work on it. She needed those notes. If she ever had a chance to exorcise Reggie, she'd have to be ready. But now all of that work was probably gone forever.

"What are we going to do?"

"About what?" came Blackstone's voice from the doorway. The man seemed to have a sixth-sense about when something interesting was happening. How long had he been listening?

Kyle explained what they'd discovered. Blackstone frowned and stood motionless for a moment. He moved to the desk and picked up the telephone handset, punching the buttons so quickly that Kyle couldn't tell what number he'd dialed.

"It's Blackstone. Someone has removed Amanda Clark's *lupusdaemon* exorcism from the archive … yes, I understand the implications … right. Feel free to check, but I'll wager the paper copy is missing as well. Let me know immediately if you find anything, but at the moment, I'm more concerned with *who* than *how*."

Blackstone hung up and turned his eyes to Amanda. "We must assume the exorcism ritual has been lost. I want you, Kyle, and Noreen to reassemble as much as you can remember about the ritual itself and any research that helped you design it."

Amanda resisted sharing a triumphant smile with Kyle. Rebuilding the ritual was exactly what she wanted to do, and having Noreen's help would be invaluable. Rather than having to work in secret with Kyle when she could find the time, Blackstone had suddenly made it their top priority. The question was, *why* did he want it to be their top priority?

"Are you worried that the dark coven will finally succeed in offing me?" she asked with a wry tone.

"That's a consideration, but it's not my primary concern."

Amanda was taken aback, but Blackstone seemed unaware of her reaction. "What *is* your primary concern?"

Blackstone blinked at her in a way that said the answer was obvious. "Why, the security breach, of course. If you are able to put together a credible replacement, we may be able to lay a trap for whoever is responsible for deleting the first set of documents. The ritual also has great value to the Order, so you would be killing two birds with one stone, so to speak."

Amanda had a private third purpose for the reconstituted ritual, but Blackstone didn't need to know about that. Whatever the rationale, his priorities and hers coincided nicely. "I'll be happy to be of service," she said sincerely.

"Good. I'll inform Noreen." He strode purposefully out of the office.

After Blackstone had left the room, Kyle's gaze met hers. "Have faith," he said, echoing what he'd been telling her since the beginning. His look and his tone admonished her for her actions the previous evening. "As Henry Ford said, 'Obstacles are those frightful things you see when you take your eyes off your goal.'"

Amanda reached out and put her hand on his arm, squeezing gently and silently thanking him for his support. He laid his free hand over hers, rubbing his thumb softly over the back of her hand.

"Okay, I get it," she said. "We're in this together, no matter what."

Kyle simply smiled back at her.

~

Amanda typed Kyle's comments into her new laptop. Across the table, Noreen waited impatiently for the chance to rattle off another of her own recollections.

Kyle sat to Amanda's right, his face scrunched in concentration as he tried to add more memories to the summary she was putting together.

The three of them were seated at a folding card table that had been set up in the moon shrine. Amanda would have preferred to work in her office, but it was too small to be comfortable for three people trying to work together.

Kyle had suggested that they start the process of rebuilding the exorcism ritual by brainstorming everything they could remember about it, regardless of what order they thought of things. He didn't want to restrict their memories by imposing any kind of structure on the process. Coming from Mr. Rational, the idea was unexpected. Noreen had approved the suggestion with as much surprise as Amanda.

Their session had been as chaotic as it had been productive. Tasked with being the scribe, Amanda had more than five pages of notes, and they were still adding ideas to the list as fast as she could type them.

Blackstone had been right to put the three of them together on the project. Noreen tended to remember the technical details of the exorcism ritual, not only because she was most familiar with that part, but because she had contributed to the ritual's design. For his part, Kyle remembered a startling amount of detail relating to the research they'd done into the Navajo shamanistic ritual that had inspired Amanda's exorcism. Amanda added her own memories as well as a full perspective on her decision process.

Amanda also came up with ideas for improving the ritual. Noreen didn't see the point since odds were low that they would have an opportunity to use it again. Amanda didn't share that her improvements were made with an eye toward using the ritual on Reggie, but Kyle knew what she was thinking. She had to be careful not to arouse Noreen's suspicions. Her coven mistress could be just as irritatingly perceptive as Blackstone.

During a momentary lull in their staccato blast of recollections, Amanda took a deep breath and sat back from her hunched position over the unsteady writing surface. The folding chairs that accompanied the cheap card table were of similar poor quality, and she squirmed to restore the circulation in her legs.

She mentally apologized to the moon shrine for intruding upon its healing process with such crass furnishings and foreign human energies. It wasn't accident or frugality that had inspired her to find second-hand wooden bookshelves and a workbench that she had re-purposed as her altar. She felt strongly that her moon shrine needed organic materials and a consistent application of her personal energy for it to resonate with her workings and function at its peak.

Noreen had helped her cleanse the space, but Amanda would be mostly responsible for rebuilding the spiritual fortifications that strengthened and protected it. When she opened herself up to the energy of the room, it was still raw and unsettled. More than anything else that the dark coven had destroyed, she mourned losing the sense of comfort and potential that used to embrace her when she entered her moon shrine.

"Earth to Amanda," Kyle said, touching her arm and drawing her out of her reverie. "You okay?"

"I'm fine. Just got distracted for a minute."

Noreen's expression softened, and she gave a slight knowing nod. "Give it time, Amanda. Your moon shrine will recover."

"Looks great to me," Kyle said, looking around. "Almost like nothing happened. It's even a little cleaner if you don't mind my saying so."

"Your eyes don't see the real damage," Noreen said in a disapproving tone. "Amanda poured much of herself into this space. That presence has been stripped away and can never truly be replaced. It will always be different now."

Amanda wanted to deny her mentor's claim, but she knew Noreen was right. She was a different woman now, and her restored moon shrine would reflect the energies of the woman she'd become.

Noreen noted her expression of disappointment. "Different can be good, Amanda. You'll be uncomfortable for a while, but what you build here will reflect a more mature and more powerful self. You'll see. In time, it will be an even better match for you than it was before."

"Hey, it could be worse," Kyle added. "The whole place almost burned down."

Amanda's initial frown at Kyle's flippant remark turned into a laugh. "Good point. I should be thankful I still have something to rehabilitate."

Kyle's encouraging smile faded and was replaced by a serious expression. "Being thankful is good, but I still have a bone to pick with whoever left that frog for you and tried to burn us up in our sleep."

Noreen leveled a stern look at Kyle. "You need to purge ideas of revenge from your head right now. Let the Order deal with them. It's what we do."

"You keep forgetting I'm part of the Order now," Kyle said bitterly. "And no one knows better than me what we're up against."

Noreen sat back and folded her arms. "You literally only know the half of it. I'll concede that your near-werewolf experience uniquely qualifies you to understand certain aspects of our enemies, but the dark coven is another matter."

Kyle seemed unconvinced. Amanda put a hand on his arm before he could argue further. "She's right, Kyle. We're contending with *lupusdaemons and* dark magic. Fighting them will take expertise in both subjects." She hoped he would catch on to her subtext: that between the two of them, they *did* have expertise in both subjects.

Kyle gave her a long look. A sly smirk would have alerted Noreen to their private communication, but Kyle was good at maintaining a neutral expression. Even Amanda had trouble reading him at times. True to her expectation, all he said was, "I understand."

Noreen narrowed her eyes at them, suspicious of Kyle's easy capitulation. Amanda sighed to herself, knowing the two of them would find something else to argue about soon enough.

Footsteps thumped up the treads of the attic stairway, and Jonathan appeared at the door to the moon shrine. "I hope I'm not interrupting anything."

"Please, do interrupt," Amanda said. Alerted by her wry tone, Jonathan glanced at Kyle and Noreen, observing their annoyed expressions. He was no stranger to their bickering.

Staying at the doorway, Jonathan appeared reluctant to intrude. Amanda guessed that Jessie might have warned him to avoid the moon shrine as much as possible while it was still being restored. She appreciated his consideration.

"The forensics team just contacted me. They have a match on the saliva in Mike's wounds. It was Fenris Kellen."

"That bastard lawyer has finally gone too far," Noreen said with venom in her voice.

Kyle appeared puzzled. "You have Kellen's DNA?"

"That's a requirement of the treaty," Jonathan confirmed. "Every paranormal submits to DNA collection as a sign of good faith."

"So what happens now?" Kyle asked. "Do you arrest him?"

"That depends upon what the director decides," Jonathan answered. His voice turned cold. "Personally, I'm hoping we have enough proof for a termination mandate."

"What's that?" Kyle asked.

"Shoot on sight."

Kyle blinked a couple of times. "We can do that? Without any kind of trial?"

Jonathan frowned at Kyle. "When we have solid evidence of a demon killing humans, a trial is at the director's discretion. Mike sure didn't get much opportunity for justice before he had his throat torn out."

"Sorry," Kyle said, putting up his hands in surrender at Jonathan's defensive tone. "I'm just trying to understand how things work. I know Mike was your friend, and I sure won't shed any tears over Fenris Kellen's grave."

Jonathan huffed out a breath in frustration. "What sucks is that the grave won't be the demon's. Killing the body only sends it back to the abyss."

"It can return?"

"Well, not easily, and probably not for a long time," Jonathan conceded.

Noreen interrupted, looking down her nose at Kyle. "See? You don't know as much about *lupusdaemons* as you think you do."

Kyle flushed, but to Amanda's relief, he didn't respond to Noreen's baiting.

"When will we know the director's decision?" Amanda asked, trying to change the direction of the conversation.

"I don't know," Jonathan answered. "Forensics submitted the case file to him, but I'll bet he'll want to consult with Blackstone before he decides on a course of action."

"No doubt," Noreen said. "Kellen is now part of a larger problem."

"That's an understatement," Jonathan said. He lowered his voice, his tone going dark. "Blackstone has no intention of negotiating with the dark coven. When we move on them, it will be a fight, and all kinds of things can happen in the heat of battle. Termination mandate or not, I don't intend to give Kellen a chance to surrender."

Jonathan's words chilled her, but Amanda didn't blame him for his attitude. He'd taken the attack on the farm personally since it had threatened Jessie's life and resulted in the death of a friend on his team. She just hoped Jonathan's thirst for revenge wouldn't impair his ability to lead his team effectively.

CHAPTER 17

Fair Warning

Marcella stood with her arms folded, staring down at her captive. Cyrus guarded the open door behind her. Cara had started to get up from her sleeping mat, but Marcella told the girl to remain seated. She wanted to retain the psychological advantage of standing over the young woman. The tactic seemed to work, as Cara returned her stare with wide eyes like a frightened mouse.

"Have you thought about my offer?" Marcella asked.

Cara squirmed, drawing her legs under her. "I would be honored to learn from you," she answered, her voice trailing off.

"But?"

"May I ask some questions first?"

"You may ask ..." Marcella responded, her tone indicating that she might not answer.

Cara opened her mouth a couple of times to speak, but clamped it shut again. She finally mustered the courage to ask her first question. "If I join your coven, won't that make me an enemy of the Order?"

Marcella's mouth twitched into a sardonic smile. "You mean, like I am? Yes, the Order have meddled in our affairs many times. We usually manage to avoid them. When we don't, they pay for it dearly."

"You aren't afraid of them?"

Marcella laughed. "The Order is not all-powerful. I'd be foolish not to respect their influence, and fear is a useful tool when it keeps you alert. However, I've learned how to deal with them. The Order tends to put down roots and settle in. The best way to stay out of their reach is to keep moving."

"Sounds exhausting."

You have no idea, Marcella thought. Her coven had been following the "keep-moving" strategy for far too long. It was time to change things, and forging an alliance with the werewolves was the first step. But to Cara, she said, "You get used to it. After a while, it feels strange to stay in one place too long."

After a moment of silence and more squirming, Cara asked, "Would I have to kill people?"

Marcella's eyebrows rose. "Only to defend the coven. The fact that you are sitting here alive is proof of that."

Cara's face turned red. "I'm alive because I *didn't* burn up in the house you set on fire."

"And then you left," Marcella answered reasonably. "That shows you weren't part of the Order's conspiracy to destroy *lupusdaemons*."

"Conspiracy?" Cara responded with a confused expression. "I don't think there's a conspiracy. The exorcism was Amanda's personal project. The Order only got involved when Kyle asked for sanctuary."

Ah, so Cara knew more than she'd been letting on. How much more could Marcella prompt from her? "And now? The Order has formed up to protect both Kyle and Amanda from the consequences of her actions."

Cara shrugged. "She's one of them. And now, so is Kyle. Of course they're going to protect their own."

Marcella liked the way Cara consistently spoke of the Order as "them" instead of "us." She had been watching carefully for slips during their conversations that might indicate Cara was not who she claimed to be. It was still possible that the Order had dangled Cara as bait and that she was really on a mission for the Order.

"What about the rest of your coven? If you weren't involved in the exorcism, why did the Order offer you sanctuary?"

"They were just being careful," Cara said, and once again Marcella had the impression the girl was leaving something out. Cara's voice went sour as she added, "They called it 'protective custody.'"

A wise precaution, considering Marcella had indeed gone to visit the residences of the Gold Ridge Coven's members, only to discover that they had already been swept up and moved to Hayworth Farm.

"All things considered, you probably should have been more appreciative of the Order's protection."

Cara sighed and looked down. "I guess. But it was too crowded, and after the fire, I felt like a sitting duck."

"I'm surprised they let you leave."

"I didn't ask for permission. I snuck out. I knew that Blackstone guy wouldn't allow it, and Noreen would find a way to talk me out of it."

The name "Blackstone" shocked Marcella like she'd touched the hot wire on a livestock fence. Her heart started pounding so hard that she could hear her own pulse. A sharp intake of breath from behind her told her Cyrus had also recognized the name. Reeling internally, she carefully controlled her voice and her expression. "Who did you say wouldn't allow you to leave?"

"Some creepy guy named Blackstone. He seemed to be the one in charge."

"Tell me what he looks like," Marcella demanded.

Cara blinked in surprise. "Okay … uh … he's tall and thin and wears black all the time."

"What about his face?"

Cara paused to think. "His eyes are blue, or maybe gray, and he has a thin beard that makes it look like he always needs a shave. His hair is dark and thinning."

"How long has he been there?"

"I'm not sure. He was already at the farm when I arrived. I heard he showed up and took over the investigation right after Amanda's moon shrine was destroyed."

Marcella narrowed her eyes at the term "moon shrine." Amanda had apparently given her altar room a name. How quaint.

"What has Blackstone been doing all this time? Did he put out the fire?"

Cara's expression grew contemplative. "Why do you care so much about Blackstone?"

"Answer the question!" Marcella shouted, taking a step forward.

Cara cowered back against the wall in response to the vehemence in Marcella's voice. "We put out the fire. I mean, my coven did. Blackstone wasn't there."

Realizing that her agitation regarding Blackstone was revealing her fear to the prisoner, Marcella relaxed her posture and quieted her voice. "Where was he?"

"How would I know? He just disappears sometimes. I've heard Noreen complain about it."

So Blackstone had been in the area for days, knowing that the Red Claw Coven was nearby. All this time, she thought she'd been playing cat and mouse with Amanda's coven and a small team of the Order's soldiers. It made her skin crawl to think about how close she would have been to Blackstone were he at the farm the night she set the fire. Luckily, he was somewhere else. But where?

Blackstone's presence changed everything. It was only a matter of time before he devised a plan of attack and came after her. She had to set up some kind of trap for him … or take a more direct approach. She'd always been better at offense than defense: her strike-and-disappear tactics were difficult to anticipate or counter. They'd certainly done a good job of keeping her alive so far, except this time she didn't want to disappear afterward. She needed time to think.

Meanwhile, Cara was giving her a speculative look that she didn't care for.

"You're running out of time to make up your mind," Marcella warned in a calm but deadly tone. "You have until my next visit to figure out what you want." She turned and started for the door.

"What happens if I choose not to join your coven?" Cara asked.

"Nothing good," Marcella answered as she exited the room.

CHAPTER 18

Under Observation

Adolphus Rutlinger poured himself a glass of red wine—his third of the afternoon. He hesitated as he raised the goblet to his lips, half tempted to throw it across the room. He sighed and took a sip instead, knowing the mess would accomplish nothing and he would only end up pouring another.

Allowing Marcella to take over was disgraceful. He should have challenged her, even if it meant losing and returning to the abyss.

No. That must not happen.

All the work he'd put into the Rutlinger Foundation would be destroyed. He needed to be patient. Marcella would make a mistake at some point, and the Order would take care of her for him.

But the wait was excruciating. In the meantime, she was undermining his authority and subverting his pack. Skyler was still his, but Fenris had joined Marcella's exorcism crusade. The lawyer's betrayal was not out of character, but his support for *any* authority figure certainly was. Adolphus sourly admitted to himself that perhaps Fenris had been waiting for the right leader. If that was the case, good riddance.

The ringing phone interrupted his thoughts. He walked to the corner table where the phone rested and lifted the handset. "Hello?"

"Adolphus. So good to hear your voice. I take it you are still allowed to answer the phone?"

Rutlinger cringed, recognizing the mocking voice of David Bonham, alpha of the Colville Pack in Eastern Washington. "News travels fast."

David chuckled across the line. "The wonders of modern technology, my ancient friend. It is a miracle to those of us who remember when the four-paws network was the speediest way to move information."

"Indeed. I sometimes miss those days. What can I do for you, David, or did you call just to harass me?"

"Come now, Adolphus. Your sense of humor is failing you. I know what you're up to, so you don't have to pretend for my sake. Your new alpha is attracting a lot of attention with her mission. If she succeeds, she'll have the respect of every pack in the world, but if she fails … well, let's just say it would be best not to be the one in charge."

Adolphus didn't think it would make much difference who was in charge. The repercussions of Marcella's actions would engulf everyone near her, guilty or not. At some point, she would call upon the entire Pack for support and suck all of them into her mad plans. A strong sense of foreboding warned him that the time was rapidly approaching.

At that moment, Marcella entered the living room with Cyrus in tow. Her unfocused eyes and a deep frown revealed that something had disturbed her.

"Marcella is here now," Adolphus said into the handset, "if you would like to speak to her."

"Yes, please put her on," David replied.

Marcella focused on Adolphus and narrowed her eyes. "Who is it?"

He held the handset out toward her. "David Bonham of the Colville Pack."

Marcella's face cleared, and she eagerly snatched the handset. "Thanks for getting back to me so quickly, David."

She glanced toward Adolphus upon hearing David's response. "The pack leaders didn't like my proposal?"

David's answer put a smile on her face. Marcella had contacted all of the northwest werewolf packs, proposing an alliance with herself as an ambassador of sorts. It was a thinly disguised bid to position herself as queen of the alliance, and it would give her all the protection she needed from the Order's hunters.

"That's good news," Marcella said. "I'm sure they won't regret their decision."

Her smile faded as David continued. "My mission benefits us all. How dare you threaten me with ultimatums!"

Adolphus cheered silently to himself. It was sounding like Marcella's northwest pack alliance had just responded to her proposal with a "do-or-die" condition. That boded well for him and his pack. If she succeeded, he would enjoy the protection of her alliance and the comfort of knowing the exorcism was no longer a threat. If she failed, that same alliance would help him get rid of her.

Marcella took a deep breath. "All right. I accept your terms. See that you live up to them." She hung up the phone without waiting for a response.

Turning to Adolphus, she said, "As you've probably surmised, the pack leaders won't commit themselves to helping me yet. However, if I can eliminate the exorcism threat, they'll accept that I have the necessary strength and skill to lead an alliance."

Careful to hide his glee, Adolphus asked, "And if you fail?"

Anger flashed in Marcella's eyes. "I'm not going to fail. And you're going to help make sure that I don't." She folded her arms and spoke in a chilling tone. "It's time the Selkirk Pack started taking a more direct role in assisting its alpha, starting tonight. Gather everyone who is staying here at the Foundation. We have no time to waste."

Her demand should have surprised him, but all it did was confirm his feelings of foreboding. Adolphus nodded slowly. "I understand."

It was a bad time to oppose her—she was focused and angry. He was better off cooperating for the moment even though that meant the entire Pack might share her fate. He would support her until he became certain that she would fail. At that point, his only hope would be to betray her to the Order and claim that she had used her powers to coerce them. It was a risky approach, but he might be able to salvage a truce. In the meantime, he would have to find subtle ways of maintaining contact with the Order without Marcella's knowledge and without truly jeopardizing her plans.

Adolphus sighed to himself as Marcella and Cyrus left the room. Duplicity was always so taxing.

CHAPTER 19
Overwhelmed

After a long day of going over the exorcism ritual repeatedly, Amanda was tired, hungry, and a little grumpy. She sat back in her chair and laced her fingers behind her head to stretch her arms. The folding chair was putting her legs to sleep, in spite of the cushion she'd found to sit on. She stamped her feet to restore some circulation. The sky through the moon shrine's cupola was darkening with the onset of dusk.

"Let's call it a day," Noreen said, rubbing her forehead. "We're just repeating ourselves at this point anyway. If we think of anything new later on, we can add it to the work we've already done."

"Sounds good to me," Kyle said with relief, pushing his chair back and standing to stretch.

Amanda saved the document with her notes and closed her laptop. "I'm going back to my office so I can get on the network and send these notes to all of our email accounts as a backup."

"Send a copy to the Order archive as well," Noreen said, "and be sure to tell Blackstone before you do. We still haven't caught whoever deleted the first set of notes, but we're watching now. If the spy tries to delete them again, we should be able to find out who it is."

"Maybe we should send a copy to the Rutlinger Foundation," Kyle said jokingly. "I'll bet that would piss them off."

"Great idea," Amanda said. "As if we don't have enough trouble already."

Noreen said nothing, but her annoyed expression said volumes.

Kyle grinned and shrugged. "Just kidding. Sheesh. You two need to lighten up. We got a lot done today."

Noreen nodded her head grudgingly. "That's true. Even if we are redoing work that was already done once before."

Kyle shook his head and spoke in an exasperated tone. "Man, the glass is always half-empty with you, isn't it?"

"Kyle ..." Amanda said in a warning tone.

"I know, I know. Sorry," Kyle apologized without much sincerity. "As my grandfather used to say, 'Don't tease the animals.'"

"Not helping," Amanda chastised.

Noreen stood and swept her hands down her skirt to straighten it. "That's all right, Amanda. It's just a shame his grandfather's good sense wasn't hereditary."

Kyle blinked at Noreen in surprise. "I think that was almost a joke. I didn't know you had it in you."

"I'm no longer surprised by what you don't know," Noreen retorted.

Amanda gave up on trying to be peacemaker. Kyle and Noreen were fine while they were on task, but, socially, they mixed like oil and water. The best strategy for keeping the peace was to separate them.

Amanda grabbed Kyle's arm and pulled him toward the stairway door. "C'mon, let's go." Her haste wasn't only about putting an end to the bickering—an uneasy feeling made her want to hurry to her office. Her laptop contained the only copy of all the work they'd done, and after everything they'd been through, that was unacceptable.

Ten minutes later, Amanda sat back with a satisfied smile as electronic copies of their day's work went out to everyone she could think of who had an interest in it. It was a relief to know that it would be a lot harder for her enemies to destroy all records of the exorcism again.

Her stomach grumbled, reminding her that lunch had been hours ago. But she had one more task to complete before she could break for the day: she had to find Blackstone and warn him that she was ready to send the exorcism notes to the Order.

Kyle looked up from the book he was reading. "All done?"

"Almost," Amanda said as she stood. "I just need to find Blackstone and—"

Amanda's voice caught as a strong sense of danger jangled across her nerves. "Wait," she said, closing her eyes and holding up a hand to warn Kyle to be quiet. She focused her awareness on her perimeter wards, but the bad sensation was fading quickly. The wards still seemed intact, but something was off.

"Amanda!" Noreen shouted from the bottom of the stairwell. Amanda apparently wasn't the only one who had sensed the disturbance. When they had reinforced Amanda's wards after the fire, the entire coven had participated, so all of the witches at the farm were sensitive to them.

Kyle dropped his book and leaped to his feet. "What's happening?"

Amanda turned toward the door and headed out of the room. "I'm not sure," she answered over her shoulder. "Something touched the wards, but it stopped."

"Do you think someone came through?" Kyle asked as the two of them hurried toward the stairwell.

"No, the wards would still be alerting me."

A boom rattled the house. At the same instant, a shock jolted through Amanda, weakening her legs. She stumbled and had to catch herself with the stairwell railing to keep from going to her knees. Kyle took her arm and helped her back to her feet.

"The wards are down!" she shouted.

Through the walls, the pop-pop of gunfire came from outside the house. She was starting down the stairs to the first floor when Noreen appeared at the bottom with Jessie right behind her. In the dining room, Jonathan was shouting into the radio, trying to get status from the tactical teams he had arranged around the house.

Noreen waved Amanda back up the stairs. "Go back up," she said. "Jonathan wants us off the bottom floor until we know what's going on."

Tanya appeared at the doorway to the room she was staying in. "What's happening?"

Noreen had reached the second floor by then and answered, "We don't know. Everyone go to the moon shrine. If it's the *lupusdaemons*, we can hold them off there."

Kyle started down the stairs, but Amanda stopped him by grabbing his arm. "Where are you going?"

"I can't do any good in the moon shrine," he answered. "I'm going to help Jonathan."

Amanda let go, nodding her understanding. She leaned forward and gave him a quick kiss. "Stay safe."

"You, too," he said before stomping down the stairs.

By the time Amanda and the other witches reached the moon shrine, the gunfire from outside had stopped. That was either good or very bad. Noreen gathered everyone around the recently cleansed casting circle and took prime position in the center. Cara's position was empty, but they were still plenty powerful as a coven of four.

Without preamble, Noreen started an incantation of protection against evil. It would shield them from demons and dark magic, but it wouldn't do anything to repel physical attacks. That was what Jonathan and his team were for.

Noreen had finished the first stanza of the spell when the sound of crashing glass came from the first floor. Lucille's scream told them the attackers had entered the house—through a window, Amanda guessed.

Shouts and sounds of conflict from below distracted Amanda as she tried to concentrate on the spell. While she chanted, Noreen gave each of the women a look that warned them to focus. Tanya shook from head to toe, her eyes wide and brimming with tears. Jessie was the most composed of them all. Her gaze held Tanya's, and she encouraged the younger witch with a tight smile.

Noreen completed the final stanza of the incantation and clapped her hands together. Amanda's energy joined the others' and began to flow into a faintly glowing protective shield that formed around their group. Noreen pushed the shield out as far as she could, extending it throughout the room. The physical pressure of the spell pushed the stairwell door closed with a solid thump.

As the door swung closed, Amanda caught a whiff of smoke. If their enemies were setting the house on fire again, the attic was not a good place to be. The room had no windows except around the cupola, which was far out of reach above. Their only escape route was through the stairwell door.

Confirming her supposition, a smoke alarm sounded from below, adding to the general din.

"Jessie and Tanya, hold the protection spell," Noreen ordered. "Amanda, you and I are going to raise a deflection shield."

Splitting their energies was risky, as was driving two different primary spells from the same casting circle. But they had little choice. The real question was whether or not they were strong enough to fend off whatever might come their way while their energies were paired off.

Amanda carefully disengaged her energy from the protection spell, giving Jessie and Tanya time to adjust. Noreen was already starting on the second incantation when Amanda reached out with her powers and added her support.

The door suddenly opened, startling Amanda enough that she dropped her connection to Noreen. Noreen stopped her incantation and let out an exasperated noise as Blackstone slipped into the room and closed the door behind himself.

"Sorry," he said, stepping away from the door, "but they're right behind me. We have to make our stand here."

The sound of claws on wood came from the stairwell and made Amanda's chest constrict in fear. There was no mistaking that sound for human footsteps. The door crashed open again, interrupting Noreen's attempt to start over with her incantation.

Fur filled the doorway, along with two sets of blazing eyes and bared fangs that gleamed wetly in the room's dim illumination. A tendril of smoke slipped into the room, as if the werewolves had brought the fires of hell with them.

The larger wolf moved forward, snarling as it encountered the protection shield. Tanya gasped and whimpered, closing her eyes against the horrors slavering at the door. If the fearful witch panicked, she'd lose her concentration and Jessie would have to hold the protection spell alone.

If their attackers had made it to the moon shrine, what was going on downstairs? Was Kyle okay? Had the werewolves gone around him or ... through him?

With a more pressing challenge right in front of her, Amanda suppressed her concern for Kyle and glanced at Noreen for direction. Should she help Tanya and Jessie? Or was Noreen going to try to raise a shield again?

Noreen took a deep breath and started the incantation. But she was too late.

Soft steps on the stairs presaged the appearance of a tall, dark-haired woman in a hooded cloak the color of dried blood. She stepped between the wolves, looking like some fairy queen of the forest accompanied by her familiars. Her lip curled in disgust when she spotted Blackstone.

Noreen's incantation trailed off. From somewhere deep within Amanda came the certainty that the woman at the doorway was Marcella Pedroso, the dark witch Blackstone had been hunting. The same dark witch who had defiled Amanda's moon shrine and tried to kill her. Dark power seemed to flow off the woman in waves.

With a bemused expression, Marcella reached a hand toward the shield. She pressed against the sparking resistance as if testing its strength.

Realizing their danger, Amanda tried to rejoin Tanya and Jessie and strengthen the protection shield. It was the only thing between them and their enemies. She assumed Noreen was doing the same thing since the coven leader had stopped chanting the second spell.

Taking a deep breath, Amanda tried to calm herself and clear her thoughts long enough to concentrate. Her power was just linking up with her coven mates' when two things happened. The dark witch spoke a brief incantation and pushed her hand forward, disrupting and draining the shield. Then Tanya cried out in response to the shock of the attack and lost her concentration. Amanda tried to shore up the failing spell and could sense Noreen doing the same, but the shield was dissipating faster than they could strengthen it. Jessie struggled to maintain the spell as it unraveled, but she couldn't hold it by herself. The spell collapsed under the dark witch's assault, and with a grunt, Jessie fell to the floor unconscious.

Marcella stepped forward with a sneer of triumph, and the wolves leaped past her legs. The larger wolf ran straight for Noreen while the smaller one lunged at Amanda. The dark witch turned her attention to Blackstone. If the fury and hatred revealed in her glare had been a spell, it would have turned Blackstone to a pile of ash in that instant.

The moment Jessie collapsed, Amanda snatched her athame off the altar. The attacking wolf was so fast that she barely had time to bring up the blade before the beast slammed into her. She swiped desperately as she was thrown backward off her feet, scoring a slice along the creature's chest that caused it to growl with pain and anger. Amanda hit the floor hard, and the breath was knocked from her lungs, the athame bouncing from her hand. Her body slid a foot or so before her head bumped hard against the wall behind her. Her vision darkened and swam with stars.

Amanda tried to catch her breath, but a heavy weight on her chest made that impossible. When her vision cleared, she was staring into the eyes of the wolf that pressed her to the floor.

From her supine position at the edge of the room, Amanda couldn't see what was happening with the other witches. She tried to move, but the wolf's growl warned her to stillness. The wolf glanced toward the dark witch and Amanda followed its gaze.

Blackstone had his hands folded in front of his chest as if in prayer. In fact, his eyes were closed, and he appeared to be whispering something that Amanda couldn't hear over the dark witch's loud incantation. Marcella was about to strike, and the best he could do was pray?

Looking up at the wolf, Amanda wondered why it was holding back. It could have torn her throat out while she was disoriented from hitting her head. She started to raise her arms to shove it away, but the beast pushed hard with one of the paws that rested on her chest and flashed its teeth within an inch of her face with a snarling bark. Amanda dropped her hands to her side and went still, trying to ignore the drop of wolf spittle that tickled the tip of her nose. Her only tiny hope was the knowledge that the wolf had chosen not to kill her so far.

Marcella finished her incantation and clapped her hands together, pointing her fingertips toward Blackstone. A twisting stream of violet lightning jumped the distance between them, and Amanda was certain that Blackstone was doomed.

Blackstone had stopped praying and had opened his eyes. As the dark witch clapped, he unfolded his hands like wings hinged at his pinkies. The lightning arced toward him and hit an invisible barrier that lit up in the shape of a satellite dish. It seemed to absorb the lightning and then spit it back out at the center. In the next instant, Marcella was zapped by her own construct.

Screaming with pain and fury, she hugged herself and sank to one knee as her spell fizzled. She glared at Blackstone with a mixture of hate and fear before rising unsteadily and taking a step backward toward the door.

Kyle appeared and grabbed the dark witch in a bear hug from behind. Blackstone paused in the middle of what looked like another prayer.

Marcella looked over her shoulder and sneered. "Just like old times, eh Kyle? Sorry, no time to snuggle today." She then twisted her torso and drove her elbow into Kyle's side, easily breaking his grip and sending him careening into the wall.

As he fell away from her, he caught sight of the wolf standing over Amanda and rebounded with impressive speed and agility. In a heartbeat, he had lifted the wolf off Amanda and flung it across the room where it crashed head first into a cabinet.

Amanda turned her attention back to the showdown between Blackstone and Marcella, but the dark witch was gone. The larger wolf that had attacked Noreen streaked past Blackstone and disappeared through the doorway. The crash of glass told her that Marcella and the wolf had chosen to exit the house by one of the second-story windows.

Kyle reached down and helped Amanda to her feet, keeping a wary eye on the still wolf form that lay in the opposite corner of the room.

Jonathan charged into the room, saw Jessie collapsed in the corner, and ran to her side. Taking her in his arms, he coaxed her to awaken. Jessie groaned and rubbed the back of her head before sitting up and accepting a hug from Jonathan.

Amanda went to Noreen, who had her back to the wall and was nursing a bleeding forearm. "Damned thing bit me," she complained, inspecting the jagged wound.

Blackstone stood with his arms folded, considering the collapsed wolf. It opened its eyes and raised its head, looking around while its ears twitched. It slowly rolled up to a sitting position. Kyle positioned himself between the wolf and Amanda while Jonathan stood at Jessie's side and pointed his carbine at the creature.

Blackstone raised his hand in a checking gesture toward Jonathan. "Something odd is going on here," he said.

An unpleasant pressure pushed against Amanda's magical senses, alerting her that the wolf was about to transform. She sighed in frustration, knowing that the dark magic that was being unleashed within the room would set her back days in her project to restore the moon shrine.

When the transformation was complete, a naked Skyler Arpin stood where the wolf had been. The wound from Amanda's knife had already closed to a thin red line. Lithe and toned, Skyler seemed unembarrassed by her nudity. When she gave Kyle a challenging smile, he gulped and stepped back to stand alongside Amanda.

Amanda noted wryly that Kyle had been perfectly willing to stand between her and a deadly wolf, but a naked woman had him backpedaling to her side. Maybe she should encourage that behavior.

"I don't have much time," Skyler said, keeping her voice low. "If I don't catch up to the others soon, they'll become suspicious."

Jonathan raised his weapon to his shoulder, sighting down its length. "You aren't going anywhere."

Skyler ignored him, focusing her attention on Blackstone. "I stayed behind to deliver a message."

"Go on," Blackstone said, nodding slightly.

"Marcella has taken over the Foundation, but some of us are not happy about that. We're looking for a way to stop her, and we're willing to work with the Order."

Blackstone looked at her askance. "You would betray your own kind?"

Jonathan took a step forward. "She's a demon. We can't trust her."

"I'm not asking you to trust me," Skyler said. "I'm asking you to let me rejoin the others and continue to prove I'm telling the truth."

Amanda connected a few dots in her mind. Someone from inside the Pack had warned Lucille about Marcella's intent to go after the entire Gold Ridge Coven. Was it Skyler?

"You're the one who called," Amanda stated. Her announcement was purposely vague, in case her guess was wrong. The demon could prove it was telling the truth by filling in a few details.

Skyler nodded. "Marcella had already begun to stalk your coven. I knew Ms. Hayworth could get the word out quickly."

Amanda was satisfied that Skyler had either made the call herself or was working with the person who did. Either way, that call had probably saved the lives of her coven mates.

Blackstone seemed unconvinced. "That call could have been a trick to gather everyone in one place for easier disposal. And here you are, participating in this raid."

"*She* was the prime target of the raid," Skyler said, waving a hand toward Amanda. "I could have torn her throat out, but I didn't. I could have turned and fought Kyle when he entered the room, but I didn't. I let him throw me against the wall and pretended to be unconscious until the others left so I could talk to you."

Blackstone's eyes narrowed. "You did not kill Amanda, but you were ready to do so. You were waiting to see how we would fare against the dark witch."

Skyler shrugged. "If Marcella had defeated you, there wouldn't have been much point in defying her. She would have killed Amanda herself, and the Order would assume the whole Pack supported her."

Amanda's mind froze as she realized how close she had come to death that evening. The wolf could have killed her a dozen times over. If not for Blackstone's unusual powers, everyone in the house would probably be dead.

"What exactly do you want?" Blackstone asked.

"I want you to know that Dr. Rutlinger and I will continue to work against Marcella as much as we can. We want things to go back to the way they were. We'll continue to give you advance warning of her plans when we can."

"Like you warned us about the raid tonight?" Jonathan scoffed.

"We didn't have the opportunity," Skyler insisted. "We didn't even know about it until earlier today. She was spooked by something her little captive said, and it made her react hastily."

"What captive?" Noreen and Amanda demanded simultaneously.

Skyler leaned back and raised her eyebrows. "I thought you knew. Marcella is holding your air witch in the basement at the Foundation."

"Dammit!" Noreen exclaimed. "That stupid girl. Now they have a hostage."

Amanda wanted to be angry too, but she was thinking about how scared Cara must be. "We've got to get her out of there."

"What spooked Marcella?" Blackstone asked.

Skyler took a step forward, looking him over in an assessing manner. "You're Blackstone?" He nodded. "Then *you* are what spooked her."

"Explain."

"You probably know more than I do. She said she's been running from you for a long time, and it was time to put an end to it."

Blackstone seemed confused. "She's had much better opportunities than this in the past. Why here? Why now?"

"Because she's a werewolf now," Kyle answered. "She threw me off too easily when I tried to grab her."

Blackstone blinked several times in stunned silence. "Then the witch I knew as Marcella is gone. The *lupusdaemon* who took her has somehow mastered her powers. How extraordinary."

"Not extraordinary," Noreen disagreed. "Impossible. Demons can't use mortal magic. If they could, they'd summon more of their kind and overrun us."

"She's right," Skyler confirmed.

"But that means ..." Blackstone mused in a disturbed tone, "Marcella has chosen to share her body with a *lupusdaemon*." It was the first time Amanda had seen him shaken by anything. He looked sharply at Skyler. "Cyrus Fleming as well?"

Skyler nodded and stepped back to the space where she had transformed earlier. "I need to go," she announced.

A shot rang out in the room, making everyone jump. Skyler doubled over with a screeching cry, clutching the side of her thigh. Everyone looked at Jonathan as he lowered his weapon back to a rest position. "That will make your story more convincing when you return to your pack."

He glanced around at the incredulous expressions of the others in the room. "What? It's just a flesh wound. She'll heal."

Leveling an angry glare at Jonathan, Skyler transformed back into a wolf. She loped off toward the stairwell with a limp, leaving a trail of blood spots. She leaped through the broken window and disappeared.

A few sniffling sobs caught Amanda's attention, and she turned toward Tanya. The young woman was curled up in the corner of the room with her legs drawn up and her hands holding her head. Amanda went over to her and knelt in front of her. "Are you hurt?" she asked.

Tanya shook her head.

"It's okay now. It's over."

Tanya looked up, her eyes filled with tears and panic. "It's *not* over," she said. "We're all going to die."

"Don't be ridiculous," Noreen's voice said from behind. "Look around you. We're fine."

Amanda knew without looking that Noreen's hand was dripping blood from holding the rip on her arm, but if she didn't think the wound was worth mentioning, Amanda wasn't about to contradict her.

Amanda stepped back when Blackstone came over to the corner. He extended a hand for Tanya to take. At first, she just stared at him. After a moment, she accepted his silent offer and stood, wiping the tears from her eyes.

"What are you afraid of, Tanya?" he asked gently.

"The dark witch," she replied almost in a whisper. "She's a demon who controls dark magic. We can't fight her."

"But we did fight her," Blackstone said. "And we won."

Tanya shook her head. "We didn't win. She'll come back."

"And we'll be ready for her."

Tanya exhaled and let go of Blackstone's hand. "She's too strong. I couldn't stop her from coming in. I failed us all."

"Nonsense," Blackstone said. "She got lucky. You can blame me if you like. I interrupted Amanda and Noreen."

Tanya obviously wasn't buying his arguments. Blackstone put both hands on her shoulders and waited until her eyes met his. "You're only looking at what went wrong. Think about what went right. We successfully repelled an all out assault of four werewolves and two dark magic users."

Amanda sent a surprised glance toward Kyle, and he nodded in confirmation. She'd get the details from him later about what had happened downstairs.

Meanwhile, Blackstone went on. "You're being too hard on yourself. What makes you think you failed?"

Tanya's gaze dropped toward her feet. "I lost my grip on the spell."

"Why did you lose your concentration?"

"I … I was scared."

"You were shocked," Blackstone corrected. "Combat magic is nothing like the orderly rituals most covens perform. The Order trains its witches to work under conditions of duress and distraction. Fear is natural and can't be avoided, but you can learn to work around it. How many times have you fought another witch who was seeking to do you harm?"

"N–Never."

Blackstone dropped his hands from her shoulders. "Then you can't blame yourself for not being an expert duelist."

"But I could have gotten us all killed!" Tanya insisted.

"But you didn't. Do you know why? Because you are part of a team. Whether we succeed or fail is not up to you alone."

Tanya blinked a few times while she considered Blackstone's remarks. He seemed to be getting through to her at last.

"I'm sorry you've been caught up in this little war of the Order's, but we really need your help. I suggest you work with your coven mates to learn some of the skills you'll need going forward. The only true failure today would be if you walked away having learned nothing."

Tanya gave Noreen a questioning look, and the coven mistress nodded her head in agreement with Blackstone's suggestion. "Okay," Tanya answered. "I'll do my best."

"Of course you will," Blackstone said in a tone of finality. "Now, I suggest we all go downstairs and see if anyone other than Mistress Thornquist needs medical attention."

CHAPTER 20
Aftermath

For privacy, Blackstone had suggested that Noreen and Jonathan join him in the back of his highly customized SUV for a strategy meeting. It had become almost impossible to find a quiet and secure spot in the farmhouse. His guests sat in the second-row passenger seats, swiveled to face the rear of the vehicle while Blackstone sat on a long bench that doubled as a bed in the rear cargo area. His left leg was resting up on the padded upholstery so he could face his fellow team leaders.

"It's a bit cramped, but we should be able to speak freely here," Blackstone commented. "After the attack, emotions are understandably running high. We need to plan our response, and I don't want to be interrupted by passionate cheerleaders for any particular course of action."

Noreen and Jonathan both nodded in response.

Blackstone had another reason for meeting privately with his team leaders that he didn't share: he wanted to assess how the attack had affected their states of mind. Could he rely on them as matters progressed?

"I think it's pretty clear what we need to do," said Jonathan. "The farm is not working out as a sanctuary. The first thing we need to do is move Jessie and Tanya somewhere safer so we can focus on dealing with the Pack."

Blackstone couldn't blame Jonathan for worrying about his wife. Jessie had suffered only a mild concussion and a few scrapes in the attack, but her injuries could have easily been much worse.

"You think Jessie will go along with that?" Noreen asked doubtfully.

"It's not her decision to make," Jonathan said with a shrug.

"I'd like to hear you say that to her face," Noreen retorted.

Technically, Jonathan was right, but Blackstone was inclined to agree with Noreen's appraisal of how Jessie would feel about abandoning her husband in the middle of the conflict. Throughout every crisis so far, she had remained stable and competent.

"With two dark witches in the mix, Amanda and I could definitely use their help," Noreen added.

Jonathan rounded on Noreen, his face set in a stubborn frown. "Tanya is terrified, and Jessie doesn't know what she's getting herself into. Neither of them is in the Order, so they don't have the training or experience they need. You'll get them both killed."

"No amount of training could prepare them for what happened here," Noreen argued. "As for experience, every one of us started without it. Besides, now they *do* have experience. Tanya is learning to overcome her fear, and you know better than I do how strong Jessie is."

"But this isn't their fight," Jonathan almost pleaded.

"It is now," Noreen said. "The enemy has Cara, and the coven has the right to defend itself. Less than an hour ago, Tanya asked me how we were going to get Cara out of the Foundation. If we give her and Jessie the choice to leave or stay, which do you think they'll chose?"

Blackstone had already made his decision on the subject. He could have stopped their argument at any point, but he thought it prudent to let them make their cases to each other. It would be best if Noreen could convince Jonathan that splitting up the coven was a bad idea, or at least a futile one. The man would accept the reality of the situation more easily if it weren't forced upon him.

Jonathan took a deep breath and let it out as a sigh. "They would chose to stay," he admitted, looking down at his hands.

Blackstone smiled. "Great. Now that we have that out of the way, let's move on to where we go from here."

"I say we call in an air strike and turn the entire Foundation into a giant crater," Jonathan said bitterly. "Let's see what dark magic can do against *that*."

The callous brutality of his remark seemed to stun Noreen. "But ... Cara," she objected.

Blackstone sensed that Jonathan wasn't being serious although his proposal held a certain appeal. It would quickly solve several difficult problems even if the political ramifications would generate new ones. And then there was the innocent captive to consider. Not for the first time, he wondered if Marcella had abducted the girl specifically to prevent the Order from employing drastic measures like the one Jonathan suggested.

Noreen's accusing stare made Jonathan blink in surprise. "I'm kidding," he reassured her.

"We understand your frustration," Blackstone interrupted. "We'd all like a quick solution that minimizes the potential for casualties. But let's focus on *practical* solutions for the moment. The hostage does indeed complicate matters."

"I'm concerned about Cara," Noreen said, "but she can be surprisingly resourceful when she wants something. We have a much bigger problem to consider."

"Marcella the demon witch," Blackstone supplied.

"Yes. Or is it *witch demon*? To work magic, Marcella must be in control. To shape change, the demon must be in control. They can't have been ... is there even a word for this? ...

cohabitating for long, so I can't imagine the handoff between two powerful egos is easy or fast. I'd sure like to understand more about the motivations behind this arrangement on both sides. To our knowledge, a *lupusdaemon* has never willingly shared a body with the original human owner beyond First Moon."

"First time for everything," Jonathan suggested.

"Maybe," Noreen allowed. "But even if Marcella is the one in control most of the time, we're in worse trouble than I imagined."

Jonathan nodded. "*Lupusdaemon* speed and strength are hard enough to fight without adding magic to the mix."

The haunted look in Noreen's eyes drew Blackstone's attention. "There's more," he prompted.

Noreen raised an eyebrow and sighed. "Isn't there always?"

"Tell me," he demanded gently.

"It's a matter of power," she answered. "We witches draw our power from the spirits. Our rituals are designed to draw light spirits to us and push dark spirits away. Dark witches do the reverse. Working together and using a casting circle allow a coven to call more spirits and strengthen the spell. Any one of us can cast spells independently and with minimal ceremony, but those spells are much weaker by comparison."

"But that's good news, isn't it?" Jonathan asked. "The dark witch attacked on her own. Wouldn't that make her weaker?"

"It *should* have," Noreen answered. "But she cut through our defenses almost effortlessly. She didn't even need the help of the warlock who was keeping the rest of you busy downstairs."

When the attack began, Blackstone had been downstairs with Kyle, Jonathan, and the tactical team, ready to defend the house. As soon as he understood that they were dealing with an all-out attack of both werewolves and dark witches, he anticipated their enemies' true objective and fell back to the moon shrine to protect Amanda. Marcella and two of the werewolves had followed him upstairs, but Cyrus and the two other werewolves had remained on the ground floor fighting the defenders.

As Blackstone had entered the moon shrine, he'd passed through the protective shield the witches had raised and judged it sufficient to repel their attackers. He had been shocked when Marcella tore it down within seconds.

Noreen's description of how witches derived their power hinted at an explanation. "You've formulated a theory?" he asked her.

"It was something Tanya said, actually. She feared we were doomed because Marcella is a demon with dark magic. That's backward, but close enough. Demons are the most powerful of dark spirits, and they attract other dark spirits. A dark adept like Marcella with constant and immediate access to a substantial pool of dark spirit support would have nearly as much power as a full coven."

"Nearly?" Blackstone asked hopefully.

Noreen shrugged. "Maybe more … I don't know. There's no way to measure these things exactly."

Blackstone sat back and thought.

"Our primary goal is to rescue Cara as quickly as possible," he finally said. "She is an innocent victim caught in the middle of an Order conflict."

"Yes," Noreen agreed. "We need to rescue Cara for more reasons than you know."

Blackstone's calm finally cracked with the addition of another unexpected complication. With an exhale of exasperation, he asked, "What now?"

"Since we learned about the demon witch, we've focused on the ramifications. We haven't seriously considered *how* it happened in the first place."

"Does that matter?" Jonathan asked.

"Perhaps," Noreen replied. "It goes back to motivations. I've been thinking about why a witch and a demon would pair up. Marcella gains incredible physical and magical powers, but how does the demon benefit? And which of them suggested the arrangement?"

"I'm still not seeing the relevance," Jonathan said, shaking his head impatiently.

Noreen stopped and gave Jonathan an irritated glare. "If you let me finish, I promise you will."

Jonathan held up a hand in apology and then waved for her to continue. "Sorry."

"Although it's possible that a *lupusdaemon* approached Marcella, it would need a powerful reason to give up full control over its current body in exchange for a back seat in Marcella's body. I think it's far more likely that Marcella initiated the bargain in an effort to strengthen her defenses against the Order."

Jonathan's brow furrowed. "Okay. But doesn't that have the same net result for the demon? Getting a *back seat* as you put it?"

Noreen paused before responding, and Blackstone sharpened his attention on what she was about to say.

"Not if she summoned a *lupusdaemon* from the abyss. The demon would have nothing to lose and plenty to gain. When you factor Cyrus into the equation, it also explains how she managed to get *two lupusdaemons* to accept the arrangement."

Blackstone suddenly understood what Noreen had been getting at. They had to rescue Cara sooner rather than later because … "You're concerned that Marcella might cast a summoning ritual with Cara as the sacrifice."

"Exactly," Noreen confirmed. "I just hope we're not too late."

Blackstone had hoped to avoid bringing up the fact that the full moon would rise that night. It would increase the perceived risk of the plan he was about to propose.

"If we're going after Cara, we're going to need backup," Jonathan said. "I can't take on a rescue mission and defend the sanctuary at the same time. Even if I leave Noreen in charge of the sanctuary squad, I don't have enough people."

"You need me on that rescue team," Noreen objected. "No one in this region has more mission experience."

Jonathan shrugged. "Hey, I hear you. But you're one of the targets, along with Amanda and Kyle. We can't very well send any of you right into their stronghold."

Blackstone shook his head. "We don't have time to get backup, and we also can't take the security risk. We have to use the resources we have available. That includes everyone at the sanctuary with skills we can use. I want to hit the Foundation at dawn."

"That's insane!" Jonathan objected. "We'd be delivering the people we've been trying to protect right into the enemy's hands. Besides, we can't possibly get ready by dawn."

Noreen's expression turned contemplative. "After our talk with Skyler Arpin, I'm not sure how much of a stronghold it is. It's possible we'll get some inside assistance."

Jonathan's face was getting redder by the moment. He was obviously not accepting any plan that put Jessie in harm's way. "You can't trust the word of a demon! You're just worried about your nomination to the Court of Elders," he accused. "It wouldn't do to bow out of such an important mission, especially when you are partly responsible for the situation."

Noreen glared wordlessly at Jonathan. Even if there was some truth to his accusation, the remark had been hurtful. Her stare seemed to make Jonathan check himself.

When he turned to Blackstone, Jonathan's voice hardened. "This is a bad idea. You talk about a security risk in one breath and then offer up the coven as a distraction the next. Now you want to storm a werewolf lair on the night of a full moon!"

Blackstone ignored the angry barbs and stared blandly. He doubted he could say anything to make Jonathan feel better about the situation. He just needed to make sure the man would follow orders.

"After dawn, the moon will no longer be an issue," Blackstone replied with confidence he didn't entirely feel. "Security is indeed an important consideration, and I believe our charges are safest if they stay with me."

"You have a pretty high opinion of yourself," Jonathan grumbled.

Blackstone held up a hand to forestall any more comments. "I know the plan is not ideal, but think about it. We could hardly assemble a better team for this mission. I understand that bringing the targets with us puts them at greater risk. That's why this mission has to be about more than a rescue. I intend to put an end to this conflict once and for all. If having the coven with us distracts the enemy, so much the better. Our witches can take advantage of that, too."

Jonathan shook his head slowly, his mouth turned down into a frustrated frown. "You're going to turn my kids into orphans."

Blackstone mentally voiced a calming prayer while he watched Jonathan. He waited until the man's gaze locked on to his. "Don't sell us short. Think about what you've seen over the past couple of days. Imagine what we can do when we are prepared and on the offensive. We face a powerful enemy, but not an invincible one."

Noreen let out a small laugh. "The blood trail Skyler Arpin left behind after Jonathan shot her was proof enough of that."

Jonathan sat back in his chair and blew out a long breath.

"I don't like it," he said, "but I can see you've made up your mind. Just promise me you'll ask for volunteers. No one should be forced to go on a suicide mission."

"I have no problem agreeing to that promise," Blackstone answered.

And he didn't. Everyone Blackstone wanted on the mission had already volunteered in one way or another. They didn't know the full scope of what he had in mind, but no one seemed interested in being left behind.

As for the full moon, Blackstone argued with himself that the odds of a *lupusdaemon* attempting a possession during the attack were slim and that attacking at dawn should eliminate the risk. Still, he had to admit that no human knew everything about *Vollmond Ritus*.

CHAPTER 21
Wrath

Marcella leaned her head back against the cushion of the couch and closed her eyes. Her entire body ached from the effects of her own damned spell. She knew that Blackstone and the other members of his special unit were able to protect themselves from witchcraft, but what she had seen went much further than that. Blackstone had somehow reflected her magic. If she had been fully human, it probably would have killed her as it was intended to kill him.

She'd never seen anything like what he'd done. She carried the power of an entire coven. Standing alone, he should not have been able to withstand her attack, much less throw it back at her. It should have burned right through any defense he could raise. The hairs on the back of her neck tingled when she recalled the alien sense of his magic and the odd way he'd invoked it … as if he'd been praying.

It would have been one thing if she had caught him in his home ritual space where he could employ powerful static protections like a casting circle. A deflection shield of the sort he'd used was normally drawn from elemental earth and anchored to a specific location.

His magic was assisted by a powerful spirit, Iledaste commented in her head.

What did that mean? How could Blackstone tap into that kind of power so quickly and easily. Was he also possessed by some form of demon?

Not a demon, Iledaste stated flatly. *His magic was of the light.*

Was he some kind of priest, then? If so, he was like none she'd ever heard of. He wore no obvious symbols of piety. His dress, while relentlessly black, did not give the impression of official vestments. One thing a priest could usually be relied upon was a dedication to the trappings of office. They were what set him apart from others and proclaimed his power.

Iledaste offered no additional opinion on the matter.

Whatever Blackstone was, he was even more dangerous than his reputation suggested. The next time they met, she would have to be better prepared.

A feminine cry of agony erupted from the kitchen, reminding Marcella of what a disaster the attack on the Order sanctuary had been. They had not only failed in their mission, but several of her team had returned injured. The sanctuary guards had loaded their rifles with silver-coated bullets. None of the injuries were life-threatening, but the silver retarded *lupusdaemon* healing magic.

Rutlinger tended to the wounds using medical equipment he kept at the Foundation. Skyler Arpin was the only patient who chose to have her bullet removed while in human form, the others preferring to rely on Rutlinger's comprehensive veterinary expertise. Either way, there was only so much that local anesthetic could do for the pain.

The phone rang and Marcella opened her eyes. Cyrus immediately rose from where he had been sitting on the couch across from her and picked it up. After a few monosyllabic responses to the person on the other end of the line, he walked over and handed her the cordless phone.

"This is Marcella."

"I hear your mission to rid the world of Amanda Clark hit a snag," responded the snide voice of David Bonham.

Marcella was stunned that he already knew of her failure. They had been back at the Foundation for less than an hour. "How did you hear that?" she snapped.

"I have sources," he answered.

"If those sources are inside the Order, I would appreciate your sharing them with me."

Her comment was greeted with mocking laughter.

"What's so damn funny?" she asked, trying to control her anger.

"I really don't see how you can expect to lead an alliance when you can't even manage your own pack," he answered.

"I don't know what you're talking about."

"Of course not. And that's the problem. You seem to have forgotten what it means to be alpha."

Marcella went still. Bonham knew something she didn't. What was she missing? She directed that last thought at Iledaste.

The demon seemed have made some sense of Bonham's cryptic needling. *Allowing the Pack to remain dispersed was a mistake. We should have insisted that everyone stay here until the work was complete.*

Why? What have the others done?

They have renounced.

Marcella didn't understand the full implications of the term, but its basic meaning was clear enough. Some of the Pack members had officially abandoned her.

"They will be dealt with," she assured Bonham.

The line was silent for a few moments. When Bonham spoke again, his tone was deadly serious. "Perhaps it's *you* who should be dealt with. Your little war is making trouble for all of us."

Do not let the challenge go unanswered, advised Iledaste.

The handset creaked as Marcella's hand tightened around it. "Bring it. Come on over, and we'll see who deals with whom."

"It may come to that," Bonham said. "But for now, it will be more fun watching your battle with the Order from afar. You've attracted the attention of a powerful enemy. It will be interesting to see how all this plays out."

A powerful enemy, indeed. Marcella wasn't yet sure how she would defeat Blackstone, but that had become her primary goal. Eliminating the Gold Ridge Coven would be a comparatively simple matter once he was out of the way.

You must project confidence, Iledaste warned her.

"The enemy is only human," Marcella said dismissively. Iledaste chuckled in the back of her mind at the irony of the statement. Without the demon within, *she* would be only human. Instead, she was super-human, and she was going to crush Blackstone at the next opportunity.

"No one in the Order is 'only human,' as I'm sure you're beginning to appreciate," Bonham argued. "I've fought them myself although it has been many years now. It was not an experience I care to repeat."

"So you hide behind the petty human lives you've adopted."

"We don't hide," Bonham said confidently. "Hiding would attract the attention of the Order. We play the human game of life, stealing a new form only when we must."

Bonham's lack of ambition disgusted Marcella. "Bah. You expect us to live petty, unworthy lives."

"It beats the existence that awaits us in the abyss."

As much as she appreciated finding out about the traitors in the Selkirk Pack, Marcella had no interest in debating philosophy with Bonham. If he wasn't going to help, she had no use for him. "Good bye, David. Call again when you remember what it means to be *lupusdaemon*." She could sense Iledaste's approval and appreciation of the irony.

"I'll be watching," Bonham warned.

"Enjoy the show," Marcella retorted before punching the off button on the handset.

Holding the phone out to Cyrus, she said, "Call the other members of the Pack, and tell them to get over here." When he tried to take the phone, she held on to it until his eyes met hers. "Stay alert. If anyone refuses, I want to know exactly what they say."

Cyrus narrowed his eyes. "You think they'd dare to refuse?"

Marcella lowered her voice so only Cyrus could hear. "David Bonham seems to think they've renounced." She would let Cyrus's own demon fill him in on what that meant. "Make sure it's true. We'll deal with anyone who refuses the summons later."

Cyrus nodded and started to bring up the first contact number, but Marcella interrupted him.

"Make the calls from the conference room," she said. "And close the door." There was no point giving Rutlinger the satisfaction of learning about the situation. It might give him ideas.

David Bonham's call had shaken Marcella even more than the failed attack on the farm. She quickly shielded her thoughts from Iledaste even though doing so would reveal her doubts. She was losing control over the Pack and the mission. That must not happen. Her bargain with Iledaste lasted only as long as she moved forward in her plan to achieve a position of dominance among the packs in the region and did her best to eliminate Amanda Clark. If she failed, Iledaste would try to take over. She doubted she could withstand a sustained attack on her consciousness from the *lupusdaemon*.

It's not over yet, Iledaste advised.

The demon had read into her mental silence. The surprise was that it was being supportive.

I agreed to this arrangement for good reasons, the demon continued. *I have no intention of failing. I will not return to insignificance. Bonham must be put in his place.*

The demon's support burned Marcella's doubts to ash and the fire fueled her anger. The Pack was not doing its part, and it was time to do something about it. Fenris seemed enthusiastic enough, and Reggie was following orders. But Adolphus was resisting her, and she had serious doubts about Skyler. Not only was Skyler sulking, but she was behaving secretively, like she was up to something.

Skyler had the misfortune of choosing that moment to limp out of the kitchen and through the living room, heading toward her bedroom.

"Skyler, a word please," Marcella said in a too-sweet voice. Skyler's face had a wary expression as she came to a halt. "I hope your injury wasn't too severe."

"No, just painful," Skyler answered. "Dr. Rutlinger said it will heal quickly now that the silver has been removed." She started to leave but stopped when Marcella spoke again.

"How fortunate the shooter's aim was off."

Skyler went still. Marcella noted the tension in her stance and the alarm in her eyes. Yes, she was hiding something.

"What really happened at the farmhouse?"

"I ... I told you," Skyler said. She tried to feign exasperation, but it was a poor job that only highlighted her underlying panic. "I pretended to be unconscious until I saw my chance to escape."

"They left you alone that whole time?"

"No, a hunter kept me covered, which was how I got shot. Fortunately, we're faster than they are."

"Yes, we are," Marcella said in a harsh tone. "So much faster that your target should have been dead within seconds."

"She fought back ... she had a knife ... and then Kyle intervened."

Skyler's half-truths stoked Marcella's smoldering rage. The cold anger and distrust combined to inspire a flash of insight that cut through Skyler's deceptions. Skyler and Adolphus had failed to kill the witches because Marcella herself had failed against Blackstone. They were playing both sides of the conflict.

Three long swift strides later, Marcella's fingers were gripping Skyler's neck. With her first step, she had started an incantation. She completed it while staring into Skyler's fear-stricken eyes. The spell immobilized Skyler, leaving her barely able to breathe and speak.

"What did you tell them?" Marcella hissed.

"N–Nothing," Skyler squeaked. "What do you mean?"

"Liar!" Marcella shouted into Skyler's face. "You are spying for them."

"No!" Skyler objected, but Marcella didn't believe it.

We must make an example of her, Iledaste interjected with an acid tone.

Skyler's betrayal was the final straw. It was worse than failing to follow orders. It was worse than renouncing the Pack. It was mutiny. Treason. And it must be crushed.

Her focused anger and the goading of Iledaste drew dark spirits to them like iron filings to a magnet. Marcella drew on the power of those spirits and tightened the grip of the immobilization spell, crushing the breath from Skyler's lungs.

Marcella gritted her teeth as she tightened the web of power that surrounded her victim. She sent pulses of power through the web, twisting segments of it, hearing and feeling Skyler's bones snap under the pressure. Skyler's eyes widened in shock and pain, but she didn't have the breath to scream as her body was shattered under the assault of the spell.

As soon as her power began to diminish, Marcella dropped the spell and let go of Skyler's neck. The girl fell to the floor unconscious, a trickle of blood escaping from her lips to form a small pool on the floor.

Marcella looked up to see Fenris watching her from the top of the stairs to the east wing. His arms were folded and his mouth was twisted into a smirk. Marcella didn't want to hear any criticism or smug comments. She pointed toward the rag-doll pile of distorted limbs at her feet. "You have a problem with this?" she challenged.

Fenris raised an eyebrow. "Me? Not at all. The bitch had it coming."

Marcella took a deep breath and let it out, her anger slowly abating. Her fury was replaced by the deep exhaustion that followed the use of strong magic.

Fenris came down the stairs and approached cautiously, keeping an eye on Marcella. He knelt next to Skyler and put a finger to her neck. "She's still alive," he said with some surprise.

Marcella waved a hand in dismissal. "Whatever. Get her out of my sight."

Fenris carefully collected Skyler's broken body in his arms, eliciting small groans from the unconscious woman. He started walking toward Skyler's room.

"No," Marcella said, stopping him. "Put her in the basement with our guest."

Fenris changed course toward the stairs to the basement in acknowledgment of her order.

It was a shame to lose another Pack member, but Skyler could not be allowed to work against them. Adolphus would have to shape up or he would receive similar treatment. That left her with only three reliable pack mates. Was it enough?

An alpha was measured by how many followers he or she had. Her standing was eroding along with the Selkirk Pack membership. Perhaps she could lure back a few of the members who had renounced.

While Marcella walked toward her bedroom to recuperate from the strenuous spell, another thought occurred to her. Fenris was putting Skyler in with the visiting air witch in the basement. Although the blonde deputy might heal eventually, it would be a long and agonizing process to repair so much damage. Skyler would be frantic to escape that agony, and the moon would be full that night.

Marcella smiled to herself. If Nemotea ("Skyler's" true demon name) could muster the strength to take the body of the young witch, she might appreciate the opportunity she'd been given to redeem herself. On the other hand, if her body succumbed to its wounds in the next few hours, well then perhaps Marcella could convince Cara to let her summon Nemotea back from the abyss, adding another demon-powered witch to her coven.

A laugh burst forth as she thought about how Adolphus would fee about *that* turn of events.

CHAPTER 22

Strike Force

The black Suburban rumbled along, its headlights illuminating an old logging road as it flattened the pine saplings and weeds trying to reclaim the abandoned track. "Hang on," Blackstone warned as the front wheels dropped into a small crevice carved into the roadbed by crossing water.

Amanda slid back and forth on the back cargo-area bench seat, bumping against Kyle on her left and Tanya on her right. The custom bench had no restraints since it hadn't been designed for use while the vehicle was in motion. Kyle's arm gripped her tightly around her waist, pinning her hips to his while he held on to a grab bar. In turn, Tanya clasped Amanda's right hand and braced herself as best she could against each pitch and roll of the big SUV.

When the rear wheels of the Suburban bumped out of the dip, the rear of the vehicle hopped, lifting Amanda and Tanya off the bench seat. Tanya gasped as her head contacted the roof of the rig.

"You okay?" Amanda asked.

Tanya nodded, rubbing the top of her head. "Just startled. I didn't hit hard."

"Almost there," Blackstone promised.

Jessie twisted around and checked on Tanya with a look of equal parts concern and guilt. She had scored one of the regular passenger seats along with her husband and Noreen.

Amanda leaned forward and looked through the rear window, watching the Jeep behind them drive through the same dip. The driver, one of Jonathan's hunters, gunned the motor on the way out, boosting the hop and making the rear end of the lighter vehicle bounce once and slip sideways a bit as it landed. Big grins split the faces of the driver and his passenger as the jeep straightened out again.

Men. At least someone is having fun, Amanda thought.

Amanda's attention was drawn to the view out the front window as the Suburban turned off the road into a clearing bordered by the remains of a large burn pile and a loose stack of rotting logs. They had reached the log landing that Blackstone said was their destination. Blackstone turned the SUV around so it was facing back the way they'd come and turned off the engine. He told everyone to close the doors quietly when they exited. "The sound of a slamming car door carries a long way," he warned.

Sighing with relief, Tanya wasted no time in opening the back door and jumping to the ground. The strong scent of cedar wafted in through the open rear door as Amanda extricated herself from Kyle's embrace and stood behind the vehicle, duplicating Tanya's full-body stretch.

The light of the incipient dawn was overtaking the residual twilight of the setting moon, but it was still dark enough that the forest around them was reduced to a jagged-topped curtain of black. A brief clench of panic shivered up Amanda's spine when she realized that the setting moon was ominously full. She calmed herself with the knowledge that sunrise would be well upon them before the team arrived at the Foundation. She glanced toward Blackstone, wondering if his choice of timing was about more than simply allowing enough preparation time.

Tanya looked around the clearing with a dubious expression. "How will we see the trail?"

Blackstone answered as he came around to the back of the vehicle with a folded square of paper in his hand. "There's no trail to speak of. We'll mostly be bushwhacking and following wildlife paths where we can find them."

Tanya frowned down at her designer jeans and white running shoes. It wasn't the best outfit for a scramble through the damp underbrush in semi-darkness, but it was the best she was able to do with the limited clothes she had at the sanctuary. Amanda had offered to lend her coven mate an old pair of hiking boots, but they turned out to be too small.

Noreen and Jessie joined them at the back of the SUV. Jonathan left their group and jogged over to his team of hunters, who were suiting up behind the jeep. Noreen carried a thin wooden case to the rear of the rig and set it on the floor of the cargo area. The case was square and about the size of a dinner plate. Amanda shifted closer as Noreen opened the lid.

The interior of the case was separated into compartments flocked with black velvet. A four-pointed star made of deep blue stone lay tucked in the center space. Gold chains were attached to each triangular point. The chains pooled in corner compartments, keeping them from becoming entangled with one another.

Noreen put pressure on the center of the star and tugged on the chain attached to one of the star points. The point came away with an audible click and dangled from her hand. Noreen held the pendant out toward Amanda. "Put this around your neck."

Fascinated, Amanda did as she was instructed. She wanted to ask what the charms were for, but she was sure Noreen would explain soon enough. Noreen handed Jessie and Tanya a pendant as well. She put the center piece, which was now square, around her own neck. A final pendant remained in the case. If Cara had been with the coven instead of imprisoned at the Foundation, she would have undoubtedly received the remaining piece.

As the others slipped their necklaces on, Amanda felt a magical charge building. Kyle distracted her from the sensation by stepping in front of her and staring down at the blue stone where it lay nestled between her breasts.

"See something you like?" she asked.

"What?" Kyle asked, blinking a couple of times. "Well, yeah," he said with hesitant confusion. A blush revealed the instant he became aware of her double meaning as well as the landscape surrounding the object of his attention. "I mean, the pendant. Can I see it?"

Amanda glanced down. "It's not hiding."

The blush deepened. "You know what I mean. Can I *touch* it?"

Amanda looked up and turned her head to the side. In a long-suffering tone, she said, "If you must."

Kyle hesitated, still confused by her teasing. Gently lifting the stone, he turned it over in his hand, inspecting it closely. "I don't see any kind of latch or magnet. How does it attach to the center stone?"

Noreen answered, switching to her instructor voice and addressing everyone. "The artifact is called a Resonance Star. The components were formed from a single kyanite specimen, and the enchantment that was used to create the Star generated a strong affinity between the pieces. As Kyle noted, the base of each Star pendant clings to the center piece, but there's no magnetism involved."

While Noreen spoke, Kyle's attention had remained on the Star pendant. His eyes lost their focus as he turned the stone and angled it in different directions. "It knows where the center piece is," he commented absently.

Blackstone stepped closer. "What do you see, Kyle?"

"The base of the triangle brightens a little when I point it toward Noreen."

Jessie and Tanya examined their pendants, angling them as Kyle had. "Mine doesn't," Tanya said.

Kyle aimed a questioning expression at Noreen, silently asking for permission to explain. Noreen glanced toward Jonathan's hunters. Addressing Tanya and Jessie, she spoke in a low tone of voice. "This relates to the subject I asked Amanda not to discuss at our coven gathering, so keep it to yourself. Kyle can see the Star's magical aura. I didn't know about the brightening effect he described, but I'll be sure to add that information to the Star's lore. We have background on how the Star was made and how it works in a controlled environment, but we don't have much practical information about how it performs in the field. Thank you, Kyle."

Amanda and Kyle stared at Noreen in shock. Her comments had been almost complimentary, and it was unprecedented for her to express any sort of gratitude toward him.

Noreen noticed their expressions. "Kyle's attention to detail is probably his best quality," she explained defensively.

Kyle raised an eyebrow and shared a look with Amanda. "She must think we're all going to die."

Amanda had to laugh, in spite of Noreen's glare.

Blackstone looked down, but not before Amanda saw a twitch at the corner of his mouth. However, Blackstone seemed to be the only other person who appreciated Kyle's humor. Jessie glanced at Tanya, whose face had paled.

"That's not funny," Jessie said with a frown. "This is serious. And dangerous."

Kyle's brow wrinkled with concern when he saw Tanya's reaction. "Sorry," he said sincerely. "Bad joke."

Tanya ignored Kyle and held up the talisman. "What does it do?"

Noreen cleared her throat and put her instructor face back on. "As I was explaining before we were interrupted"— she cast a meaningful glance at Kyle who had apparently demoted himself to nuisance status again—"the Resonance Star is so named because the individual pieces resonate with one another. The full explanation is somewhat technical, but the bottom line is it connects us almost as if we were working together in a casting circle."

"That's ... so cool," Amanda said and looked down at her pendant. "How do we activate them?"

"You don't," Noreen answered. "They're always active. As soon as you draw on your own power for a spell, the amulet will draw from the rest of us. It basically pools our power and makes the entire resource available to whoever needs it."

"What about the spirits?" Jessie asked.

Amanda was wondering the same thing. One of the reasons her coven used ritual circles was to protect their magical workings from the mischief of dark spirits while attracting the assistance of light spirits.

"The beauty and the curse of the Star," Noreen responded, "is that the spirits seem to have no influence on it. You could say that it creates a private network of power that can be accessed only by the pendant wearers. However, you still have to take the usual precautions. The Star won't attract spirits, but the spells you cast using its power will."

"What if a pendant falls into the wrong hands?" Kyle asked.

Noreen's lips thinned, and she nodded, as if she'd been expecting the question. "That depends on whether the person who acquires it is a witch and recognizes it for what it is. The Star doesn't discriminate, so any witch who joins the network has access to all of our power." She held up the pendant she was wearing. "Also, this center piece is special. To continue the metaphor, it's the hub of the network. None of the other pieces will work unless someone is wearing this one."

"We need to get moving," Blackstone interrupted. "Noreen would have explained all of this earlier, but the Star isn't very complicated, and she wasn't sure her request to borrow it would be granted until it arrived by courier not long before we left."

Kyle addressed Blackstone. "So it doesn't change our strategy—it just gives us an extra edge?"

"Precisely," Blackstone confirmed. He looked over at Jonathan's group and waved them over.

Amanda joined the others gathering around Blackstone. They'd all been through the plan multiple times, but she didn't want to miss the chance for a final review. Unfolding the papers, he revealed a copy of the three maps he'd given to everyone on the team.

Blackstone addressed the group. "We don't know if they'll be expecting us, and we don't know if they'll have sentries posted. We must assume yes to both and that the Pack will be prepared for our arrival. We will remain together as a group for as long as possible and break up into teams only after we determine that it's safe to do so." He flipped to a map that showed a topographical representation of the surrounding area and pointed. "We're here, about a mile from the facility. I've scouted a path that we will take us all to the perimeter." He flipped the page over, showing an overview map of the grounds. A red X was marked at two points along the perimeter fence. "The Xs are the best places to cross over." He pointed at one of the marks. "The Order sent a rescue team through this entry point once before, so we will go in the other way this time."

Amanda was a member of the team that the Order had sent to rescue Kyle and his former girlfriend Sherry from the Foundation. It had been only a couple of months ago, but it seemed like a lifetime. She and Jonathan had sneaked into the Foundation compound at a place where the barrier wall joined with a rocky ridge—the spot indicated by the first red X on Blackstone's map. Once inside the perimeter, they'd followed a wildlife trail toward the facility when they encountered Kyle coming the opposite way with Sherry draped over his shoulder. He'd essentially rescued himself.

However, Kyle's disappearance had not gone unnoticed. Skyler had tracked him in her wolf form and unsuccessfully tried to prevent his escape. The Pack knew that Kyle was familiar with that route and would probably share his knowledge with the Order. They would undoubtedly be watching that entry point closely.

Blackstone quickly summarized the duties of each team and then folded up the maps. "That's it. If you have any last questions, ask them now. There will be no chatter on the trail." When no one responded, he said, "Let's go."

For the trek up the hillside, Jonathan and Blackstone led the way with two of Jonathan's men right behind them. Kyle and the remaining two tactical hunters took a rear-guard position, putting the witches in the center of the group.

Amanda stayed back with Kyle, growing more tense with every step that brought them closer to the Foundation. Would Reggie be patrolling the grounds? The team carried a single tranquilizer gun in case they got the drop on a sentry, but no one knew how well the drug would work on a werewolf or how long it would last. If they were attacked, the tactical team wouldn't hesitate to use their regular rifles with silver-jacketed bullets. No one was sure if Reggie had been one of the wolves who had attacked the sanctuary just hours ago. If he had been, perhaps he was resting and out of harm's way.

Her concerns were interrupted when Blackstone signaled another halt and made the group backtrack a bit. On a previous scouting mission, Blackstone had marked the clearest path through the forest with thin white-paper flags. They wouldn't last long, but they weren't meant to. Unfortunately, the flags were a little too subtle, so Blackstone occasionally missed a turn. They kept up a good pace in spite of that and reached the perimeter wall within about fifteen minutes.

Blackstone signaled everyone to stop alongside the block perimeter wall. A few yards farther along, a sharp ridge cut through at an angle. The masons had integrated the rocky obstacle into the border rather than try to build over it.

Jonathan and Blackstone silently climbed up onto the ridge, choosing their handholds and footholds with care. Near the top, they hunkered down and peered over the wall with binoculars. After a few moments of spying, Jonathan waved the tactical team forward and disappeared over the ridge into the compound.

Amanda's senses sharpened when she crossed the ridge and set foot behind the wall. It seemed like they'd literally and figuratively crossed a line by entering the Selkirk Pack's domain. Their objective was only minutes away.

The tactical team fanned out and scouted the immediate area. A moment later, they all returned, giving the all clear signal.

As the team formed up for the final march, Amanda glanced at Tanya and was arrested by her wide brown eyes. Tanya was trembling, and her lips were pressed into a bloodless line. Amanda was instantly sympathetic and berated herself for letting the girl talk them into bringing her along. She lacked the Order training that would have readied her mind as well as her physical body for the kind of danger they were about to face.

As if her distress had summoned him, Blackstone appeared in front of Tanya and placed his right palm on her forehead. The image reminded Amanda of a tent evangelist conducting a healing. The young witch closed her eyes and swallowed hard. When he took his hand away, she opened her eyes and returned his encouraging smile with a thankful one. When Amanda checked to see if Kyle had witnessed the exchange, his raised eyebrow communicated his own intrigue.

More than ever, Amanda wanted to know what kind of powers Blackstone possessed. The man deflected every question in a way that discouraged further inquiry. It wasn't like he was being rude or mysterious, simply private. Noreen might know his secrets, but she ignored questions about Blackstone and whatever past they might have shared. Both of them had to know that their secrecy was breeding all sorts of wild rumors. In the absence of information, people make up stories. But neither Blackstone nor Noreen seemed to care.

Blackstone returned to the front of the column. Seconds later, everyone started forward.

The trail they followed was well trodden, but irritatingly overgrown. To deer and wolves, it was probably a leafy tunnel. For the intruding humans, making progress was an irritating exercise of walking stooped over and avoiding the slap of branches swept aside by the person ahead. Amanda guessed that the rustle and swish of their march through the woods announced their presence to every forest denizen within a hundred yards.

After a short distance, the path angled away from the perimeter and took them to within a hundred feet of the Foundation. The team stopped just before the trail exited the forest and melded into the pathways around the building.

Amanda made her way to the front of the line. As the Team Three leader, she would coordinate with Blackstone and Jonathan, leaders of teams One and Two, respectively. When Blackstone gave a thumbs-up signal, she and Jonathan duplicated it. Everyone was ready. Blackstone pointed at his watch and flashed the fingers of his right hand twice. They would all approach the building in ten minutes, which would give Jonathan's team enough time to reach his target entry point on the opposite side.

Jonathan eased back through the line collecting the rest of his team as he went. Jessie, Tanya, and one of the tactical hunters followed him into the forest toward the back of the building.

Amanda moved back to where Kyle waited for her with Joel, another of the tactical hunters.

Blackstone would lead the remaining team members, including Noreen and the last two tactical hunters.

On Amanda's signal, Joel took the lead, scouting a path through the forest that would take them closer to the Foundation's east wing.

The walk didn't take long. Within about two minutes, Amanda was peeking through the trees at the two doorways she had to choose from. According to the blueprint, the door on the right entered a huge dining room near the kitchen and was closer to the building's central atrium section. The door on the left also entered the dining room, but it was at the end of the wing right next to a stairway that went up to the second floor. Unless she saw good reason to do otherwise, her intent was to choose the stairway door so her team could sneak upstairs.

When they'd gone over the plans with Blackstone earlier, Kyle observed that the Foundation's architect designed the place with two exits for every area of the building. It seemed

206 *Daniel R. Marvello*

like a reasonable safety precaution, but it made the building more vulnerable from a security standpoint. The Order's rescue team were hoping to exploit that vulnerability.

The sun hadn't made much progress above the horizon, so many of the Foundation's interior lights were still on. Amanda watched for activity while keeping an eye on the time. Thanks to the remote and private location, none of the common-area windows had curtains or blinds.

The earpiece Jonathan had assigned her crackled, and she cupped her hand over her ear to block out ambient sounds. The noise was followed by silence. Random static? Or a sign of trouble? She wasn't familiar enough with the device to know how common it was to get interference.

Her wristwatch showed that the allotted ten minutes had passed. Jonathan's team should have reached the other side of the building. Right on schedule, she heard footsteps on the gravel garden path as Blackstone's team headed for the front door.

Blackstone's objective was to appear at the front door and demand Cara's release, luring Marcella and her henchman Cyrus into the entryway area of the atrium. Amanda's team would flank the entryway by going through the east wing. Meanwhile, Jonathan's rescue team would sneak into the basement through a stairwell located in the west wing.

But they didn't dare enter the building until they knew that Marcella had taken the bait. When Blackstone greeted her by name, that would be the signal for Amanda and Jonathan to enter the building.

Amanda was about to signal her team to cross the open distance between the edge of the forest and the building when Fenris Kellen limped through the dining room and disappeared into the kitchen. *Damn.* If he happened to leave the kitchen at just the right time, he might see them approaching the building or encounter them as they went in.

Amanda waited for a moment. Fenris might leave the kitchen immediately if he was only there to get a cup of coffee. If he was after something more, she'd probably have time to cross. After a long fifteen seconds, she decided to risk it.

Amanda gave Joel the signal to move. She and Kyle followed him, stalking forward in a crouch and using the low garden shrubs as cover. Fenris was still in the kitchen when they reached the door. As long as they hugged the building, he wouldn't be able to see them through the dining-room windows.

Through her earpiece and as a delayed echo in her other ear, Amanda heard Blackstone knock on the front door. It was almost time to go in.

She gently tried the handle of the door and discovered it was locked. She'd expected that. Gripping the door lever tightly, she fingered her pentagram earring with her free hand and softly started an incantation.

She faltered before she'd managed more than a couple of phrases. The subtle sense of building energy that normally accompanied a spell casting was missing. Momentarily confused, Amanda wondered if Marcella had set up some kind of ward or trap that prevented the casting of magic. At the same time, her energy started to drain as if she *had* cast the spell. It was an eerie sensation, like having her car suddenly speed up even though she hadn't pressed on the accelerator.

When the feeling passed, she looked down at the pendant. One of the other witches must have cast a spell. Noreen said that the entire coven was connected and that any one of them could tap into the collective pool of power. Based on the way her own spell had been interrupted, Amanda guessed that the artifact allowed only one of them to cast at a time. Noreen should have warned them about that.

Amanda started her incantation again. The second time, the power flowed effortlessly. Too effortlessly. The lock made a loud click from the telekinetic force she applied to the interior turn button. As Noreen had mentioned, drawing power through the Resonance Star was like working with her coven in a circle, so she'd have to adjust the oomph she put into her spells accordingly.

Amanda paused and glanced questioningly at Kyle, who was keeping an eye on the kitchen door through the window. Had Fenris heard the click of the lock? Kyle gave her a thumbs-up.

The seconds dragged on while Amanda waited. Finally, Blackstone's voice spoke through the earpiece. "Hello Marcella."

CHAPTER 23
Helpless

"My poor Skyler," Rutlinger said in a whisper as he knelt by the broken body of his friend and co-conspirator. He didn't dare touch her because every inch of her body appeared to be bruised or broken. She shook from the pain of her injuries, and Rutlinger wasn't sure her healing abilities were up to the task of returning her to health. She needed food and comfortable rest. More comfortable than the small sleeping pad that cushioned her from the cold, hard concrete floor.

"What did you do to her?" a fearful voice queried from the opposite corner of the room.

"This is Marcella's work," Rutlinger responded. He turned to the young witch who cowered away from his gaze. "What happened when they brought her down here?"

"It was the lawyer," she answered. "He stomped in here and yelled at me to move off the pad." She gingerly touched a bruise on her cheek. "I wasn't fast enough for him."

Rutlinger moved a lock of hair away from Skyler's face. She opened one swollen eye and moaned but didn't focus on him. For the first time, he wondered if *lupusdaemon* healing powers could be a curse rather than a blessing. A human would have died from the injuries within minutes if not instantly. With so much damage to repair at once, her recuperation would be slow and excruciating. Given the lack of proper medical care, it was unlikely her recovery would be complete. She'd probably seek a new body as soon as she was able.

The thought gave him pause. Glancing over at the witch, he narrowed his eyes. Yes. Marcella would be that cruel. She had dumped Skyler in with the witch hoping it wasn't too late for *Vollmondritus*. Had Skyler been subdued enough by the near-fatal beating to swear allegiance to Marcella in thanks for a second chance in a new body? Marcella's twisted mind probably expected that. And she might be correct.

He wasn't sure what time it was, but it had to be near dawn. Being in the basement extended the window of opportunity, but soon the sun would erase any chance for *Vollmondritus* until the next full moon. Skyler was far too weak to take the young witch on her own.

Rutlinger turned a speculative gaze toward the witch. She seemed to sense what he was thinking and squirmed, packing herself tighter into the corner. She shook her head in denial of the horror he contemplated.

Under other circumstances, he wouldn't have hesitated. However, the last thing he needed was to create another pawn for Marcella. If he could be sure Skyler would credit him with her rescue from agony, he would give her the witch in a heartbeat. But Skyler was the newest and weakest member of the Selkirk Pack, and he couldn't be sure her loyalty to him would survive Marcella's intimidation.

He was still debating the situation when the door to the storage room opened. Turning slowly, he expected to see Marcella or Cyrus checking up on him. Instead, he found himself staring down the barrel of a rifle.

CHAPTER 24
Wards

After Blackstone's cue to move out, Amanda gave Kyle a quick glance to verify that Fenris was still occupied in the kitchen. He gave her a nod of confirmation, and she signaled Joel to lead on.

As the door cracked open, the loud rumble of a full blender explained why Fenris hadn't reacted to the lock click or the knock at the front door. She was impressed at how thoroughly the thick walls of the Foundation had muffled the loud noise and amused herself wondering what kind of smoothie a werewolf would make. Probably best not to speculate.

Amanda followed Joel through the door. Keeping an eye toward the kitchen, she evaluated their options. They had originally planned to sneak through the living room and position themselves at the far end where the east wing connected to the entryway. But that would put Fenris behind them. The contingency plan was to go upstairs and come down into the atrium. If they didn't get caught along the way, the route would drop them behind everyone in the entryway.

The noise of the blender stopped. They had to get out of sight immediately, so Amanda motioned toward the stairs. Joel nodded his acknowledgment of her decision and led the way upward.

Slowly and silently, Amanda followed Joel down the hallway in the east wing's upper level. Copying Joel's example, she moved on the balls of her feet and stayed close to the wall, alert for squeaky sub-flooring or anything else that might give them away. The blueprint had shown four rooms, two on each side of the hall, and all four doors were closed. It was impossible to tell whether the rooms were empty or occupied.

Blackstone's conversation with Marcella buzzed in her ear. It sounded like he was doing a good job of distracting the dark witch. As much as Amanda wanted to stop and listen in, she had to focus on her part of the mission.

As she passed one of the closed doors, a strange sensation tickled at Amanda's magical sensitivity. She came to a sudden stop. Closing her eyes, she placed the palm of her hand on the door. It seemed to vibrate with energy. A ward? Could this be Marcella's room? Why ward it unless it contained something valuable? Could the exorcism papers and the wolf skull be inside?

Amanda and Kyle had talked about the possibility of stumbling across the stolen exorcism ritual and the totem at the Foundation, but they hadn't considered it likely. The better bet was that Marcella had destroyed both.

Amanda would love to get her hands on the original exorcism papers. She could use them to verify the work she'd done with Kyle and Noreen. But what really made her itch to enter the room was the thought that the wolf skull might be inside. Would she ever get a better opportunity to steal it back?

While she pondered, Blackstone's conversation with Marcella caught her attention.

"The Order wants the violence to end," he said. "We understand your concerns regarding the exorcism ritual, and we're willing to ban its use. If you release Cara LeCouteur and allow us to arrest Fenris Kellen on murder charges, we can put an end to the bloodshed."

Amanda's mouth dropped open. Ban its use? When had *that* been decided? If the Order banned the exorcism, how could she help Reggie? She listened for Marcella's response, but heard nothing. Was the dark witch considering the offer seriously? A small part of her hoped Marcella would accept. Having a dark witch out to kill her had not done much for her sleep lately. But that was selfish. Reggie needed her, and the key to helping him was probably inside the warded room.

She glanced at Kyle, and he gave her a questioning look in return. He was probably wondering why she had stopped. She wanted to talk to him about what she was thinking, but they were supposed to keep quiet, and they didn't have time for a discussion. Or an argument, more likely. She had to make a command decision. Would she try to save Reggie even if the Order banned the exorcism?

Yes.

Amanda reached for the doorknob and turned it.

Kyle's hand shot out to stop her. His hand gripped her wrist just as her fingers wrapped around the doorknob. He was too late.

A powerful shock shot up Amanda's arm, and the next thing she knew, she was on the floor with her back resting against Kyle's chest. Kyle was sitting up, shaking his right hand as if to restore circulation.

Joel had moved to cover them with a wild look in his eye, pointing his gun down the hall in first one direction and then the other. He settled down after a few moments when no one came to investigate the commotion.

Amanda rolled off Kyle and stood up. She held out her hand to help him, more in apology than because he needed it. He took her hand, but mostly rose on his own. He gave her a well-deserved "What were you thinking?" look.

That was stupid, Amanda thought with a sigh.

She often wove an alert component into her wards. If Marcella did so as well, then she had just revealed her team's presence in the east wing. She paused to listen, but all she heard through the earpiece was the unintelligible buzz of a conversation between Marcella and someone other than Blackstone. Perhaps luck had served where wisdom had failed.

They didn't have time for her to tear down Marcella's ward, assuming she could manage to do so. Amanda ignored Kyle's disapproving frown and waved Joel forward. She could explain what she was thinking—or not thinking—later. She hated to leave the room behind, but she didn't know for sure the wolf skull was inside, only that there was *something* worth protecting.

The left wall of the hallway fell away and a banister took its place as the walkway continued into the atrium. Joel stopped to listen at the corner where the wall ended. The entryway was just below his position.

A confusion of arguing voices carried up to them from the entryway. It sounded like Fenris Kellen had joined the discussion, and it wasn't going well. She doubted he was interested in the idea of being "turned over" to the Order.

Muffled gunshots made Amanda freeze. When shouts from the entryway ended in two more loud gunshots, she ducked reflexively. It sounded like the both of the other teams might be in trouble.

Amanda was about to signal the advance when a familiar voice from behind made her jump.

"Well, look who's here," said Reggie.

CHAPTER 25
Human Shield

Looking past the barrel of the gun aimed at him, Rutlinger recognized the rifleman standing in the basement-room doorway as Jonathan Pesce, one of the Order's hunters. A tall blonde woman behind the man spied the misshapen form on the floor and cried, "Cara!" She pushed into the room, startling the hunter.

"Jessie, no! Get back!" Jonathan shouted.

The woman seemed to realize her error and stopped half-way between Jonathan and Rutlinger. But that was close enough.

Rutlinger leaped to his feet and grabbed Jessie faster than anyone could react. She squeaked with pain as he twisted her arm around her back and turned her to face Jonathan, his forearm across her windpipe. The hunter would know that his werewolf strength would allow him to instantly crush her throat. Jonathan immediately lowered his weapon, but a second hunter just outside the door kept his rifle raised and aimed. A dark-haired young woman stood behind the second rifleman, literally wringing her hands, her eyes darting between Jessie and Skyler.

"So, the Order finally decided to do something useful," Rutlinger said.

"Let her go," Jonathan demanded.

"Not until I clear up a little misunderstanding," Rutlinger said. They were obviously there to liberate Marcella's little witch prisoner, Cara. The horrifying spectacle of Skyler's broken body commanded all of their attention, so none of them had yet noticed that Cara was sitting in the opposite corner.

A sudden weight on his back informed him that he'd underestimated the little witch. As he twisted his face down and away from her clawing hands, the hunters hesitated in confusion.

Hoping to take advantage of their bewilderment, Rutlinger shoved Jessie to the side and reached over his shoulders to grab Cara by the arms. With a duck and twisting heave, she was airborne. She crashed into Jessie, and both women landed in a heap on top of Skyler. He grimaced at unintentionally adding to Skyler's pain. He would have thrown the women toward the hunters, but he couldn't afford additional congestion at the doorway.

Jonathan started to raise his rifle again, but Rutlinger's werewolf speed made it seem as if everyone else was moving in slow motion. He raced forward, grabbing the rifle and shoving it against Jonathan's chest as he pushed the man backward into the second armed hunter. The dark-haired woman was apparently a witch because she was fingering a pendant and muttering what sounded like an incantation. A well-placed, flat-handed blow to her upper chest toppled her backward, interrupting her spell as he ran toward the basement stairwell.

The hunters had time to fire a couple of shots before he ran far enough up the stairwell to be out of sight. One bullet splintered the wood of the banister, and the second scored a burning path along the side of his calf. Rutlinger hissed at the acidic sting of silver that polluted the wound.

During his flight, Rutlinger's thoughts raced through the implications of the rescue attempt. The Order wouldn't have risked the entire operation on a team of four hunters. It was possible the hunters in his basement were operating independently, but that scenario didn't fit Jonathan Pesce's reputation. No, it was more likely that additional teams of Order personnel had already invaded the building.

At the top of the stairs, Rutlinger stopped at the door to the entryway and listened. Voices ... Marcella's and a man's ... Blackstone. Rutlinger remembered Blackstone's eerily calm and confident tones from their encounter at the Hayworth Farm. *Good.* Perhaps the senior hunter would be easier to negotiate with than the trigger-happy bunch in the basement.

CHAPTER 26
Collateral Damage

Amanda turned to fully face Reggie. Whatever trouble Blackstone's team was having at the entryway would have to wait.

Reggie stood next to an open door with his hands loose at his sides. He'd probably been drawn out into the hallway by the gunshot sounds from below. As Kyle and Joel turned to face the new threat, Reggie's eyes and coiled stance mirrored the excitement of a cat poised to pounce on a mouse. Kyle edged closer to Amanda, and Joel adjusted his aim to point his rifle toward Reggie.

"If it isn't the little girl behind all this hysteria and angst," Reggie said. "I'll bet all the problems go away if you go away."

"Stay back," Joel warned, but Reggie was on the move before the hunter spoke the second word.

Kyle slammed into Reggie before Amanda had time to do anything more than flinch in response to Reggie's lunge. The two combatants moved so quickly that Amanda heard the blows they traded more than she saw them. Joel raised his gun but didn't dare shoot for risk of hitting Kyle.

Amanda found herself back-pedaling from the ferocity of the duel. Her eyes had trouble making sense of what she was seeing. She'd watched Kyle during a couple of his sparring sessions with other Order hunters, but in those bouts, he had to hold back his strength and speed. There was no holding back against Reggie—an opponent who matched or exceeded his abilities.

One of them would momentarily get a grip on the other before the fight would resume at full speed, giving their fight a stop-action strobe effect. Grunts and flecks of blood emerged from the shifting whirlwind as their blows took a toll on each other. It was as if the cartoon whirlwind of the Tasmanian Devil had come to life.

When the motion finally stopped, Reggie had Kyle bent over the banister. His hands gripped Kyle's neck while Kyle clung desperately to the railing to keep from going over. Kyle's face turned red as Reggie strangled him, but if he let go of the rail to pry at Reggie's hands, he'd plummet to the tile floor below. Reggie grinned, knowing he'd won.

"Reggie, stop!" Amanda cried uselessly.

Reggie was only a few feet away at that point, so Joel took advantage of the moment to aim his rifle. As the barrel came up, Reggie took one hand from Kyle's neck and swiped it to the side. He snatched the rifle from Joel's hands and threw it down the hallway in the same motion. Stunned, Joel looked at his empty hands.

As Reggie turned his attention back to his opponent, Kyle did something unexpected. He let go of the banister and threw himself backward. He pinched Reggie's waist between his knees and carried the werewolf over the rail with him. Already unbalanced from leaning over Kyle, the additional leverage launched Reggie off the walkway, his arms windmilling.

Amanda screamed Kyle's name as a body thumped sickeningly on the floor below. Then she noticed hands gripping the bottom of the metal balusters.

She ran to the railing and peered over the side. Kyle's battered face looked up at her with a grim smile. She reached her hand out to him, but he shook his head. He gathered himself with a deep breath, walked his hands up the supports, and hauled himself over the rail. He groaned as she hugged him tightly, but when she tried to step back, he wouldn't let her go.

Joel was staring over the rail at the floor below. "That had to hurt," he said.

Amanda didn't want to look, but she had know.

Reggie lay in an unmoving heap on the tiles below, dark blood pooling near his head. Could even a werewolf survive such an injury? She couldn't tell if he was still breathing.

"Reggie," she said softly. Her stomach clenched, and she had to fight an urge to vomit. So this was how it ended. All that research. All that work. In an instant, her brother was lost to her forever.

She ran down the stairs to where her brother's body lay, only belatedly realizing that the voice in her earpiece was no longer echoing from the entryway. As she knelt next to Reggie, she looked toward the front door. The entryway was empty. Both Marcella and Blackstone's team were gone.

Amanda reached toward Reggie's still form, her hand stopping just short of touching him. Did she want him to be alive or dead?

If he was dead, her brother could rest in peace, and her mission was over. It didn't matter that the Order were going to ban her exorcism.

If he was alive, her struggle continued, and she'd have to find a way around the Order's ban.

Kyle knelt next to her, watching her face. "I'm sorry, Amanda. I didn't mean to kill him."

Amanda blinked in surprise. "Kyle, I don't blame you. You were fighting for your life." She looked at Reggie's face, and her eyes filled with tears. She blinked them away and rested her hand on his chest. "Maybe it was supposed to end this way."

Thump, thump. Thump, thump. Her palm detected the slow beat of a heart and the slight movement of an extremely shallow breath.

She jerked her hand back. "He's still alive!"

Amanda's voice expressed both horror and relief, reflecting her torn emotions over her seemingly doomed mission to save her brother. For a second, she considered the unthinkable. The werewolf who occupied her brother's body was helpless. She could end the ordeal right there and ensure the release of her brother's spirit. But as soon as she started to think about how she would go about such a dreadful task, her mind recoiled in disgust and shame. She couldn't destroy her brother's body even if it was possessed by a *lupusdaemon*.

Kyle was still watching her and seemed to know what she was thinking. He put a supportive hand on her shoulder. "We'll find a way."

Having no earpiece of his own, Kyle didn't know about the Order's proposed ban on the exorcism. Finding a way was about to become much harder.

"Amanda, I think you need to get over here," Joel said from the entryway. He had retrieved his weapon and joined them on the ground floor. The front door was wide open, and a second interior door was ajar as well. According to the Foundation floor plan, that second door led down to the basement.

Amanda stood and took a last look at Reggie. Fate would decide whether he lived or died. She would have to deal with the consequences, however it went.

As she stepped up from the sunken living room into the entryway, Amanda realized that Joel was looking down at another body. It was Fenris Kellen. She didn't need to check for a pulse. The open-eyed stare and bullet hole between his eyes made his condition clear. He'd apparently resisted arrest after all.

Fenris's werewolf abilities made him fast, but not fast enough to dodge a silver bullet to the brain. The tactical hunter who'd taken that shot must be exceptionally skilled.

Although she was sick of the bloodshed that continued to flow from the events she'd set in motion, she had no pity for the dead lawyer. A world without Fenris Kellen was a better place.

The sound of voices rising from the basement indicated that was where everyone else had gone. And since there were no screams or gunfire, she guessed Blackstone and Marcella had reached some kind of agreement.

Joel raised an eyebrow, waiting for Amanda to decide what to do next. With a hand flourish, she invited him to lead the way into the basement.

The cold gray concrete basement echoed with conversation as Amanda stepped off the last stair. Across a large open space supported by square columns, two groups kept a wary distance from each other. Tanya had a hand on Cara's shoulder, leading her coven mate out of a room with a heavy metal door. Cara looked shaken but otherwise okay. When Jonathan exited the same room supporting a battered Jessie who was pressing a hand to her head, Amanda broke into a jog.

All conversation ended the moment the others spotted Amanda's team.

Amanda went straight to her friend. "Are you okay, Jessie? What happened?"

Cara huffed and glared. "Don't mind me. It's not like *I* wasn't abducted and thrown around like a rag doll."

Amanda ignored Cara and looked to Jonathan for an answer to her question.

Jonathan nodded toward Rutlinger with a glare. "The good doctor threw her against the wall. She has a few scrapes and a nasty bump on her head, but she'll be fine."

A shape behind Jonathan caught Amanda's eye. It took a moment to figure out what she was seeing. It was Skyler, contorted in ways that shouldn't have been possible. "Oh, my God," she said. Kyle came to her side to see what she was exclaiming about and gasped when he saw Skyler's distorted form.

Rutlinger pushed roughly between the two of them and entered the room.

After checking for a pulse, he hung his head and sighed. Then his nostrils twitched, and he looked intently at Skyler's hand.

Amanda stepped forward, wondering what had caught his attention.

Rutlinger noticed her movement and held up a hand in a stop gesture. "Please leave."

She deserved his scorn. Demon or not, Skyler's death was another to lay at her feet. "I'm sorry," she said.

"I doubt that," was his bitter retort.

Kyle took her hand and squeezed it in support. She turned with him and left the room, but not before she'd moved close enough to see the blood on Skyler's fingers. The blood could easily have been Skyler's own, but the majority of the damage to her body appeared to be internal. If it *wasn't* Skyler's blood, the possibilities were disturbing.

Marcella was speaking to Blackstone when Amanda and Kyle rejoined them. "We have a deal, so you can get off the property now and take your little commando force with you.

As long as the Order bans the exorcism as promised, we have no need to defend ourselves against its practitioners."

Blackstone's response was cold and direct. "Don't think this agreement gives you blanket immunity. Using dark magic has the same consequences as always. If you persist in using it, I shall return."

Marcella sneered and folded her arms across her chest. "I got what I wanted." Then she cut a chilling glance toward Amanda. "Mostly."

Now that the immediate danger seemed to be past, mention of the agreement fanned Amanda's disappointment and anger over the exorcism ban. "When were you planning on telling me about this little agreement?" Amanda asked Noreen tersely.

"That agreement is the only thing keeping you alive right now," Marcella stated.

"Shut up, Marcella," Noreen spat. Addressing Amanda, she answered, "We didn't want you to be distracted from the mission." With a glance toward Blackstone, she added, "And we honestly didn't think the offer would be accepted." Her tone suggested that she and Blackstone had hoped it wouldn't.

"Whatever," Jonathan said dismissively. "We need to get out of here and get medical attention for Jessie and Cara." He started moving toward the stairwell up to the entryway.

The Order people followed Jonathan out of the basement, watching the werewolves over their shoulders as they left. Marcella and Cyrus waited for them to leave with smug expressions. Rutlinger stood at the holding-cell doorway, looking exhausted in body and spirit.

When they reached the entryway at the top of the stairs, Noreen tilted her head toward Fenris's corpse. "Now, there's a lesson. Fenris expected Marcella to back him up when he attacked, not knowing she was willing to sacrifice him to achieve her goals, whatever they may be. I think we're crazy to trust her."

"I *don't* trust her," Blackstone said. "But our orders were to make the offer, and our hands are tied as long as she honors the agreement."

On the return trip to the vehicles, Amanda tried to find out more about Cara's and Jessie's injuries. The bloody marks on Cara's arm were worrisome—they looked distinctly like fingernail scratches. Jessie had a bleeding abrasion on her cheek and a bruised shoulder from where she had fallen against the wall. She didn't want to alarm her friends, so Amanda tried to be circumspect with her questions.

"How did you get hurt?" she asked them.

Cara was quick to answer. "That bastard Rutlinger used Jessie as a shield, so I jumped him. But he was too strong and fast. He threw both of us on top of what was left of Skyler." She shuddered at the memory.

"Yuck," Amanda agreed. "Being hurled onto a dead body must have been unnerving."

Cara shrugged. "She wasn't dead at the time. She cried out when we landed on her, but that might have been what did her in."

"Is that when you got scratched?"

Another shrug. "I honestly don't know if it was her, Jessie, or Rutlinger who scratched me. It all happened so fast."

Cara was silent for a moment, and then her eyes widened. She glanced at Amanda before looking up toward the cloud-obscured sun and then back toward the west. The clouds to the west were broken up enough to show that the moon had dropped below the horizon.

Cara turned back to Amanda with pale panic on her face. "You don't think ... but the sun was up! It's only on the *night* of the full moon."

Amanda patted her coven-mate's shoulder reassuringly. "I'm sure you're right. It was already sunrise when we arrived at the Foundation. Skyler's demon has gone back to the abyss, I'm sure."

Cara stared back at her. "But you aren't sure, are you? Last night was the full moon. That's why you're asking me all these questions."

"I didn't mean to scare you. Like you said, the sun was up. I'm sure the window of danger had passed."

Cara stumbled down the trail silently for a few moments before commenting, "I hope you're right. The Order just banned your exorcism ceremony. If Skyler's demon is inside me, I'm screwed."

Amanda put her arm around Cara, who had fallen silent. As they continued along the trail, she said, "Don't worry. I'm sure you're fine. But no matter what, I won't abandon you."

Cara looked up, seeming more vulnerable than ever before. A glimmer of hope eased the worry in her eyes. "Thanks, Amanda. I appreciate that."

Had she just lied to Cara? Could she really defy the Order's explicit ban? If she did, her time with the Order would be over, and they would probably punish her in some way.

Kyle would insist on helping. She'd get him in big trouble as well. All for an improbable chance of rescuing her brother, who might already be beyond saving.

Looking over her shoulder, her eyes met Kyle's. His knowing gaze and shallow nod told her he'd heard everything she said to Cara and that he agreed. His willingness to help her was a measure of the trust he placed in her. It was time she acted responsibly and worthy of that trust.

For the rest of the hike, she kept her face averted from the others. Tears spilled down her cheeks in memory of the brother she was giving up on. She had tried for so long and so hard, but the obstacles had become insurmountable. Her only remaining hope was that Reggie's body would die, releasing his spirit and sending the demon that had possessed him back to the abyss where it belonged.

CHAPTER 27
Despair

A week later, Amanda woke up with Kyle's arms around her, gently stroking her head. "It's okay, babe. It was just a bad dream."

He meant *another* bad dream. She had been having them nightly. Sometimes more than once a night.

Most of the nightmares were a variation on the one where Reggie tried to cross the chasm to reach her. As before, he failed every time. Sometimes, she tried to jump across to him. Those were the worst because she invariably woke up screaming, escaping the dream as she plummeted to her death. In the latest version, she stood on the top platform of a tall rock spire with the canyon surrounding her. She was helpless to do anything but call Reggie's name.

She was sick of waking up screaming, crying, or both. It was exhausting. The sleeping pills she'd tried didn't stop the dreams—they only made her feel fuzzy brained and depressed.

She returned Kyle's embrace and buried her face in his chest. "I'm sorry. Thanks to me, neither of us is getting any rest."

"Maybe you should see someone," he said softly.

She pushed back from him. "You mean like a psychiatrist? They would lock me away if I told them about my failed mission to save my werewolf brother."

"Doesn't the Order have psychiatrists?" Kyle asked. "They must have alternatives to normal shrinks for stuff like this."

"I honestly don't know. I'll ask Noreen about it. But even if they do, I doubt they'd happen to have one in Sandpoint."

"How about a regular MD? A doctor could probably prescribe something stronger than that over-the-counter stuff you've been taking to help you sleep."

Amanda rolled onto her back and let out a big sigh. "I'm sure you're right although drugging myself senseless every night so I can get some rest doesn't seem like a good long-term solution."

"The dreams might go away with a little more time."

"That's what I keep hoping, but no luck so far. You know what's weird? I thought for sure I'd be having nightmares about what happened to Reggie at the Foundation, but I'm not. It's always those dreams where I try to reach him but can't."

Kyle thought about that for a moment. "At the Foundation, you thought he was dead. That would be a very different kind of dream …"

Amanda nodded. "I think I see where you're going. Dreaming he was dead would probably mean I had accepted that he was gone—or at least beyond my help."

Kyle raised an eyebrow in response, having nothing more to add. They were guessing, and it was getting them nowhere.

"Whatever," Amanda said, shaking her head. "I just want a decent night's sleep." She threw the covers to the side and headed toward the bathroom.

A few minutes later, she found Kyle in the kitchen standing next to the coffee maker, which was gurgling through its cycle.

Noting that it was still dark outside, Amanda glanced up at the clock and did a double-take. "Oh, my God, it's four AM!"

Kyle captured her in his arms. "Good morning to you, too." He tried to kiss her, but she put her hand over her mouth.

"Later, lover boy," she said from behind her hand. "Morning breath."

Kyle smiled and released her. She sat at the kitchen table, resting her elbows on the surface and holding her head in her hands. "I swear I'm trying to let go. All the signs say it's over."

"Signs?"

She ticked them off on her fingers. "The Order banned the exorcism, we don't know where the wolf skull is, and Blackstone has gone back to wherever he came from." A note of exasperation crept into her voice. "You know, I get that the werewolf treaty is important, but it pisses me off that they totally caved and gave Marcella everything she wanted."

Kyle carried two cups of coffee over to the table and sat down. "You and me both. And Blackstone too. You could tell he wasn't happy about Marcella's pardon or the ban. Take me out of the picture, and it's like the exorcism never happened."

"Except we did manage to rid the world of one *lupusdaemon*."

Kyle's eyes met hers. "Yeah, not so much."

"What are you talking about? Clarissa is dead and I sent her demon to the abyss."

Kyle fiddled with is cup for a moment before speaking. "That's true, except I think the demon is back." When Amanda didn't respond, he continued. "I've been trying to find a good time to tell you this although I'm not sure it really matters. Marcella teased me about snuggling 'like old times' when I grabbed her in the moon shrine."

"But you've never met her before," Amanda concluded with a slow nod.

"Exactly. I think the demon that shares Marcella's body is the one we once knew as Clarissa."

Amanda sat back, unsure of what to think about Kyle's revelation. If he was right, his exorcism had been half wasted. The half that saved his life was no small thing, but the return of Clarissa's demon made their current situation that much more frustrating. It also explained why Marcella had tried to kill her multiple times.

But as Kyle said, it didn't really matter anymore. She looked over at him, but he kept his attention on his cup. He was probably feeling either guilty or embarrassed.

She leaned forward and caught his eye. "You're going to have to show more restraint, you know. You can't keep going around hugging werewolves. It's dangerous."

He smiled at her ribbing. "What about witches? Are they off limits too?"

"All except this one."

"I can live with that. I'm sorry I didn't find a way to tell you sooner. As far as I'm concerned, the exorcism was a smashing success. I think that what really burns me most is that your exorcism saved my life, and now it can't be used to help anyone else."

Amanda sighed. "The Order has always tolerated *lupusdaemon* possession as a sort of gray area related to the treaty. When I came up with the exorcism ritual, they weren't sure what to do with it. The Order never interfered with First Moon in the past partly because they didn't have a way to do so. Before the exorcism, their only options were to imprison or kill the werewolf. That wouldn't bring the human spirit back. All it would do is start a war with the werewolves."

"It still feels wrong to me," Kyle grumbled. He took a careful sip from his hot mug. "What about Cara?"

Noreen and Amanda had been keeping a close eye on Cara since her rescue. Other than a few moments of panic that turned out to be nothing, Cara was having none of the side effects that Kyle had experienced after being possessed by a *lupusdaemon:* she wasn't having weird dreams, and her aerobics practice hadn't revealed anything noteworthy about her physical abilities.

"She's fine," Amanda said. "She alternates between relief and disappointment when she shows no evidence of becoming Super Girl."

Kyle laughed and shook his head. Then his tone turned serious again. "Maybe you're reading the signs wrong." He copied her method of ticking off his own points on his fingers. "The *lupusdaemon* known as Reggie survived that fall. I'll bet anything that the wolf skull is tucked inside Marcella's room at the Foundation. And, finally, you're still dreaming about saving Reggie. You have motive and means. All we need is opportunity."

"That we have the means is debatable," she argued. She appreciated Kyle's support, but she couldn't believe he still thought they had a chance. "Are you seriously suggesting we try again all by ourselves?"

"Well, not *today*. Give the situation time to cool down. In the meantime, we'll gather all the information we can about their behavior patterns. All we need is fifteen minutes when no one is in the east wing to retrieve the wolf skull. Depending upon where it's hidden, we might even be able to take it without anyone knowing it's gone. Then we figure out the best place to tackle Reggie. He's already back at work, which increases his exposure."

Wow. Kyle had obviously been thinking about this. "You sound like an assassin planning a job," she said half jokingly.

Kyle sipped his coffee with a thoughtful look. "Yeah. Kyle Nelson, Demon Assassin. I like it."

For a minute, Amanda thought about what Kyle was proposing. Could she get her hopes up again? Could she defy the Order and use the exorcism? Even if a miracle happened and everything fell into place, would the exorcism work to bring her brother back? Or would that be expecting too many miracles?

She let her breath out slowly. Kyle talked about retrieving the wolf skull as if it were just a step in a process, but it wasn't. They couldn't even be sure it was at the Foundation. If she'd been smart, Marcella would have destroyed it the moment she acquired it. Although Amanda's exorcism had worked on Kyle, that meant little when it came to Reggie.

"We need to stop wasting time on this," she concluded. As the words left her mouth, a weight lifted from her shoulders. "There are too many unknowns. At some point, it doesn't make sense to risk both of our lives for a chance to help Reggie when the exorcism probably won't work anyway."

Kyle squinted at her with a look that said he didn't trust what she was saying. He probably thought she was going to try leaving him behind again and continue on alone. "None of that is new news," he said. "What changed?"

She stared at him for a second before answering, putting as much sincerity into her tone as she could muster. "I'm sick of this mission. There are too many obstacles and unknowns. I somehow have to accept that Reggie died two years ago and someone else is walking around who happens to look just like him."

Kyle sat back in his chair with both eyebrows raised. "Okay. What will you do instead?"

The question took her by surprise. All she had thought about for the past couple of years was saving Reggie. She'd put all of her spare time into it and trained her magic skills around it. Her job had been nothing more than a necessary distraction that covered expenses.

"I have no idea," she admitted in wonder.

A loud knock at the door brought Kyle to his feet. "Don't go anywhere," he said.

Amanda picked up her coffee cup and smiled. "I've nowhere to go."

Kyle started toward the front door. "Yeah, that's what we still need to talk about."

Amanda sat and sipped her coffee, feeling at loose ends for the first time since she could remember. She could do anything she wanted. Maybe start a hobby or put some effort into her career.

Kyle reappeared at the kitchen entryway. Jonathan and Jessie stood beyond him. Strain and worry deepened the wrinkles around Jonathan's eyes and mouth. He had his arm around Jessie, who was as pale as a ghost and appeared to be shivering. It looked like she was about to cry or throw up or both.

"We have a problem," Kyle announced in a tone that suggested his words were a serious understatement.

⁓

Jessie huddled against Jonathan on the living-room couch while Kyle made a fresh pot of coffee. Amanda sat in a chair opposite the desperate couple.

"How did you figure out Jessie was ... in trouble?" Amanda asked.

Jonathan gently caressed his wife's hair as he answered. "It started with bad dreams, but we didn't think much of that, after everything that happened at the Foundation. But then yesterday, Teddy, our youngest, threw a toy car at his older sister. Jessie had been facing away from the children at the time, but she turned and snatched the car out of the air at full-arm extension. A major-league baseman couldn't have caught that line drive."

"The kids both giggled and applauded," Jessie said with a sob. "But I knew what it might mean, and I nearly fainted. Now, I feel sick every time I look at their little faces and think about what I might become."

Amanda had been worried about Cara while Jessie was the unfortunate victim all along. But Jessie had no obvious bite or scratch marks at the end of the rescue mission. Her only bleeding wound had been a scrape on her cheek. Which, Amanda suddenly realized, was completely healed. They could check one more symptom off the list. Still, without a scratch or bite, it didn't make sense—unless they didn't know as much as they thought they did about *lupusdaemon* possession.

The unhappy couple were watching her process the situation. "How?" was finally all she could think to ask.

"We don't know," Jonathan answered. "The sun had to be up by then, so being underground must have made a difference. I doubt Skyler had the strength to scratch or bite, but Jessie already had an open wound and had been knocked unconscious. We're guessing that Skyler touched the wound with her fingernails and that was enough contact."

Jonathan's description brought an image to Amanda's mind. "Yes! Dr. Rutlinger was looking at something when he checked on Skyler and found her dead. I think she had blood on her fingertips, but he chased me out before I could get a clear look."

Kyle came into the room with filled mugs and handed them out before sitting down. The house was small, and the kitchen opened up into the living room, so he had been able to hear the conversation. "I'm sorry, Jessie," he said as he handed a mug to her. "I know exactly how you must be feeling right now."

"Thanks, Kyle," Jessie said. "At least you had the prospect of a cure."

"True," he allowed. "But that cure didn't exist until practically the last minute, and we didn't know it would work."

"Now we know it works," Jonathan interrupted bitterly, "but we can't use it."

Everyone was silent for a minute.

Jonathan took a deep breath and then said, "Which brings us to why we're here."

"You haven't told the Order about this yet," Kyle guessed.

"No, we haven't," Jonathan confirmed.

"Because you need our help," Amanda said.

"Exactly," Jonathan confirmed again. "I'm not going to argue with the Order about the exorcism ban. We don't have time for that, and I won't risk putting the Order on alert so they can try to stop us. It will be hard enough as it is. But no matter what, Jessie is not going to become … one of *them*."

Jessie locked eyes with Amanda. "I don't have the right to ask you to get involved," she said, "but I have to get this thing out of me." She rubbed her husband's arm. "Jonathan is speaking as if you have already agreed to help us. I may not be sworn to the Order, but I understand what he's asking of you."

"Of course I'll help," Amanda said without hesitation. How could she not? Jessie's condition was yet another consequence of her mission to save Reggie. This was her fault even if indirectly. She could see in Jonathan's eyes that he thought so as well. His unspoken accusation and expectations were irksome, but not unfair.

"I'll help too," Kyle said.

Jonathan smiled for the first time since he'd arrived. "Thanks, Kyle. I knew we could count on you. No one could understand what Jessie's going through better than you."

"I do have one request, however," Kyle added.

"Name it."

"Help us find a way to use the exorcism on Reggie as well."

Amanda turned her head quickly to look at Kyle. It wasn't his request to make, but he must have known she wouldn't bring it up herself.

Jonathan gave Amanda a sly smile. "You were planning to ignore the ban anyway, weren't you."

"No, actually," Amanda answered truthfully. "Just before you arrived, we agreed that Reggie's cause was hopeless. I *thought* we had given up on that idea," she said pointedly to Kyle.

Kyle waved a hand toward their guests. "This changes everything. Once we help Jessie, we'll have everything we need to try with Reggie."

"Except for Reggie," Amanda pointed out.

Kyle tilted his head toward Jonathan. "Our odds of dealing with that part of the problem just went up astronomically."

Jonathan nodded his agreement. "As long as Jessie is the priority, I'll do whatever I can to help you with Reggie."

Amanda looked around the room at her friends. "Just to be clear, Jessie *is* the priority because we *know* we can help her. If we can arrange it so I can try the exorcism on Reggie afterward, so much the better."

"Then I'm in," Jonathan said.

"*We're* in," Jessie said, squeezing Jonathan's arm.

Amanda took a deep breath and tried to organize her thoughts through a storm of emotions. After days of despair, she had finally accepted that Reggie was beyond her help. Now she had to face the horror that Jessie's life was at stake and yet her friend's misfortune had also resurrected her hope for her brother's return.

Jonathan had been right not to tell the Order about Jessie's condition. Their new mission to exorcise her would be difficult without the backing of the Order, but it would be next to impossible if the Order interfered. They would have to be careful about how they moved forward.

Amanda wondered if she could enlist anyone else to help. Who could she trust with this information? Noreen would be a valuable ally. But would her loyalty to a member of her coven supersede her loyalty to the Order? There was no way to know. Tanya wasn't in the Order, but she also wasn't exactly courageous. Cara might be willing to help, out of revenge against Marcella if for no other reason. But Cara wasn't much of a team player.

It might be up to only the four of them. Somehow, they had to break into the Foundation again and steal the wolf skull from Marcella's room without her knowing about it. Then they had to perform a banned exorcism ceremony on Jessie. And maybe Reggie, too. The mission had to be completed in less than three weeks, and they had to make sure the Order didn't discover what they were planning.

CHAPTER 28

Hostile Takeover

Now what does she want? Adolphus Rutlinger wondered as he followed Cyrus to the Foundation's conference room. Marcella had become insufferable since the incident with the Order the week before. He still couldn't understand how she had managed to parlay the near disaster into such a strong influence over the local packs.

He entered the conference room, noting that Reggie and Marcella were already seated. The meeting table consisted of three folding tables arranged in a "U" shape against an exterior wall. Cyrus took the seat at Marcella's right, as usual. Adolphus sat across from them, as far away as possible. Reggie sat along the base of the "U" between the two unfriendly parties.

"Don't pout, Woreblin," Marcella said. "It doesn't become you."

"Never call me that," Adolphus demanded. "Names have power, and you never know who is listening."

"I suppose you're right, Adolph," she replied sourly. "But you seem to have forgotten what you are, and a reminder was due."

He didn't bother correcting her diminution of his name. It would only give her the satisfaction of having irritated him. "You have no business reminding *me* of what I am, witch. What do you want?"

"I called this meeting to make an announcement. The northwest packs have responded favorably to my plans for an alliance, so I've invited the pack leaders to visit and discuss details."

She had to know that was a dangerous proposition. Even Reggie squirmed in his chair at the suggestion of putting the region's alphas together in one room. Some of their feuds had been going on for decades.

As if she were reading his mind, Marcella continued. "To work together, the alphas need strong leadership, and that's where I come in."

"You're delusional," Adolphus said. "What makes you think they'll accept your leadership?"

"The packs respect power, and I've shown myself to be the most powerful of all. I forced the Order to halt the biggest threat our kind has ever known."

"That's a rather charitable view of what happened. You acted for your own good, not the good of our kind."

"I'm a dark witch and a demon," she snapped in response. "You expect my motivation to be altruistic? I won, and that's all that matters to the alphas. You would understand that if you weren't so humanized."

Humanized. Iledaste must have supplied that particular term. It was meant as a grave insult, but Adolphus had to admit that there was some truth to the accusation. He enjoyed playing human—apparently even more than the dark witch who had given up her humanity. It had been a long time since he had indulged his thirst for power and control beyond the Foundation. Doing so attracted too much attention and invited a swift journey to the abyss. It was a miracle that Marcella had managed to avoid that fate so far. He sincerely hoped her luck would run out soon.

Marcella looked around the room. "We'll have to rearrange this space to accommodate more visitors. I want the rest of our pack to join us here more often as well. I'm about to become the leader of the entire region, and that prestige will benefit everyone. It's about time they showed some appreciation for what I've done for them. This place is about to become very busy."

When the former members of the Selkirk Pack had renounced, Adolphus had taken it as a statement of support for his leadership versus Marcella's. Then, two days ago, she delivered the news that they wanted to return to the Pack. His humiliation was doubled by the gloating smile she wore as she informed him.

He had no reliable allies. Skyler was gone, and in spite of the way Marcella had tortured the man, Baldur Peri was among those who wanted to return and had agreed to swear allegiance to her. Allies or not, he had to stand up for what he had worked a human lifetime to build.

"Before you get too far with your redecorating plans," he said, "you should consider another venue for your great convention of alphas. This facility is dedicated to supporting those of us who need help during the *Erste Mond* transition and who need a sanctuary when conditions turn against them. It is not your personal conference center."

Marcella raised an eyebrow and folded her arms. "This place may be called the *Rutlinger* Foundation, but it isn't *yours*. The Foundation owns the land and the building."

"Correct," Adolphus agreed. "And *you* aren't a member."

"That's easily remedied. Your bylaws allow an existing member to sponsor anyone who can cough up twenty grand for membership. In fact, the language is so sloppy that a *human* could theoretically join."

Adolphus could feel his face heat as he saw where she was going. "That provision was designed to make it easier for us to return after we'd moved to a new body."

"And to admit new members of the Pack into the Foundation, right?"

"Yes."

"Okay, then. I want in, and Cyrus is joining with me."

Adolphus looked over at Reggie. "I suppose you have agreed to sponsor them?"

Reggie shrugged in a "why not?" gesture.

"That still leaves the matter of membership fees."

Marcella glanced at Cyrus and shared a private smirk with him. "We're working on that."

So, they didn't have the money, but they had come up with a way to get it. He doubted the source of funds would be legal, considering how little inclination either of them had shown for anything resembling a career. Putting "Dark Witch" in the experience section of a resume wouldn't score points with prospective employers.

"Becoming members doesn't change what the Foundation is about," Adolphus declared stubbornly.

"Oh, but it does," the witch cooed. "Members can vote to change almost anything, and I expect plenty of support for my proposals. Your charitable mission for disadvantaged werewolves is sweet, but it's a terrible waste of the Foundation's potential."

Adolphus was speechless with anger. He wanted to argue that the membership would never support her proposals, but he was no longer sure of that. He wanted to defend his original vision for the Foundation, but her denigration of that vision suggested his words would fall on deaf ears. She was planning to corrupt the organization to fit her agenda. An organization that *he* had founded and that bore *his* name.

His hands tightened into fists in his lap as he struggled to resist the urge to knock the smug smile off her face, but that would be suicide. A challenging glint in her eyes showed she was ready and waiting for him to make such a move.

Iledaste had always chafed under his leadership, but as Clarissa, she'd never had the guts to challenge his authority like this. Instead, she had brooded at her cottage in the valley and distracted herself with an endless string of sex partners. Now, with the dark witch leading their collaboration, she could enjoy the benefits of working with an ambitious and confident manipulator.

He had to bide his time. Marcella was ruthless, but she was also reckless. An opportunity to take her down would appear eventually. All he had to do was be patient and remain vigilant.

CHAPTER 29

Volunteers

Amanda settled into her favorite chair in Noreen's living room, but she was far from comfortable. The coven had gathered for their regular meeting. Everyone was in their usual seats with Cara arriving late and taking the last space on the couch. The reality of Jessie's condition made the normal meeting preparations seem almost surreal.

Catching Jessie's eye, Amanda offered an encouraging smile. Her friend smiled back and took a deep breath. As much as Jessie wanted to share her dilemma with the coven, Noreen's Order affiliation complicated matters. They couldn't be sure she would support their efforts to defy the Order's ban.

Noreen carried in a tray of beverages, and everyone busied themselves with pouring their drinks and making small talk.

"I won't be able to host our next meeting," Noreen announced without preamble. "I have to stand in review before the Court of Elders. However, I'd like for you all to meet without me. I suggest you make arrangements by the end of our meeting today."

"So is this it?" Cara asked. "Is this where the Court decides whether or not you'll be joining them?"

"Almost," Noreen answered. "The review is important, but not the final step. The Court will use the review to recommend a candidate, and then the entire Coven Conclave will vote."

"But if the Court recommends a candidate, isn't the Conclave vote pretty much a formality?"

"Not at all. The politics of the election can be … extreme. The Court's recommendation is only one factor among many."

"Good luck on the review, then," Jessie said. Amanda, Cara, and Tanya echoed her sentiment.

Amanda didn't envy Noreen's dive into coven politics. Although she was starting to warm up to the idea of leading her own coven some day, that was as far as she wanted to go. It was difficult enough to juggle the rules of the Order and the Coven Conclave. Rising to leadership in either would put her right in the middle of managing disputes between the two organizations and their differing priorities.

Noreen picked up a familiar wooden box from the coffee table and held it in her hands. "I'll have to return the Resonance Star before too long, but until then, I thought we'd do some more experimenting with it. The lore associated with the Star seems a little deficient on the operational side, as Amanda's observations revealed."

She was talking about the problem Amanda ran into at the Foundation: when one witch was casting, the others were prevented from casting.

Noreen continued. "We'll take turns using the center piece and try casting different spells together and separately. We'll document what we learn, which is the excuse I gave for hanging on to it a bit longer."

Excuse? That was an interesting choice of words. Did Noreen want to keep the device around a bit longer for other reasons? Maybe Amanda was reading too much into it.

"Let's start with you," Noreen said as she tossed the box to Jessie.

Jessie was sitting back on the couch with her juice glass in her left hand. She had been paying attention to Noreen, but still could not possibly have been ready for the box to come flying toward her. Regardless, her right hand caught the weighty spinning object as if it had been handed to her.

Amanda froze for a second. She wasn't surprised at Jessie's catch because it wasn't so different from the test she'd given Kyle so many months ago when she'd tipped over a water glass that he'd caught before it spilled. Was Noreen testing Jessie in a similar way?

She watched while Noreen poured herself a glass of juice and sat back in her chair, behaving as if nothing unusual had happened. Cara and Tanya both stared at Jessie with round eyes, but quickly recovered their composure and pretended to be interested in their drinks.

Jessie slowly set her drink down, and then opened the latch on the box. She cleared her throat and finally let her eyes meet Noreen's. The coven leader's face was bland, revealing nothing about what she was thinking.

"Go ahead and pass out the Star pendants," Noreen instructed, waving her glass toward the box.

Jessie did as she was told, and Amanda slowly let out the breath she'd been holding as the tense moment passed.

For the next hour, Amanda and the rest of the coven worked with the Resonance Star, plumbing its depths and documenting what they learned. Cara and Tanya both stole concerned glances at Jessie. When Amanda caught their eyes, she did her best to convey caution. They seemed to get the hint because they said nothing about the earlier incident.

The time passed so quickly that Amanda was surprised when Noreen announced, "Well, that's it for today." She held out her pendant for Amanda to take. "Amanda, I want you to keep the Star at the farmhouse so you can use it again at the next gathering. Be sure to write down anything new you learn, and I'll add it to my notes."

Amanda collected the pendants from the other witches and stored them in the box. Holding the box in her hands, she considered what a valuable tool it would be for her developing plans with Kyle. She and Jessie would be able to share their powers when it was time to retrieve the wolf skull from the Foundation.

After the gathering, the witches filed out of the house and walked toward their vehicles. Cara and Tanya hurried to catch up with Jessie.

"Jessie, wait," Cara said.

Jessie's face showed a look of reluctance as she turned around.

"You have to let us help," Cara insisted. Tanya nodded vigorously in agreement.

"Help with what?" Jessie said, but her voice revealed that she knew her denial was pointless.

"You know what," Cara answered. As Amanda joined the cluster of women, Cara gave her an accusing frown. "You both know what. We want in on whatever you have planned."

Jessie let out a sigh and looked to Amanda for help.

"It's really dangerous," Amanda said. "It wouldn't be fair to involve you. There's a good chance we'll get in serious trouble even if we succeed."

"We don't care," Cara insisted, once again eliciting a confirming nod from Tanya. "It's not fair to leave us out." Cara lifted her arm and looked at the healing scars from where she'd been scratched. "It was almost me," she said in a quiet voice.

Amanda focused on Tanya. "This isn't your battle, and if you got hurt, I'd never forgive myself."

Tanya shook her head and looked at Jessie. "Jessie is my friend and coven-mate. I know that if I were in trouble, she wouldn't take no for an answer."

Amanda had no argument for that. They all knew it was true.

"Thank you," Jessie said, her voice breaking with emotion. She reached out with both arms and pulled the two volunteers into a tight hug. Amanda saw her own surprise mirrored on Cara's and Tanya's faces. The spontaneous hug was an unusual move for Jessie, who was normally so calm and collected.

Amanda glanced toward the house and saw Noreen step back from the picture window. She went deeper into the house until Amanda couldn't see her anymore.

How much did she suspect? Probably everything. She couldn't acknowledge or support what they were doing because of her position in the Order. Amanda looked at the box in her hands. Noreen had given them an edge, though. With Cara and Tanya on board, the Resonance Star would be more useful than ever. And Amanda was having a few ideas on how she could keep Cara and Tanya safe while still letting them contribute in an important way.

Tucking the box under her arm, Amanda said, "Okay. This changes things. I'll get in touch with you soon, so do what you can to stay available."

As they all got into their cars and left, Amanda turned her thoughts to what would happen next. Kyle and Jonathan would undoubtedly have mixed emotions about Cara and Tanya joining the team, just as she and Jessie had. But the truth was they were going to need all the help they could get.

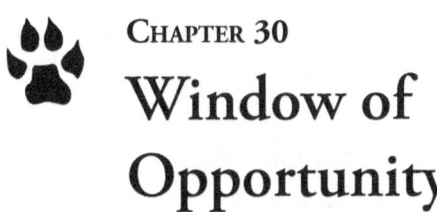

CHAPTER 30

Window of Opportunity

The sedan rolled out of the Foundation's gateway and accelerated as the gate automatically closed behind it. Two occupants rode in the front seats, their silhouettes a good match for Marcella and Cyrus.

"Let's go," Amanda said, turning back toward the forest trail behind her. All morning, they had watched the werewolves leave the Foundation one by one. Reggie was first, heading off to his job with a logging company. Rutlinger was next, going to his veterinary clinic in town. Marcella and Cyrus were last, as was the case every day they'd been watching.

Amanda wondered what Marcella and Cyrus were up to. They left in the early afternoon and didn't return until some time after the last surveillance shift ended at 6:00 PM. Not that it really mattered. All she cared about was that the Foundation was consistently unoccupied long enough for her team to get in and out. If the werewolves followed the pattern her team had observed over the past week, they had several hours to work with, which was far more than they needed.

The center pendant from the Resonance Star dangled between her breasts with unaccustomed weight, and she silently thanked Noreen for loaning it to them. With four members of the coven on the mission and the Star to concentrate their power, Amanda believed they'd be able to counter any passive magic Marcella might have left behind.

They approached the Foundation near the same side door Amanda had used for Cara's rescue. It was the closest point of ingress to the warded room, and unlike the front door, no cameras monitored it.

Crouching outside, she waited for a couple of minutes and listened. Since they hadn't been watching the place 24 hours a day, it was possible that a guest had arrived without anyone on her team knowing.

"Déjà vu," Kyle whispered. Amanda smiled in response.

She put her hand on the door handle and whispered the incantation that would open the lock. She was careful to adjust the strength of the spell, accounting for the additional power she received through the Star. The lock made satisfyingly little noise when it clicked. Although she wasn't particularly concerned about being silent, an echo of Noreen's voice in the back of her mind reminded her that she should maintain precise control over her magic at all times. One never knew when precision would be critical.

Pushing open the door, Amanda swiftly led the way up the stairs to the second floor. Kyle, Jessie, and Jonathan followed her. She glanced back before the door closed, catching a last glimpse of Cara's and Tanya's tense faces. They would remain outside and watch for any unexpected arrivals, with Cara reporting to Jonathan through a walkie-talkie.

Amanda and Jessie had experimented with the Star's range and determined that it became more of a detriment than an advantage at about a hundred yards. At that distance, the power it shared was minimal, but it still interfered with their ability to cast spells individually. However, as long as Cara and Tanya stayed nearby, the entire Foundation building was well within the Star's range.

As Amanda approached the bedroom door that had been warded previously, strong magic brushed against her senses again. It said something that Marcella kept the room warded even after the threat from the Order had passed. Either Marcella was naturally paranoid, or she didn't trust her pack mates. Or both.

The first thing Amanda did was to look for physical evidence of the ward's components. Any residue from the ward spell might give her a clue about how to dismantle it. Kyle boosted her up so she could check the top of the door frame, but she found nothing useful.

"Do you see anything?" she whispered to Kyle.

"No. But last time, I didn't see the ward's magic until you touched the door handle."

"And we know how *that* turned out," she said mostly to herself.

How was she going to defeat the ward and get into the room? She knew from experience that the brute-force method wouldn't work. Just turning the door handle had knocked both her and Kyle on their asses.

She had to assume the spell was layered and dismantle it one layer at a time. She also had to hope Marcella was far enough away not to detect her efforts.

Amanda already knew something about the first layer. Marcella would have drawn from the air element to power the shock. According to Cara, Marcella was an air adept, so that made sense.

The ward delivered a powerful shock, but it probably couldn't sustain that power indefinitely. It would take time to recharge although there was no way to know how long. Regardless, she wasn't too excited about taking the direct approach to draining it. Been there. Done that. Got the rug burns.

Amanda rubbed her hands together. Her element, earth, was a good match for the challenge. She stretched her palms toward the door and started an incantation with an appeal to the spirits of the light.

Nothing happened.

When she reached out with her senses, she immediately understood why. The Foundation was home to demons, and the place was thick with dark spirits. She needed help. "Jessie, could you perform a purification before I try to work on the ward?"

"With pleasure," her friend answered. Amanda waited while Jessie started her own incantation. As a water witch, Jessie was the best in the coven at purification. After a few seconds, Jessie stopped with a look of surprise and disgust. "Yuck. This place is a sewer."

Amanda nodded ruefully. "Now you know why I need your help."

Jessie squared her shoulders and started again.

After a few moments, the suffocating darkness lifted somewhat. Amanda took over the incantation from Jessie, relieved when the Resonance Star smoothly shifted its power flow back to her.

Tentatively probing the ward, Amanda detected a web of energy along the interior of the door. Turning the door handle would put it in contact with the web, and anyone who did manage to get the door open would walk straight into it.

But what powered the thing? Passive wards like the ones she used at Hayworth Farm required little energy. The shock Marcella's ward had given her had to have come from somewhere. Tracing the edges of the web, Amanda found a link to a nearby electrical outlet.

Marcella had tied the ward into the building's electrical system! How diabolically ingenious.

Amanda shook off her curiosity, wishing she had time to examine the ward further. Mixing magical and mundane powers took a lot of skill. However, she had limited time to accomplish her mission, and she didn't know what other obstacles they might face. She might not know exactly how the ward was constructed, but she had a good idea of how to defeat it: the ward's strength was also its weakness. With just a small bridge of her own earth power directed right about there ….

A muffled pop from inside the room startled the rest of the team until Amanda waved her hand in a calming gesture. She ended her spell after verifying that she had successfully shorted out the web of energy and that the door was clear of other dangers.

Glancing at Kyle, she gave him a "here-goes-nothing" look before reaching out and grasping the door handle. She turned the cold handle slowly and cringed at the memory of her last attempt to enter the room. This time, the door unlatched and swung open on silent hinges.

Eager to find the wolf skull, Amanda hurried inside and then froze in place. Kyle, not expecting her sudden stop, bumped into her from behind and mumbled an apology that he cut short with a gasp.

The room seemed to resist the light that seeped through the window curtains. Deep shadows lurked in every corner, and a thin dark fog dimmed Amanda's view, like the atmosphere in a smoky old jazz bar. She rubbed her eyes and looked for the source of the fog, finding nothing obvious.

Suppressing a shiver of revulsion, Amanda stalked over to the window and yanked the curtains aside. Although the sun was on the opposite side of the building, the additional natural light was a tremendous relief. When she turned around, it was as if the strange fog had never existed. The room was still menacing but nowhere near as oppressive.

Kyle stared at the floor in one corner of the room. When Amanda followed his gaze, she spotted the casting circle that held his attention.

Amanda stepped forward with her fists clenched. The dark witch had desecrated her moon shrine, and here was her chance to return the favor.

It was obvious that the casting circle was designed to be portable. It consisted of a metal band set on edge in the shape of a ring. Four candle bases were attached to the outside surface at evenly spaced positions. The ring was maybe three feet in diameter—not much more than standing room for one person. It could probably be carried in the trunk of a car and would take just a few minutes of alignment before it would be ready to go.

The temptation to destroy Marcella's casting circle faded and was replaced with a desire to steal it instead. That would show the bitch. It was probably heavy, but Kyle was strong. He could lug the thing back through the forest to her car.

Kyle appeared at her side. "Cool," he said.

"Yeah. I want it."

"Bad idea," Jessie said from behind. "You think the moon shrine was a mess? It would take months to consecrate that thing."

Amanda sighed. Jessie was probably right. Who knew how much dark magic had passed through that circle? The spiritual stain might be impossible to fully cleanse. She'd be better off starting from scratch with raw materials.

"Yeah, but still," Amanda mused out loud. "I wish we'd had this when we put out the fire at the farm. It's just a tool, and even tainted, it would have magnified our powers. We should at least consider stealing the idea and making our own. The coven could perform powerful ceremonies just about anywhere."

Jessie seemed to accept Amanda's suggestion, and her expression turned contemplative as she stared at the device.

Amanda shook her head in frustration. She was letting herself get distracted again. Turning away from the casting circle, she started searching the room for the wolf skull. Jessie and Kyle helped while Jonathan kept watch in the hallway.

Kyle was searching through the bottom drawer of the desk when he let out an "aha" of triumph and held up a familiar looking folder. Amanda took the folder and quickly paged through it, verifying that he'd found her notes.

She handed it back to him with a satisfied smile. "Good job."

However, they still hadn't found the wolf skull. Amanda and Kyle continued to look in and under every stick of furniture while Jessie muttered something about being thorough and went into the bathroom.

The sight of a small trunk gave her a moment of hope, but when she opened it, she found it was filled with the dark witch's spell-casting implements. No wolf skull.

Several minutes of searching later, Amanda stood side by side with Kyle and Jessie. All three of them stared at the door to the closet—the only space they hadn't checked.

"Do you think she'd bother to put a ward within a ward?" Jessie asked.

Amanda shrugged. "I guess we're about to find out."

~

Amanda opened her eyes and lifted her hands off the surface of the closet door. If it was warded by magic, she couldn't detect it.

"Anything?" Jessie asked.

Amanda shook her head, hovering her hand over the doorknob. She tapped the doorknob with her index finger as if checking for static. When nothing happened, she gripped the knob decisively and turned. The closet door swung toward her a couple of inches.

Nothing blew up, no sirens went off, and she wasn't dead. So far, so good.

Amanda opened the door the rest of the way and turned on the light switch. The closet was too small for anyone else to help. As she searched the shelf above the hanging clothes, her heart skipped a beat. A set of wicked white teeth gleamed at her.

Reaching up, Amanda grabbed the wolf skull with both hands and carried it out into the room. She smiled at Jessie. "Got it!"

Jessie closed the distance between them and ran a finger over the symbols etched into the skull. "It's so ... primal ... and savage."

"I know," Amanda agreed. "It seems fitting, doesn't it?"

Jessie nodded, continuing to stare at the skull.

Kyle was looking over Amanda's shoulder into the closet. "What about the cash box?" he asked.

Amanda held up the skull. "Who cares? We found what we came for. Let's get out of here before our luck runs out."

Kyle stepped around her and took the box down from the shelf. "It's locked. What do you suppose could be so important that she'd bother to lock it up *inside* her ward?"

Amanda was about to tell Kyle to leave the box alone when Jonathan leaned into the room from the doorway. "I'm with Amanda. We should go."

"No," Jessie stated, finally taking her eyes off the talisman. "I want to do this now."

"The exorcism?" Amanda asked incredulously. "Here?"

"Yes. We have everything we need, we should have plenty of time, and I don't want to take the chance that we'll lose the skull again."

Amanda looked around the room. "It isn't safe to stay here. What if one of them comes back early today?" Her eyes lingered on the casting circle. "And do you really want to trust the ceremony to *that* thing?"

Jessie glanced at the circle. "It's not ideal, but like you said, it's just a tool. Don't you want a chance to return the favor after what she did to your moon shrine?"

Amanda was aware that her friend was appealing to her sense of vengeance in an attempt to manipulate her, and truthfully, she *was* tempted. If Amanda's coven used the casting circle, the work they did with the spirits of the light would "defile" it, at least temporarily, for the dark witch's purposes.

"Nice try," Amanda said in a wry tone. She took a step toward the door and beckoned with the skull. "Come on. We'll go straight to the farm and do this where we'll be safe."

Jessie folded her arms and shook her head. "You know as well as I do that we won't be safe anywhere. Marcella is going to discover our theft as soon as she gets back, and the farm will be the first place she goes. Even if we finish the ceremony before she can stop us, we'll get Lucille in trouble with her *and* the Order."

Amanda sighed with exasperation. "We've been over this. Lucille already gave her blessing, but okay, fine. We'll go to your house."

"We can't. The kids are there, and it would take too long to set up anyway," Jessie said stubbornly. Then her tone turned pleading. "Amanda, we have to do this now while we still can. I'm scared to death that someone will stop us before we can get this vile thing out of me. I'll kill myself before I let it take me from my family."

Kyle looked over from the desk where he was fiddling with the lock on the metal box. "I can relate to *that* feeling."

Jonathan's face fell when he heard his wife's heartfelt plea. The expression he turned toward Amanda gave his support for whatever she might decide.

Amanda had no more arguments to present, and she couldn't deny the validity of her friend's fears. The clock was ticking, and the only thing that really mattered was completing the ceremony. "Then we'd better get on with this," she said, her voice tinged with annoyance. She went over to the casting circle and dragged it away from the wall so there'd be more room around it.

"Jonathan, call Cara and Tanya up here. I'll need them at the circle with me."

"But we won't have anyone keeping watch outside," Jonathan objected.

"You can keep an eye on things from the window in the entryway," Amanda suggested.

"No way," Jonathan replied, shaking his head. "I'm not leaving Jessie at a time like this."

Amanda was tired of losing arguments. "Fine. I guess it doesn't really matter. If any of the Pack returns while we're in the middle of this, we're screwed anyway."

"Ow! Shit!" Kyle yelped, leaping back from the desk so fast that he overturned his chair. He shook his right hand and then stared at it, flexing his fingers. On the desk, the metal box sat open.

"What happened?" Amanda asked.

"I guess I triggered some kind of trap when I opened the box. It zapped me and burned my hand."

Amanda snatched the toppled chair and thumped it down in the center of the casting circle. "Dammit, Kyle. You're lucky Marcella didn't ward the box with something really nasty." Grabbing his wrist, she checked the reddened skin on the back of his hand. It wasn't much worse than a sunburn. "She was probably trying to mark anyone who was poking around." Releasing his wrist, she added, "You've been caught red handed."

Kyle rolled his eyes. "Very funny," he said as his attention strayed back to the box. "But it makes me even more curious. If Marcella put that much effort into hiding something, we might be able to use it against her." Lifting out a notebook, he started perusing the pages.

Amanda blew out a breath of irritation and left Kyle to his snooping. The damage was done. Going back to her own task, she rummaged through the trunk of magical supplies. The dark witch had to have candles somewhere.

"Huh," Kyle muttered as he thumbed through the notebook.

"What now?"

"I'm not sure. I think they were spying on someone. And there's a bunch of cash in the box."

Jessie looked over Kyle's shoulder at the notebook. "I see what you mean. It appears to be a journal of dates and times with notes about people's movements."

Amanda stood up from the chest with a candle in each hand, her curiosity piqued. What was Marcella up to?

"The notes are for a sequence of locations," Kyle added, flipping forward and backward through the pages. He glanced at the stack of bills. "I think she was casing these places. I'll bet this money is stolen."

That wasn't a surprise. In her past, Marcella had been in trouble for committing crimes with dark magic. But that was before the *lupusdaemon* took over ... or was it? "How recent are the dates?"

Kyle thumbed forward to the last pages that had writing. "Pretty recent. Like, yesterday."

Too bad Blackstone wasn't still around. He'd undoubtedly be interested in Kyle's find. Maybe Amanda would try to send the master hunter a message when she returned to Hayworth Farm. Cara and Tanya walked into the room, reminding her that it wasn't their immediate problem.

"Kyle," she said firmly, waiting until she had his attention. "I need you put that back the way you found it and do something else for me."

"Sure, what do you need?" He returned the journal to the box and repositioning it carefully before closing the lid. "Not sure I can get it locked again."

"Don't worry about that. I want you to go downstairs and keep watch from the entryway."

Kyle sighed as he put the metal box back into the closet. He was obviously disappointed that he'd miss out on the action, but he understood that someone had to make sure they weren't taken completely by surprise.

Chapter 31

Foreboding

Flipping through the Spokane Yellow Pages, Marcella considered their options. They needed another target that would have plenty of cash on hand and that wasn't open 24 hours. And they needed a bigger score.

The last few hits had gone perfectly, but they couldn't expect their luck to last indefinitely. Although she and Cyrus had spread their efforts across three states, the cops would eventually work together and recognize a pattern. That was one major advantage of working from North Idaho: Washington and Montana were each only an hour away.

"I want this to be the last job for a while," Marcella announced over the rock-and-roll music playing from the radio.

Cyrus turned down the volume. "Why? I thought things were going pretty well."

"Better than I had hoped," Marcella agreed. "But I want to get this stupid membership issue out of the way so I can keep the momentum I've built with the packs. The conference has to happen as soon as possible."

"Why don't you just hold the conference anyway? Rutlinger can't stop you."

"Appearances. When the pack leaders arrive, I want to be in full control of the Foundation. I want them to see me operating from a position of strength with the full support of the Selkirk Pack."

"Except for Rutlinger."

Marcella made a derisive noise. "No one will credit the sour grapes of a deposed alpha."

Cyrus pursed his lips. "Probably not. How much more do we need?"

"We're close. Just a couple thousand more, I think," Marcella answered while she dug into her canvas carry bag. "Crap. I forgot to bring the job journal."

Cyrus squirmed in his seat. He straightened his back and glanced over at her bag. "You left it at the Foundation?"

"Don't worry, the wards are in place, and I didn't exactly leave it sitting out on my desk."

Cyrus focused on his driving and didn't say anything more, but his wrinkled brow told Marcella that he was still concerned. "We don't need it today," she reasoned. "We're casing a new job, so we'll just pick up another notebook. We'll merge them later."

"We should *burn* them later," Cyrus countered.

"Sure," Marcella said with a shrug. "Once the Foundation is ours, we won't need them anymore."

Members of the Foundation had full access to all of its resources, including several homes and properties around the area. For a while, Marcella would stay at the Foundation building and solidify her power base. After that, she would leave the commune lifestyle behind and move into a place of her own.

She glanced over at Cyrus. He'd proved to be a reliable lieutenant and an adequate, if unimaginative, sexual partner. Perhaps she'd take him with her.

About an hour into their drive toward Spokane, Cyrus slowed the car and pulled into a travel center near the town of Post Falls, Idaho. They weren't particularly low on gas, but it was their habit to start the evening's stakeout with a full tank, just in case it became necessary to leave quickly and travel far. "This place has a large convenience store," he pointed out. "They might have a notebook."

Marcella opened her door. "I'll check."

She wandered through the store, impressed by the quantity and variety of products available. It seemed to cater to the trucker crowd with all kinds of automotive supplies, snacks, and coffee. She had no trouble locating a spiral-bound notebook. Cyrus joined her at the checkout with an energy drink he favored.

Back in the car, Cyrus popped open his beverage and took a deep swig. When he set the can down to start the car's engine, the lightning bolt on the side of the can caught and held Marcella's attention.

Her chest tightened inexplicably, and her hands closed into fists. It was like real lightning had struck close by. Her heart pounded, and she couldn't seem to get enough air.

Cyrus looked over, concern tightening his features. "What's wrong?"

"I don't know," she answered. The feeling grew into a panic that made her close her eyes and throw herself back in her seat, her body rigid with tension. She felt like screaming.

After a few seconds, the unexpected sensations subsided, and her breathing slowed. She opened her eyes, aware of a lingering sense of foreboding.

"Turn around," Marcella instructed in a firm tone. "We're going back to the Foundation." Cyrus didn't question her. He turned back onto the highway and put Post Falls in the rear-view mirror.

Marcella tried to sort out the odd experience she'd just had and what it might mean. The only thing that made sense was that someone had tampered with one of her wards. But could she sense that from so far away? Had joining with Iledaste amplified her abilities that much? What disturbed her more was that she only remembered putting an alert on the cash box ward. That meant someone had already defeated the main ward on the door and was inside the room poking around.

Cyrus accelerated to well over the speed limit, correctly interpreting her tense silence. Marcella put her hand on his arm. "Let's get back as quickly as possible, but I don't want to get pulled over." Cyrus nodded and slowed the car to just above the speed limit. "I think one of my wards has been compromised."

Cyrus narrowed his eyes at her. "You can tell from here?"

"I'm as surprised as you are. And, no, I can't be sure, but it feels right."

"Who? Why?" Cyrus asked.

"That's what we need to think about. When we get back, we need to be prepared for whatever might be going on."

CHAPTER 32

Skyler's Plea

With Kyle downstairs and Jonathan keeping watch at the doorway, the witches had more space to move around the room. Amanda sat Jessie in the chair at the center of the casting circle and instructed the others to take their customary positions.

"Okay, here's what we're going to do," Amanda said. She went on to explain her plan for conducting the exorcism. All of the women had studied Amanda's revised exorcism notes, so they knew basically what to expect.

"This is going to be weird," Jessie said, squirming in her seat. "Just sitting here while the rest of you do the work."

"We don't know what will happen when we cast out the demon," Amanda responded. "But I'm pretty sure we don't want you involved in the spell at that point."

"I know, I know. It still sucks. At least I get to drive away the troublemakers."

Jessie was unarguably the best purifier in their coven. As a water witch, purification came naturally to her, but she had strength that could not be explained by her elemental affinity alone. She would need every bit of that strength to drive away the dark spirits hovering around the dark witch's room and the casting circle. Amanda and the other witches would lend their strength to Jessie while she did her thing.

Amanda smiled to herself. Marcella would be furious when she next went to use her casting circle and discovered the light spirit taint from Jessie's purification. She might even figure out that they'd used her own equipment to perform the exorcism. Not that Amanda was thrilled with the idea of handling the dark witch's tools of the trade. No soap was going to remove *that* spiritual grime. But Jessie was right— they were just tools. Although they wouldn't amplify her abilities as well as her own equipment would, they'd do the job.

Amanda took several deep breaths and cleared her mind in preparation for the ceremony. She heard the others do the same.

She was about to signal Jessie to begin the purification when she remembered that they were all still connected through the Resonance Star. Jessie would have direct access to all of their power, which would be fine at first. But later, each of them would need to work independently to support the exorcism. Besides, having Jessie connected to the rest of the coven while they cast out the *lupusdaemon* seemed like a Very Bad Idea. Amanda removed the Star's square center pendant from around her neck. It was the hub, so none of the other pendants would work without it.

As she severed the connection to her coven-mates, Amanda experienced both regret and relief. The sense of strength the Resonance Star granted was seductive, but it was also a violation of sorts. Amanda was much more comfortable being in full control of her own power and having the discretion to use it when and how she wished.

Tanya, who had her eyes closed, immediately opened them and touched her hand to her pendant. She looked toward Amanda, frowning with confusion. When she saw Amanda tucking the hub pendant into a pocket, comprehension dawned on the fire witch's face. She started to remove her pendant as well, but Amanda stopped her.

"Keep it on," Amanda suggested. "Just in case. Then all I'll have to do is put mine back on to link us up again." Tanya released her pendant with a nod.

At Amanda's bidding, Jessie started her incantation to purify the room and push away the remaining dark spirits that infested it. Her voice sharpened with intensity as she fought against far more resistance than she was accustomed to. What would have been an easy task at Noreen's house or in the moon shrine was more difficult from inside the dark witch's lair.

For a large casting that involved the full coven, the normal sequence of events started with the water witch purifying the workspace and the air witch protecting it. The prime, usually Noreen, would then cast the primary spell while the fire witch added strength to it and the earth witch stabilized it.

However, Noreen wasn't there. Amanda was prime, which meant her earth-borne stabilizing influence would be diluted by her efforts toward the exorcism. Cara would have to work extra hard to maintain her protections and Tanya would have to be sensitive to where her strength was needed the most. It would be a delicate dance, and Amanda honestly didn't know if the coven could pull it off. They had trained together under many scenarios, but nothing like what they were facing.

In spite of the resistance, Jessie succeeded in clearing the room. As soon as she did, Cara joined the working and wove her protection spell to keep the dark spirits at bay. Within moments, a shimmering column of energy swirled around the circumference of the casting circle.

As soon as the protections were up, Amanda started the exorcism incantation. Distracted by their uncomfortable circumstances and the worry that one of the werewolves might show up at any moment, her first few phrases were weak and halting. Jessie's slump of disappointment and frustration slapped Amanda back into focus. She shut out the distractions and spoke the next phrases clearly and forcefully.

After sealing the casting circle against the *lupusdaemon's* escape, Amanda held up the wolf skull and summoned forth the demon.

Amanda sensed Marcella's casting circle augmenting her power, and she was surprised at how much of a boost it gave her. In that moment, she understood why she had succeeded where many priests had failed. To sever the *lupusdaemon's* strong magical bond with the victim's physical body, it had to be *summoned* before it could be cast into the abyss. Demon-summoning was not exactly a priesthood favorite. Among witches, summoning was gray magic at best. It all depended upon what you did with the demon once you controlled it. Regardless, the dark witch's casting circle was in perfect tune for questionable magic.

Jessie's eyes rolled back in her head, and she slumped forward. When her head came back up, her eyes darted around in panic, and she jumped to her feet.

"No! Don't do this. I tried to help you. Don't send me back to the abyss." She slammed the base of her fist against Cara's protections, but to no avail.

It was a shock to hear Skyler's words coming from Jessie's mouth. The *lupusdaemon* seemed to instantly understand what was happening. The abomination of her presence put steel into Amanda's response. "You think we'll let you send Jessie in your place? Forget it!"

"There may be a way for us to share this body until I can find another one. That's what Marcella and Cyrus have done. Just give me a chance to try."

A "chance to try" meant someone else would be sacrificed instead. The cycle had to stop. "No," Amanda said. "You don't belong here."

Skyler screamed in desperate fury and pounded both of her fists against the circle of protection. Amanda glanced at

Cara, wondering if the demon might break through, but Cara's sneering smile said she was having no trouble keeping Skyler in check.

This was getting out of hand. She should have tied Jessie to the chair before they started. Kyle had been able to keep the demon from taking over full control during his exorcism, but he'd had a lot more experience with fighting it by then. Amanda altered her incantation to bring Jessie back.

Jessie dropped her hands to her sides and collapsed back into the chair with one hand to her head. When she looked up, her frightened expression told Amanda that her friend had returned.

"What happened?," Jessie asked. "I was ... nowhere. It was horrible."

"I couldn't pull the demon into the skull," Amanda answered. "It took over your body instead."

Jessie's hands gripped the chair arms. "What's wrong? Why isn't it working?"

Amanda thought back to Kyle's exorcism. They had changed the spell somewhat since then, but the changes should have made it stronger, not weaker. The main difference was that Amanda wasn't inside the circle with Jessie as she had been with Kyle, so she couldn't hold the wolf skull directly over Jessie's head during the summoning. But what could she do? The circle was too small to hold both of them.

She turned to Cara. "What do you think will happen if I reach through the protections with the wolf skull?"

Cara seemed surprised to be asked her opinion. She blinked a couple of times and then furrowed her brow in thought. "I'm not sure. If it were just your hands, I don't think it would hurt anything, but I don't know about the skull."

Amanda focused on Jessie again. "This isn't going to be easy. You have to let the demon come forth but stay in control of your body. Can you do that?"

Jessie shook her head in bewilderment. "I don't know. I'll try."

"You must," Amanda insisted. "I have to reach in there and hold the skull over your head. If Skyler takes over again, she'll interrupt the spell, and I don't know what happens after that."

Jessie visibly gulped. "Okay," she said in a small voice.

Amanda addressed Tanya. "Watch the protections. If they start to weaken, help Cara with them."

Tanya nodded, accepting the instructions. At the same time, Amanda hoped it wouldn't come to that. If Tanya aided Cara, Amanda would be on her own with the exorcism. She'd had Noreen's considerable support for Kyle's exorcism. Did she have the strength to complete the summoning and banishment by herself?

There was only one way to find out.

Amanda resumed her incantation. She altered it slightly, asking the spirits to help Jessie stay in control. The additional phrases felt right as they fell from her lips. It was as if the earth spirits approved of the stabilizing influence.

Before she reached the part where she would call the demon forth, Amanda slowly moved her hands toward the space over Jessie's head. Her hands tingled as they pushed through the protective barrier. She paused and nearly drew them back, afraid of dropping the skull. Before she could decide whether to go forward or pull back, the tingle quickly spread up her arms and over her body.

Her view of Jessie cleared, and she gasped, thinking the protections had failed. Then Amanda realized that the tell-tale shimmer vibrated around them both. The protections weren't down—they had enveloped her, effectively putting her inside the circle with Jessie.

The change in configuration must have strained the protections because Tanya added her voice to Cara's.

Amanda held the wolf skull above Jessie while she called forth the demon. Jessie clenched her teeth and groaned as the demon fought her for control.

Jessie's hands suddenly came up and clamped onto Amanda's wrists. The eyes that looked up into Amanda's were not Jessie's, and she could feel the struggle for dominance between the demon and her friend.

Straining to keep the skull positioned over Jessie's head, Amanda moved on to the part of the incantation that would draw the demon into the skull. After several attempts, she could tell it wasn't working. She wasn't strong enough.

"Try again," Tanya said.

When Amanda repeated the key phrases of the summoning, she could feel Tanya's strength adding to her own. As the final phrases left Amanda's mouth, Jessie's hands dropped back to her lap, and she tilted her head back to let out a scream that stunned Amanda to stillness. Then Jessie slumped to the side, nearly falling out of the chair. From within the wolf skull came a keening howl.

Amanda called upon the spirits of the light to banish the *lupusdaemon's* dark spirit back to the abyss. The spirits responded, and silver lightning flashed from the protection barrier to strike the skull, cutting off the howl of the trapped demon.

Amanda let out a shuddering breath of relief. The *lupusdaemon* was gone. Jessie was free.

"What the hell?"

The exclamation came from the doorway, and everyone turned their attention to the source. Jonathan, who had moved into the room during the drama of his wife's exorcism, turned and dropped into a crouch, aiming his weapon toward the speaker.

Reggie took in the scene, his eyebrows rising as he figured out what was going on. When his gaze met Amanda's and he saw the speculative look she was giving him, he turned and ran.

CHAPTER 33

Access

Adolphus Rutlinger sat at his desk reviewing patient records in preparation for making afternoon phone calls to clients. The call-backs would be less dreadful than usual because all of the pet owners were receiving good news that day.

It was a relief to be done with the exorcism crisis so he could go back to his regular schedule at the vet clinic. His work at the clinic also gave him a break from the drama at home. Thanks to Marcella, the Foundation had become a place of strife rather than solace.

He was picking up the telephone handset to place the first call when Britney, his assistant, knocked on his open door.

"Sorry to interrupt, Doctor, but a Mr. Blackstone is here to see you."

He let the handset fall back into its cradle. What was Blackstone doing here? His face must have revealed a lack of enthusiasm at hearing the visitor's name.

"Should I tell him you're busy and can't see him right now?"

Adolphus doubted Blackstone would accept such an obvious excuse, and there wasn't much point putting off the meeting.

"No. It's fine, Britney." Adolphus said. "Please show him in."

The young woman nodded her blonde head once and bustled her rounded figure back toward the reception area.

A moment later, she ushered Blackstone into the office. She softly closed the door behind him in response to Adolphus's subtle head tilt.

The tall hunter was, as ever, dressed from head to toe in black. His expression revealed nothing about the nature of his visit.

Adolphus started the conversation. "How may I be of service, Mr. Blackstone?"

After a quick glance at the closed door, Blackstone answered in a low voice. "I apologize for interrupting your work, but I have a proposal for you, Dr. Rutlinger."

Adolphus's initial thought was *forget it*. It might be a case of blaming the messenger, but Blackstone had been the one to deliver the Order's pardon of Marcella, leaving the witch in control of his pack. To be fair, Blackstone had also delivered the Order's exorcism ban, but Adolphus wasn't convinced of the Order's commitment to that new policy.

It was still too early to tell for sure, but Adolphus thought it possible that Nemotea, his one reliable supporter, might have successfully transferred from Skyler's broken body to one of the witches during their entanglement on the basement floor. The true test of the exorcism ban would come if the witches learned that one of their own had been possessed.

Hmm. Perhaps they had. And that might have something to do with Blackstone's visit. If so, the hunter was about to be disappointed.

"I'm listening," Adolphus finally acknowledged.

"I've been investigating a series of robberies involving dark magic. Marcella Pedroso and Cyrus Fleming are my prime suspects."

Blackstone's direct statement was unexpected, so it took a few seconds to process. When the pieces fit together,

Adolphus had his explanation for where Marcella was getting the Foundation- membership fees for her and Cyrus.

"Is that so?" Adolphus said, folding his hands on his desk. "What do you need from me?"

"Access," Blackstone answered. "If you give me permission to search for evidence, preferably at a time they aren't around, I can charge Pedroso and Fleming with using black magic against the mundane."

The arrest of Marcella and Cyrus would be a dream come true. Their plans to take over the Foundation would disappear with them.

If only it were that easy. The Order had let him down before. "You seem certain that you'll find this evidence you seek."

"Do you doubt that I will?"

Adolphus considered his visitor for a moment. He didn't really know much about Blackstone, except that Marcella seemed to fear the man. Could the hunter truly deliver what he promised? Adolphus didn't doubt evidence existed, but he was less convinced that Blackstone would be able to locate and retrieve it.

"If there is evidence to be found," Adolphus said, "it will be in her room, which is heavily warded. I haven't been in there myself since she took up residence."

"Leave the wards to me," Blackstone said.

The hunter's confidence was irritating. He would not have to face the fallout if he took down Marcella's wards and then failed to find this evidence he wanted so badly. Marcella would know Adolphus had been party to the violation of her privacy.

"You are asking me to take a considerable risk," Adolphus said.

280 Daniel R. Marvello

"I understand. You must weigh that risk against the potential benefits, of course. Besides, it seems to me that you face risks either way."

Indeed. Doing nothing would allow things to progress in the intolerable direction they were already going. The opportunity to be rid of the two demon witches was too good to pass up.

"I agree under one condition," Adolphus said.

"Name it."

Adolphus stood. "We go now. Marcella and Cyrus have been leaving in the middle of the day and returning in the late evening. I don't know how long that pattern will continue."

Blackstone smiled. "Thank you for that bit of information. It makes me even more certain I'll find the evidence I need."

"Let us hope that you do," Adolphus said, picking up the call-back paperwork. "I need a moment to hand these calls off to my assistant, and then we can go. Reggie will be at work, so we should have the Foundation to ourselves for a while."

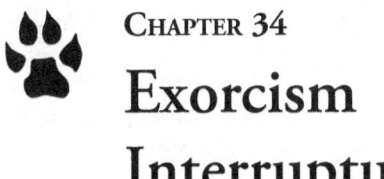

CHAPTER 34

Exorcism Interruptus

Jonathan ran out the door after Reggie, but Amanda knew there was no way he could catch the stronger and faster werewolf. Where was Kyle?

An "oof" and the sound of a scuffle ended in a thud and a grunt of pain. Kyle and Jonathan dragged an unconscious Reggie into the room by his armpits. After setting Reggie down, Kyle said, "Sorry. I didn't see him arrive. He must have come in through one of the side doors."

Jonathan tilted his head toward Jessie. "She's okay now, right? We'd better get out of here."

He was right. With Skyler gone, Amanda had been about to release the spirits and end the exorcism anyway. If Reggie was home, they were running out of time fast. Then she glanced at her watch and hesitated. "He's early. I wonder why?"

"Does it matter?" Kyle said. "We should get going before anyone else shows up."

Jessie stood and touched Amanda's arm. "I'll help, if you want to do it now."

As she looked into her friend's eyes, Amanda blinked back tears. Jessie knew exactly what she was thinking. Like Kyle, Jessie understood what her brother might be experiencing.

"Everything is ready," Jessie continued. "There will never be a better time."

Well, that wasn't exactly true. Although she had the backing of her coven this time, Amanda's first time through the ritual had still been tiring. "Do we have the strength?"

Looking at Tanya and Cara, Amanda tried to judge how much energy the two had left. Neither said anything, but both looked bright eyed and eager. Amanda understood what they must be feeling. This was the first major working they'd ever attempted without Noreen at the helm, and they'd all performed amazingly well. She hoped that their pride wasn't making them overconfident. On the other hand, the coven had never managed to fully deplete Tanya's reserves, and Jessie was still relatively fresh.

Amanda could hardly believe it. The one-in-a-million chance she and Kyle had talked about had arrived. How could she be hesitating? "Okay, let's do it," she said.

"No!" Jonathan shouted, stepping forward. "We've done what we came to do. It's time to go."

Kyle glanced at his watch. He looked at Reggie. "It's risky," he warned.

Was it really? Their spying had revealed that Reggie was the most likely resident to return home while they were skulking around the Foundation. Well, they got that one right. Dr. Rutlinger wasn't expected until after the clinic closed, which gave them at least another hour. Marcella and Cyrus hadn't been returning to the Foundation until much later in the evening.

As Jessie had said, there would never be a greater opportunity.

While Amanda considered the risk of proceeding, Jessie signaled Cara to drop the protections and let her out of the circle. She went over to Jonathan and hugged him fiercely. After a moment, she pulled back and looked him in the eyes. "You don't know what it's like." Her gaze went to the werewolf's slumped form. "We have to do this. For Amanda and for Reggie."

Jonathan let out an exasperated sigh. "Is the small chance we can help Reggie worth all of our lives? Maybe orphaning our children?"

"He's right, Jessie," Amanda interrupted. "You two have your kids to think about. I think I can do this with Tanya and Cara's help. You can wait for us back at the cars if you want."

"Right," Jessie scoffed. "Abandon you after all you did for me." She turned toward her husband. "Honey, you do what you have to. I owe Amanda my life, so I'm seeing this through."

Jonathan stepped back as if she'd slapped him. "I wouldn't leave without you."

"Then it's settled," Jessie said, turning her back on him. She returned to the circle. "Let's do this."

During Jessie's and Jonathan's standoff, Kyle had been exploring the closet. He came out with a coil of shiny black rope. "Here, we can tie him to the chair with this."

Kyle had apparently reached the same conclusion as Amanda—that the subject of the exorcism should be restrained during the rite. Amanda took the rope from him and ran her fingers over it. "How strange. This feels like silk." She gave a section of it an experimental tug. "Should be strong enough. Where'd you get it?"

Kyle dipped his head, blushing. "I found it in a chest of ... toys. There's a felt-lined set of handcuffs if you think they'd be a better option."

"Felt lined?"

"Yeah, I guess we shouldn't be surprised that Marcella has a kinky streak."

Amanda handed the rope back to Kyle, touching it only with her thumb and forefinger. "Eew."

With Jonathan's help, Kyle used the rope to immobilize Reggie and anchor him to the chair. Amanda observed nervously, certain that Reggie's strength could easily shatter the chair if he managed to get any leverage.

As soon as Reggie was secure, Jessie purified the circle again, having a much easier time of it the second time around. In fact, with the four witches working together, all of the preliminaries went smoothly and quickly. Amanda's confidence in their chance of success grew.

Out of the corner of her eye, Amanda saw Jonathan turn and speak to Kyle. "You should go back down to the entryway and keep watch."

"Don't bother," Marcella said from outside the doorway.

Marcella's voice shocked Amanda into immobility. Cyrus took advantage of everyone's surprise, streaking past the dark witch into the room. He went for Jonathan first, knocking the hunter into the wall with a straight-armed blow to the chest. Jonathan dropped his rifle as he slid down the wall, stunned and with the breath knocked out of him. Kyle grabbed at Cyrus, but the wiry werewolf twisted away, swinging a back-handed blow that barely missed Kyle's jaw.

While Cyrus distracted Kyle and Jonathan, Marcella uttered a rapid incantation and thrust her hand forward. Cara's protections dropped so quickly that she gasped and collapsed to her knees.

With the exorcism interrupted, Amanda turned her thoughts to defense. The dark witch was going to fry them all if they didn't protect themselves. She reached into her pocket for the Resonance Star pendant. Individually, they couldn't match Marcella's strength, but together they might be able to hold her off until they could figure out a way to fight back.

Marcella wasted no time following up after she dispelled the circle's protections. With a few quick phrases and a casual wave of her hand, she hurled a blow of force that knocked Amanda off her feet. The pendant flew from Amanda's hand and rebounded off the wall before sliding under the dresser.

Well, Amanda thought, *we can always link up the old fashioned way.* She rolled next to where Cara was kneeling and grabbed her hand, glad to see that Tanya was already holding the other one. Nodding to Cara, she confirmed the questioning look the air witch gave her. Any of them could cast a shield, but Cara's were the best.

Cara's shield was barely formed when Marcella's attack flared against it. A hot blast of air ruffled Amanda's hair as the shield deflected the bulk of the spell.

Marcella's eyes narrowed with calculation, and she started another incantation. She seemed to be taking her time to build a stronger attack that would probably blow right through Cara's shield.

Jessie had stepped away from the circle to check on Jonathan who seemed to be recovering. The struggle between Cyrus and Kyle surged in the space between Jessie and Marcella, keeping her out of the magical line of fire. When the dark witch started her new, more lengthy incantation, Jessie took the direct approach. Grabbing a heavy crystal from the trunk of magical paraphernalia, she stepped out from behind Cyrus and Kyle and hurled the stone at Marcella.

Hoping Jessie's distraction would give her a few seconds, Amanda turned her head to look for her piece of the Resonance Star. From her position lying on her side, she could see light glint off the dark blue stone at the edge of the shadows under the dresser. Marcella's grunt of pain told her that Jessie's missile had struck home, which probably bought her another few seconds. Amanda slid her fingers under the dresser to retrieve the pendant, careful not to push it under further.

From behind her came a new unwelcome sound: Reggie stirred with a groan.

Amanda hooked her finger on the pendant's loop of chain and pulled the stone out from under the dresser. She slid the pendant over her neck and turned to check on Reggie.

Reggie had raised his head and opened his eyes, struggling to make sense of the chaos around him. After a failed attempt to move, he looked down at his bindings and then at Amanda. Bright panic shone in his amber eyes. When he closed his eyes again and relaxed back into his seat, Amanda knew they were about to have a problem. Reggie was preparing to transform. His wolf form would probably slip free of the bindings, and then he'd either escape or attack.

Amanda's hand tightened around the pendant. Her instinct was to block Reggie's transformation somehow, but she didn't know if such a thing was even possible. She turned her attention back toward the greater and more immediate threat.

Marcella glared at Jessie as she side-stepped Cyrus and Kyle. She aimed her hand with her fingers curled like claws and started another incantation.

Jessie hastily brought up a shield and rushed through phrases that would reinforce it. Amanda prayed that the Star would give Jessie the power she needed. Could the coven last long enough to wear down the dark witch? There was no way to know.

Jonathan staggered to his feet. He glanced from Marcella to Jessie and seemed to be thinking about interposing himself.

"No!" Amanda shouted, but Jonathan had already drawn the dark witch's attention. She shifted her aim toward him instead. Jessie's mouth dropped open with shock. While Marcella could change the target of her attack right up to the moment she released the spell, it wasn't so easy for Jessie to alter her shield on the fly.

Jonathan had to know he was in grave danger. Still, he launched himself away from the wall toward Marcella. His only hope was to tackle her before she could finish her spell.

A blur flew in through the doorway and toward Marcella before Jonathan could complete his first step. Marcella and her new assailant crashed into the dresser and rolled to the floor.

Before Amanda could sit up and see who had tackled Marcella, Blackstone appeared at the doorway. His eyes narrowed when he spotted Reggie, and he raised his hand, palm forward. He spoke a few words in what sounded like Latin.

With Marcella distracted, Jonathan tried to help Kyle with Cyrus. That turned out to be a mistake. Kyle had been gaining the upper hand, but he had to step back when Jonathan entered the fray. Cyrus took advantage of the distraction to strike, using his magic to strengthen a blow to Kyle's solar plexus. Kyle's breath whooshed out, and he doubled over, staggering backward. He lost his footing and crashed to the floor, coughing and retching. Jonathan got one good blow in to Cyrus's head, but the werewolf merely shook it off and came back with a roundhouse punch that made Jonathan's head snap around. He collapsed to the floor next to Kyle.

Jessie took a half-step toward Jonathan when he hit the floor, but she couldn't go to him without dropping her shield. There was no mistaking the promise of retribution in her gaze when she locked eyes with Cyrus. He answered with a mocking smirk and a casual attack spell that sparked against the shield, as if to test its strength.

Cyrus effectively had Amanda and her coven mates in a standoff. As long as the witches were connected through the Star, they couldn't act individually. All of their energy was powering Jessie's shield, which they didn't dare drop.

Amanda stood up and was surprised to see that it was Dr. Rutlinger who had tackled Marcella and was rolling around on the floor with her in a tangle of limbs. Although it seemed that he was stronger, she was clearly more vicious. The doctor's face was bleeding from several scratches, and he couldn't seem to restrain the dark witch for more than a second. Rutlinger seemed to finally be getting the upper hand as he straddled the dark witch. He had a grip on both of her hands, but every time she started an incantation, he had to release one hand to slap her and interrupt it.

The crystal Jessie had thrown at Marcella had fallen to the floor near where the two werewolves were struggling. The next time her hand was free, Marcella's hand flashed out and grabbed it. Before he could dodge, Marcella struck Dr. Rutlinger on the side of the head with the stone. The doctor toppled off of her and rolled onto the floor.

Marcella leapt to her feet. She took in the situation with a quick glance around the room, her attention settling on Blackstone. With an expression that said bad things for his future, she started an incantation, forcefully spitting out the phrases.

Amanda thought quickly. Was there any way to help Blackstone? The Star was their greatest strength and their greatest weakness. To help Blackstone, they would have to drop the shield, and then they'd be defenseless against Cyrus.

Blackstone turned his attention from Reggie to Marcella when she started her incantation. He spread his arms wide and closed his eyes as if welcoming her attack, and then tipped his head back and began speaking Latin-sounding phrases again.

When Marcella's spell struck, Blackstone wavered on his feet. The violet lightning that flowed from her hands to his body arced all over him, making his hair stand on end and fluttering his clothes as if he were standing over an air vent. The storm of electricity never seemed to actually touch him although small trickles of blood appeared under his nose, ears, and eyes. Marcella shouted and then screamed the words of her spell as she poured more and more energy into it.

Amanda had never seen such a display of power in her life. She hoped Cyrus wasn't that strong, or she and her friends were all doomed. She glanced at Reggie, wondering if he would try to transform now that Blackstone was otherwise occupied. But Reggie was transfixed by Marcella's attack on Blackstone.

Better transfixed than transformed, she thought.

Blackstone's voice had dropped to a strained whisper, and Amanda thought he was about to succumb to the onslaught. Then his body started to glow as he swept his hands slowly forward. The glow brightened as his hands moved closer together. It became so bright that Amanda had to avert her eyes. When his hands came together, a searingly bright stream of light sucked all of the energy that twisted around him into a beam that slammed into Marcella. It seemed to enter her and light her up from the inside, her skin glowing a translucent red. Marcella screamed and her body shook violently. When the beam of light suddenly stopped, she dropped like a marionette with cut strings.

Blackstone's hands fell to his sides, and he bowed his head, breathing heavily. When he looked up again, he fixed his attention on Cyrus.

Cyrus was staring incredulously at Marcella's still body and her unblinking skyward stare. He sensed Blackstone's gaze and looked up into eyes that watched expectantly from a blood-streaked and stony countenance. When Blackstone eased sideways to give clear access to the doorway, Cyrus accepted the subtle offer by streaking out of the room.

~

After Cyrus left, Jessie dropped the shield. Amanda went to Kyle's side while Jessie checked on Jonathan. Both men came around quickly.

Dr. Rutlinger sat up as well, gently touching his head where Marcella had struck him. Amanda squared off against him, uncertain of what he would do next. Seeing her wariness, he held up a hand in a gesture of peace. He slowly got to his feet, using the dresser to steady himself, and looked at Marcella with a dour expression.

"It seems you won't need that evidence after all," Dr. Rutlinger said to Blackstone.

"I will," Blackstone disagreed, "but for different reasons now."

"Would the Order truly hold you responsible for her death?" Dr. Rutlinger asked.

Blackstone took out a handkerchief and started wiping the blood from his face. "Probably not," he answered. "But it's always good to be able to show justification."

"She tried to kill you," Amanda said. "What more justification do you need?"

"I need to justify why I was here antagonizing her in the first place." He raised an eyebrow. "As will you."

Amanda looked at Jessie and smiled. "My justification is right there," she said.

"So Skyler is gone?" Dr. Rutlinger asked in a heavy voice.

Amanda turned to him with narrowed eyes. "You knew?"

"I suspected."

Amanda's jaw clenched in anger, but her ire faded when she couldn't think of a way to blame him. He hadn't harassed Jessie in any way. In fact, none of the Selkirk Pack had approached her, which indicated he'd kept his suspicions to himself. Given the exorcism ban, Marcella would surely have gloated over Jessie's plight.

A rustle from behind her caught Amanda's attention. Reggie was alternately struggling with the ropes and stopping to concentrate on transforming. He was making no headway with either endeavor. After a failed attempt at transforming, he glared at Blackstone. "What did you do to me?"

Blackstone tucked the bloody handkerchief into a pocket and folded his arms. "To be honest, I'm surprised my ward is still functioning. The casting circle must be aiding it somehow."

"Release me!" Reggie demanded of Blackstone. He then glared at Dr. Rutlinger. "Untie these ropes and make them leave."

Dr. Rutlinger glanced at the others in the room but said nothing and made no move toward his fellow werewolf. Even if he'd wanted to help Reggie, the odds were stacked against him. He'd have to take on a group that had just defeated two powerful *lupusdaemon* witches.

Blackstone also ignored Reggie's request. He turned his attention to Amanda. "So this is the opportunity you've been waiting for. Do you still have the strength to take advantage of it?"

"You aren't going to stop me?" Amanda asked.

"My mission is to deal with practitioners of dark magic," Blackstone said. "Although your exorcism has been banned by the Order, that doesn't make it dark magic. On the other hand, if you proceed, you must be prepared to accept the consequences."

"You can't let them do this!" Reggie pleaded with Dr. Rutlinger. "I'm a member of your pack. It's your duty as alpha to protect me."

Dr. Rutlinger folded his arms, his eyes showing his anger. "So, *now* you support me as alpha. I've been unimpressed by your loyalty lately, and Skyler has paid the price for your betrayal."

"That wasn't my fault," Reggie insisted. "You're the one who let Marcella take over. I had no choice but to support her."

Dr. Rutlinger glanced around the room at opponents who were ready and waiting for him to make a move. His gaze settled on Amanda, and Kyle moved to her side protectively. He let out a sigh of frustration. "Against all odds, it seems you have finally earned your chance, little witch. Forgive me if I hope you fail, but I don't see how I can stop you." He turned and walked to the doorway.

"You bastard!" Reggie shouted. "End this now, or I'll come after you, either here or in the abyss."

Dr. Rutlinger paused at the doorway with his hands closed into fists, but he didn't turn around. "Goodbye, Oholepsu," he said over his shoulder before disappearing into the hallway.

Blackstone closed the door behind the departing werewolf and leaned his back against it.

Reggie's face had gone ashen, and his eyes were wide with disbelief. "No," he said in a near whisper.

Amanda closed her eyes and repeated the name Oholepsu in her mind until she was sure she wouldn't forget it. She didn't know how much difference it would make to have the *lupusdaemon's* true name for the exorcism, but it couldn't hurt. As for the consequences Blackstone warned against, she'd been ready to trade those for a chance to get her brother back for a long time.

It was good to have a name for the demon that had taken her brother's body. Referring to it by Reggie's name had always been painful.

As Amanda walked back to her position at the circle, Oholepsu said, "If you let me go now, we can pretend this never happened. But if you try the ritual and fail, I swear I'll hunt you down and tear you to pieces."

Amanda looked at him soberly. She didn't doubt he'd make good on his threat. One way or another, she was about to join her brother. Then she looked at each of her coven mates and Kyle. Although she was willing to risk death for herself, she had to consider the others. "Then I guess I'd better not fail," she said.

Amanda started to remove her Star pendant. "Leave it on," Blackstone suggested.

"I can't. Only one of us can cast while the Star is active. We can't maintain the protections and work the ritual at the same time.

"The dark spirits won't interfere," Blackstone said confidently. He gestured toward the body of the dark witch. "They scattered upon her death and won't return while I'm here."

"Why is that?" Kyle asked, voicing Amanda's own question.

"I think I scare them," Blackstone said with a wink.

Well, you are *pretty scary*, Amanda thought.

Taking a deep breath, Amanda tried to evaluate the condition of the coven. Even with the Star, did they have the power to do this? They were stronger than they'd ever been, due to the intense practice they'd been doing lately.

But they'd already pulled off one exorcism and held a shield against both Marcella and Cyrus. It would be heartbreaking to come close to succeeding and then fail because they didn't have the energy to finish the job.

Tanya interrupted her cycle of indecision. "Amanda, this is it. You have everything you need."

She was right. Amanda smiled at the fire witch, amused that the roles of doubter and cheerleader had been reversed for a change. "Thanks, Tanya. I needed that."

Amanda took a moment to collect herself and then began the incantation for the prime casting. It seemed strange to get right into it without the usual air wall of protection swirling around the casting circle. On the other hand, she didn't sense the dark-spirit interference that had plagued them earlier.

As soon as she started the spell, Oholepsu redoubled his struggle to free himself from the chair. He gritted his teeth, and his face went red as he strained at the ropes. If he broke the bonds or the chair, they were all in big trouble. But Marcella's silken rope proved to be more than decorative and held up to the assault.

During her many preparations, Amanda had created two versions of the exorcism. The one she used on Jessie summoned the demon forth so she could trap it. Removing the demon allowed Jessie's spirit to regain control.

Reggie's exorcism was a different proposition. The demon was already in full control of the body, and Amanda had no idea where her brother's spirit might be. She had altered the ritual to call Reggie forth so he would be "nearby" when she purged the demon from his body. If she couldn't make contact with Reggie's spirit, the departing demon was probably going to leave behind either a zombie or a corpse. It was one of the many risks she'd debated with Kyle over the past several weeks.

Taking an extra-deep breath, Amanda held the wolf skull above Reggie's head and summoned her brother's spirit. Her hands twitched when the skull did something it hadn't before. It started to glow white. The glow flickered and then extended down over Reggie's head, surrounding it with a white aura.

While Reggie's body continued to twitch and jerk against the bindings, his head held steady and his face cleared, giving him an almost sleepy look. The incongruity between his expression and the thrashing of his arms and legs was unsettling.

Reggie's eyes rolled around for a moment before he managed to focus on Cara. She smiled encouragingly, but he didn't react. His gaze floated back and forth between the witches in his field of vision until it stopped on Amanda.

"Mandy?" he whispered.

The word instantly brought tears to Amanda's eyes. No one but her brother had ever called her Mandy. She *had* brought him back! "It's okay, Reggie. Just hold on. You're almost home."

A low groan escaped Reggie's lips. "Let me go," he whispered. The glow faded, and his gaze sharpened. The demon behind them snarled at her.

Amanda blinked in surprise. Had Reggie been arguing with the demon controlling his body or asking *her* to let him go? This all had to be confusing for him. He'd be fine once he was back with her.

Amanda continued her chanting, calling on the spirits to help her remove the demon Oholepsu from her brother's body. The demon screamed in fury and agony, its struggles to escape making the chair wobble.

Once again, the wolf skull began to glow. The glow grew painfully bright and then flowed over Reggie's body. When the glow withdrew, the skull was lit from within with a white light mottled by shifting dark shadows. Reggie's body went still and slumped against the bindings holding it in place.

The demon that had stolen Amanda's brother from her was literally in the palms of her hands. If she'd known how, she would have crushed it right then and there so it would never bother anyone again. Sending it back to the abyss was the best she could do.

She called on the spirits once again to help her banish the demon back whence it came. Nothing happened. She repeated her call several times before she understood that her words weren't gathering the magical force she normally sensed. She stopped chanting and turned her attention inward, realizing at once that her own reserves of power were almost completely drained. And if she was drained, *all* of the witches were drained.

Amanda swallowed hard. What would happen now? Could the demon return to Reggie's body? Could it attack someone else in the room?

Amanda felt a warm hand on her shoulder. Blackstone had come to her side. He reached his other hand toward the skull and placed his palm on the front, like a faith healer ministering to the infirm. In a calm but commanding voice, he spoke several phrases and then bumped his hand solidly against the skull.

With a screech that hurt Amanda's ears, the mottled light streamed out of the top of the skull. Rushing upward, it scattered against the ceiling like a fountain.

The sound and brightness suddenly cut off, and Amanda found herself panting and staring at the wolf skull's toothy grin. The artifact seemed to be pleased with itself.

Blackstone gave Amanda's shoulder a squeeze. "Nice work," he said. "Now, let's see what you've wrought."

Amanda handed the wolf skull to Kyle and knelt in front of Reggie. He was so still that she was afraid her efforts might have been in vain. She checked his neck for a pulse and found a slow but steady beat. His chest moved gently up and down with each breath. Okay, the lights were on, but was anybody home?

She lifted his head off his chest, cupping his face in her hands. "Reggie. Reggie, wake up. I've missed you so much. Please come back to me."

Reggie's eyelids fluttered. When he opened them, it took him a several seconds for his eyes to focus on Amanda's face. He lifted his head and drew in a shuddering breath. "Oh, Mandy. What have you done?"

CHAPTER 35

Careful Wishing

"Follow me," the nurse said, coming around from her station with a folder under her arm. "I have to go that way anyway."

Amanda hurried to keep pace with the swift-footed woman. At her side, Kyle was humming something familiar. When Amanda realized what it was, she stopped and stared at him.

"You aren't seriously humming 'Ding, Dong, the Witch is Dead?'"

He grinned and urged her to get moving again. "Why not? Marcella's death took a big weight off my mind." He then sang, "Ding dong, the demon witch is dead."

The nurse frowned over her shoulder at them, and Amanda elbowed Kyle in the ribs. "Shh. This is a hospital." Amanda's attempt to be serious fell on deaf ears.

"So what? No frivolity? I'd think the patients would enjoy a little entertainment to brighten their day."

"Maybe if someone else were singing it."

"Ooh, ouch."

The nurse paused at a door and waved a hand toward it before continuing on. Amanda peered in through the door's window. Reggie was sitting up in his bed, reading. Amanda opened the door and went inside.

"Hi," she said, walking to the side of the bed. "How are you feeling?" she asked as she put her hand on his.

"Better, thanks." Reggie answered. He started to pull his hand away but then let it be. "The doctor says he'll release me tomorrow."

Amanda was disappointed by his guarded tone. It was like he didn't want to talk to her. "That's good news," she said, forcing cheer into her tone. "Do you have somewhere to go? I'm sure Lucille would be happy to have you stay at the farm for as long as you want."

He looked away from her and fussed with his bed sheets. "Thanks for the offer. I'm not sure what I'm going to do yet."

What was wrong with him? Of course he needed a place to stay. He had no money and no transportation. "Do you know what time you'll be released tomorrow? I can come get you."

"We'll see," he said.

Kyle shifted from one foot to the other. He undoubtedly sensed that something was amiss.

"What's going on? Why are you being like this?" Amanda asked.

"Don't push, Mandy. I have some things to figure out."

"Like what?" she insisted. "Aren't you glad to see me? Aren't you glad to be back among the living?"

He looked up at her then and squeezed her hand. "Yes to the first. I'm not so sure about the second."

"I don't understand."

"You should have let me go."

His words pierced her heart like a knife. She lowered her head. "I couldn't let that thing walk around in your skin. It was torture every time I saw it."

"Oh, you were right to destroy the demon," he said with conviction. "As long as my body lived, I was trapped in a dark space with the promise of the light just out of reach. It was … a kind of purgatory."

Kyle had been right after all. Reggie was trapped in the abyss that whole time. "That sounds horrible," she said.

"It was. But all this," he waved his free hand around vaguely, "ain't a whole lot better. The demon left behind … memories … and impressions. Some of them are seriously disturbing."

Amanda's heart crept into her throat. What had she done? Tears filled her eyes. "You'd rather be dead?"

He was silent for a moment. "It's hard to explain. When the demon pushed me into the abyss, I was terrified at first. All I could think of was getting my body back. Over time I reconciled myself to the idea that the life of Reggie Clark was over and it was time to move on. But I couldn't move on. My spirit was still somehow tethered to my body. After a while, all I could think about was finding a way to move into the light."

"And then I snatched you away from it," Amanda concluded.

"Exactly," he responded gently.

"I don't know what to say. Maybe I'm being selfish, but I'm not sorry I brought you back. I missed you so much. But I'm sorry if you're unhappy."

They were both silent until the moment grew awkward.

"Maybe it wasn't your time to go," Kyle suggested.

To Amanda's surprise, Reggie responded positively to the philosophical remark. "That's what I've been pondering," he said.

"You're coming from a unique perspective on the 'Why are we here?' question," Kyle continued. "I've been where you were, briefly, so I can relate to the initial terror, but you've gone where only the fully possessed have been before."

Reggie gave Kyle an approving look. "Yes. I think you understand. And it bugs me that others are still trapped like I was."

Amanda shook her head sadly. "I'm not sure what we can do about that. At the moment, the Order still has a ban on the *lupusdaemon* exorcism. And that was before we knew it could be used after First Moon. The werewolves must feel more threatened than ever now that they're *all* vulnerable."

Reggie's brow creased with concern. "Doesn't that make you a target?"

"To some degree," Amanda said. "But I learned my lesson from the first time around. I published the new ritual as soon as I got home yesterday. Besides, we don't know if having the demon's true name plays a critical role in the ritual's success. If it *is* essential, the werewolf community can rest a little easier. They don't generally share their true names with humans."

"Unless one of them is feeling vindictive," Kyle added.

"Well, Dr. Rutlinger *is* a demon," Amanda pointed out. "Vindictive probably goes with the territory."

"Which is why we're still watching your back," Kyle said.

Amanda agreed with a nod and turned her attention back to Reggie. "Anyway, I think you should come to the farm, get your bearings, and take your time figuring out what you want to do with yourself."

"I'm sure that's good advice," Reggie answered.

"But you're not going to take it," Amanda said, sharper than she intended.

"Like I said, I'm pondering. The Hayworth Farm is still an Order sanctuary, right?" Amanda nodded. "You know how I feel about that bunch. I'm not too excited about becoming their latest subject of study."

Kyle shrugged. "It's not so bad. It's been interesting to work with them."

"I'll take your word for it," Reggie said wryly. To Amanda, he said, "Leave me your number. I'll call you later to let you know what time I'll be released tomorrow."

It *sounded* like he was agreeing to let her come and get him, so that was progress. Amanda had come prepared for the request. She slipped a business card out of her pocket and handed it to him.

"Great," Reggie said with a smile, setting the card on the rolling table next to his hospital bed. He adjusted his pillow and eased himself lower on the bed. "Now, if you don't mind, I'd like to catch some Zs."

Amanda rubbed his arm lightly. "All right, you get some rest. Just give me a call later, okay?"

"Sure thing, Sis. Good seeing you again, Kyle."

Kyle nodded and offered a parting wave.

Amanda rubbed her forehead as she and Kyle walked down the hallway away from Reggie's room. "Why do I get the feeling he's not going to call?"

Kyle put his arm around her shoulder. "He'll call. He has nowhere else to go."

~

Amanda grabbed an armful of clothes from her dresser drawer and dropped them into the open box on the bed. Kyle worked at her desk, filling another box with books.

"I'm so mad I could spit," Lucille said from where she stood at the doorway to Amanda's room. Her arms were folded across her chest and her expression was a thundercloud of frustration.

"Don't worry about it, Lucille," Amanda said with a sigh. "They did what they had to do."

"I disagree," Lucille snapped. "What did the Order expect you to do? Let your friend turn into a werewolf while you had the means to prevent it?"

"If it had ended with Jessie, they might have put me on probation like they did Kyle and Jonathan. It was the second count of breaking the ban that did me in."

"Fine. Then let me put it a different way. Were you supposed to let a demon keep your brother's body while you had the means to do something about it?"

"Apparently," Amanda answered in a droll tone. "I don't think they want me setting a precedent or, worse, having the werewolf packs think I'm setting a precedent."

Lucille shook her head. "I don't know what angers me more. That they dismissed you for helping your friends or because they needed to make a political statement."

Amanda shrugged. "Either way, it's done."

Lucille was silent for a moment. She was looking back and forth between Kyle and Amanda, chewing her lower lip. For her, it was an unusual show of indecision. "Are you sure moving in together is what you want? It's not your only option, you know."

"Thanks for the vote of confidence," Kyle said with a laugh.

"It's nothing against you, Kyle. The circumstances should not make *either* of you feel forced into something your relationship isn't prepared for."

Amanda stopped packing and looked Lucille in the eye. Lucille had become like a second mother to her over the time Amanda had lived at the farm. Most of the time, Amanda appreciated it. "I know I have other options," she assured the older woman. "Kyle and I talked it over pretty thoroughly. I'm taking over the second bedroom, so I'll still have my own space." She didn't think Lucille had any business knowing that she probably wouldn't be *sleeping* in her new room.

Lucille's raised eyebrow told Amanda that the woman had reached that conclusion on her own. "Okay, Amanda. If you're happy, I'm happy."

The words made Amanda pause and consider. Was she happy?

When the Order canned her, she was surprised to discover more feelings of relief than despair. The Order had always been a means to an end for her, and that end had finally been accomplished. She was going to have to find a new mission for her life without the Order.

Not that her mission to save her brother had gone as she'd hoped. As she'd feared, Reggie never called her that afternoon. When she gave up on waiting and called the hospital to find out for herself when he'd be released, she learned that he'd checked himself out an hour before. A week later, she still hadn't heard from him.

He probably just needed time to get used to his restored life. At least, that was her hope. She couldn't accept that he'd abandon her entirely.

Her thoughts were interrupted by a hand on her arm. "You okay?" Kyle asked.

She shook herself and went back to packing. "Yeah, I'm fine. Just thinking about Reggie again."

"Give him time," Lucille suggested. "He'll come around."

"That's what I keep telling myself. But I'm worried that he hates me now. I never imagined he wouldn't want his life back. Everything I went through, everything I put us *all* through, was for nothing. Worse than nothing."

"You did what you thought was right," Kyle reassured her. "I've been where he was, and I thought you were doing the right thing, too."

"Thanks, but we both know you warned me that I might be making a mistake. I should have listened."

"Too late to second-guess yourself now," Lucille admonished. She looked like she was about to say more, but the ringing of the kitchen telephone interrupted her. The phone in Amanda's room was on a separate line, so Lucille had to leave them to answer.

"Lucille's right," Kyle said, moving close and putting his arms around her. She returned the light embrace. "Reggie might be looking for a new purpose in life and come back to you on his own terms. In the meantime, one good thing did come out of everything we went through." Then he kissed her.

"True," she said with a smile. "You've been very supportive—even when I was wrong."

Lucille appeared at the doorway. She was moving slowly with a preoccupied expression. Kyle and Amanda both dropped their arms to their sides. "What is it?" Amanda asked.

At the same time, Kyle jokingly asked "Who died?"

Lucille gave Kyle a sardonic look. "Dr. Rutlinger, actually. He was murdered."

"Murdered?" Amanda said. "How is that possible?"

Dr. Rutlinger had the speed and strength of a werewolf. Any burglar who attempted to steal from the Foundation would be in for a big surprise. It was unlikely a human could kill a werewolf unless that person was extremely stealthy or armed with a machine gun full of silver bullets. Perhaps he'd been attacked by another werewolf.

"A member of his pack found him in his living room, sitting on the couch." Lucille explained. "His throat had been cut, nearly severing his head."

"Grisly," Kyle said, shuddering.

"That's a good word for it," Lucille agreed. "The Selkirk Pack is livid and demanding answers. Given recent events, you two should expect to be questioned by an Order investigator."

"Do you know when it happened?" Amanda asked.

"No. The call was from a friend in Paranormal Investigations who wanted to give me a heads-up. She was repeating scuttlebutt and didn't have access to the case file."

"Probably within the past twelve hours," Kyle guessed. "I'm betting he didn't show up at his clinic today and someone went up there to check on him."

"Sounds reasonable," Lucille said. "Well, I'm going to make some lunch. We can expect an investigator to show up at any time, and who knows when you'll get a chance to eat."

Typical Lucille, Amanda thought. *Mother hen to the end.*

"Thanks, Lucille," Amanda said as the woman departed.

She lowered her voice after her friend and mentor had descended the stairs. "Not just anyone could get the drop on Dr. Rutlinger in his own living room."

Kyle followed her lead and lowered his voice as well. "Agreed. It was probably someone he knew."

"Someone who could match a werewolf's strength and reflexes," Amanda added.

Kyle nodded. "Yeah, like another werewolf."

"Or someone like you," Amanda said pointedly.

"I'm not worried," he said with a dismissive wave. "We've been here with Lucille for the past day, and before that, we were sitting in front of an Order tribunal."

"It's not *your* alibi I'm thinking about."

Kyle's eyes went distant as he considered her implication. "Reggie? Why would he have a grudge against Dr. Rutlinger?"

Amanda shook her head. "Maybe not *specifically* Dr. Rutlinger ..."

Kyle's brow furrowed. "You think he's after the entire Selkirk Pack?"

"For starters."

"That's crazy," Kyle scoffed. "One man, even one who's a physical match for them, couldn't expect to take *all* the werewolves out."

"Think about what he told us," Amanda insisted. She was becoming more sure of her theory with every moment. "It bothered him that every werewolf represents another human spirit stuck in the abyss just like he was. He told me I should have destroyed his body instead of bringing him back to it."

"Oh, wow."

"Yeah. *Wow.* And the Order knows about him. They weren't happy when they found out he skipped out of the hospital. Like you, his strength and speed make him a paranormal being, and they want to keep tabs on him."

Amanda waited quietly while Kyle stood with a distant look in his eyes, digesting her theory. Inside that nerdy brain of his, he'd be tearing it apart, putting it back together fifteen different ways, and following additional ramifications to entirely new conclusions. She'd learned to let the wheels grind through their full cycle without interruption.

"We have to find him and fast," Kyle finally stated. "If you're right and he kills again, all hell will break loose. The werewolves will hunt him and hold the Order responsible for doing the same. They'll also hold *you* responsible for unleashing a serial killer." Kyle squinted and shook his head. She could tell that something didn't add up for him.

"What?" Amanda prompted.

"Assuming we aren't making all this up, how can he possibly expect to get away with it? Without a *lupusdaemon's* innate magic, he can't heal like the werewolves can. If any of them catch up to him, he'd never survive."

"You did."

"Once," he said, holding up a finger for emphasis. "And it almost went the other way. I wouldn't want to rely on that kind of luck."

"Maybe he doesn't intend to survive. Every werewolf he takes out is one more spirit freed. If he dies fighting his jihad, he gets what he wanted all along."

"He'll free his own spirit," Kyle said softly.

Amanda nodded. "Win, win."

Kyle shuddered and then blew out a breath. "We're getting ahead of ourselves. We don't know that any of this speculation is true."

"Okay. What are we supposed to do? Wait for another werewolf to turn up dead?"

"Point taken. Well, now that the dust has settled, I'm sure you want to find Reggie anyway. And no one will be suspicious about you searching for your missing brother. Who knows? Maybe we'll find him selling beads on the boardwalk in some seaside town, and all this speculation will have been the product of our imaginations."

"Selling beads on the boardwalk?" Amanda said with a lift of her eyebrow.

"Sure, why not?"

Amanda took Kyle's arm and steered him toward the doorway. "Come on, Mr. Imagination. Let's take Lucille's advice and get something to eat before the investigator arrives."

Kyle's stomach growled right on cue. He rubbed his hand on his abdomen. "I think that was an agreement. We'd better eat up. We've got our work cut out for us."

Amanda squeezed his hand with hers in acknowledgment.

Kyle was right that she wanted to find her brother. She couldn't help but feel that he owed her an explanation for disappearing even if he probably didn't see it that way. His sudden disappearance was what fed all of this ominous theorizing.

Of course, they might have it all wrong, but Amanda was pretty sure of one thing: when they found Reggie, he wouldn't be selling beads on the boardwalk.

Thank You for Reading

Thank you for dedicating some of your reading time to *Demon Witch*. I hope you enjoyed the adventures of Kyle and Amanda and that you look forward to more tales of the Ternion Order.

If you would like to be notified by email when I release a new book, please subscribe to the New Releases list at my blog: www.DanielRMarvello.com/releases. I only use the list for release announcements, and you may unsubscribe at any time.

I know that not everyone likes to write book reviews, but if you are willing to spare the time to write a sentence or two about what you thought of *Demon Witch*, I encourage you to post a review at your favorite book vendor site or recommend the story to your social networking friends.

I love hearing from fans. If you would like to share your thoughts with me privately, you can reach me through the contact page on my blog: DanielRMarvello.com/contact. I look forward to meeting you.

Happy reading,
Daniel R. Marvello

ACKNOWLEDGEMENTS

My thanks go out to my readers and my family for supporting my writing career. I couldn't have done it without you.

Thanks also to my beta readers, who helped me make *Demon Witch* a better book than it would have been without their feedback. I sincerely appreciate their time and effort:

- Susan Daffron (author of the Alpine Grove Romantic Comedies and Jennings & O'Shea mysteries)
- Becca Mills (author of the Emanations series)
- Nancy Brashear (contributing author of the *Grimm & Grimmer Volume Two* anthology)
- Paul Sheriff (author of the PDSA programming series).
- Ken Rahmoeller
- Cynthia Daffron
- Melanie Griffin

ABOUT THE AUTHOR

Daniel R. Marvello writes fantasy adventure stories from his log home on forty acres of forest and meadow in the North Idaho panhandle. The scenic beauty of his surroundings inspired the settings for the Vaetra Chronicles and Ternion Order book series. Daniel shares his home with his loving wife of 20 years and several wonderful animals.

Books by Daniel R. Marvello

The Vaetra Chronicles

- *Vaetra Unveiled*
- *Vaetra Untrained*
- *Vaetra Unleashed*

Find out more at www.vaetra.com

The Ternion Order

- *First Moon*
- *Demon Witch*

The Western Geomancer

- *Geomancer's Bargain*

Visit Daniel's blog at: www.DanielRMarvello.com

www.ingramcontent.com/pod-product-compliance
Lightning Source LLC
Chambersburg PA
CBHW020333120726
47904CB00002B/395